The Peacock

Books by JON GODDEN

THE BIRD ESCAPED

THE HOUSE BY THE SEA

THE PEACOCK

The Peacock

by Jon Godden

RINEHART & CO., INC.

NEW YORK

To my Father
who first took me there

Part One

The River

The River

CHAPTER I

THE river flowed round the bend, in under the high
bank, and out again to the long pool above the rapid. On
the right bank, facing the hills, in the beginning of February
1948, Murray Coombes made his fishing-camp.

The river was small for an Indian river and for almost
the whole of its course it was wild and quick and undisturbed.
It rose in the swamps under the foothills, wandered in hidden streams through thick jungle and emerged to the forest
and the plain. No bridges crossed it and on its banks were no
buildings larger than a grass-thatched hut, a fisherman's
home built on stilts at the edge of the water. Fishing lines
were sometimes set in its pools, fish-traps of stakes and nets
set across it and, in its lower reaches, dams made of mud and
branches attempted to control its course. But these were
made by men who were nearly as wild as the river, as wild as
the otters who played in its water or the monkeys who, in

their untidy way, threw sticks and fruit skins down from the trees onto its pools. The river ran for itself and for the fish in its bed and for the birds and animals who lived in the long grass and under the trees on its banks.

Under the high bank below the camp the water was almost black. The trees dropped their leaves onto the water and the leaves were seized and spun round and sent sailing out to the end of the pool. Exposed tree roots waved above the swift sliding surface and the bank was riddled by the bee-eaters who drove their long tunnels into the earth and made their nests deep in under the trees. These birds, green and rich blue, flashed their arrow-tails all day across the pool. Until the camp was made it was always quiet here by the river; the only sounds were made by water or by birds; but the forest road ran behind the trees, a few hundred yards from the bank above the pool.

This rough earth track marked by cart ruts was the only road in many square miles of country. It ran from the small town or village of Hokgaon, where there was a police station and a post office and the Divisional Forest Officer's bungalow, through fifty miles of reserved forest and grassy open plain to the border. It was used by bullock carts, bands of pedestrians walking together for safety, forest rangers and guards in their khaki uniforms, runners who carried the mail down miles of lonely road with only their spears crowned with bells to protect them, ponies whose harness too was alive with bells. Bicycles, lorries, even a car or two, had raised its dust, but for the greater part of the day and for all the nights the road was undisturbed; tree shadows lay thick across it and, at night, fireflies swarmed in starry clouds in the long grass at its verge. Where the road bent, following the bend in the river, grew a large belu tree. This tree was a landmark on the road. When the traveller saw its enormous pale buttressed trunk, he knew that he was half way between Hokgaon and the border and, if he were a regular user of the road and if the time were evening and dusk was about to fall, he would look round anxiously and hurry by, listening to the silence. It was known that here, on many evenings, the old Ganesh, the single tusker, crossed the road.

All day this solitary aged elephant grazed and roamed and slept in the heavy jungle and at sunset returned to the river, crossing the road and vanishing into the trees again. This Ganesh, called after the God of Wisdom and venerated by Hindus, as single tuskers are, had been seen many times. Tales were told in the district of his great size and of the single sacred right tusk, and it was rumoured that there were the marks of old shackles on his legs. It was certain that he crossed the road in the evening a few yards above the huge pale tree, raising a cloud of dust that persisted for some time after he had gone.

One day, early in February, a car and a 15cwt truck were parked under the tree, a tent was pitched and fires lighted and the sound of axes was heard through the forest, but the elephant saw no reason to change his habits. He made his evening appearance, and the tent and the truck were moved hurriedly back down the road. Because of him the line of the new track leading to the river was altered. But no one interfered with him and he interfered with nobody. Every evening he crossed the road and the camp was made on the bank above the river.

§ 5 §

CHAPTER II

A small elderly man carried a folding chair from his tent and set it up on the bank facing the hills. Dr Murray Coombes had bathed in the canvas bath behind his tent, and put on clean clothes and mosquito boots. He had been up since dawn and hard at work on the camp all day; when it grew dark he would eat his supper and go straight to bed. Now he sat down, resting his hands on his thighs, and looked towards the hills. The gorge breeze that blew every evening down the river touched his newly shaved old cheeks and his hair that was as thick and fine and white as a white bird's crest. Sitting alone on the bank above the river under the sunset sky with the dark forest behind him, he looked small and inconspicuous, not much more to be remarked than the night heron who, a few minutes before, had taken up his evening stance on the other side of the pool.

Evening sounds came from the camp behind him: someone emptying a bath, the water-carrier filling his tins at the edge of the river, a laugh from the cook-tent, a squeal from the elephant pickets, the low notes of a sleepy bird from the trees and, under all the other sounds, the sound of the river running below the bank. The evening camp smells rose into the air: woodsmoke from the different fires, cooking curry, a whiff of kerosene, the smell of newly turned earth and cut wood and bruised leaves, and the river smell that is wild and damp and unmistakable. The old man was not alone. The camp with its many inmates was behind him. He had made it and he knew it all from the rough perimeter of felled trees

§ 6 §

and branches to the last bamboo walled-latrine in the trees. It would have given him pleasure to know that his camp, which from the river looked a wide clearing in the forest, from the air, if seen at all, would be only a minute bare spot on the vast dark pelt of trees.

This old man had made many camps, large and elaborate as this one was, or small and simple to the point of discomfort. There is satisfaction in living as the forest hunters do, sleeping on the ground, eating rough monotonous foods, bathing in the quick forest streams; but it is also good after long hard days in the sun to come back to cooked food, warm baths, soft beds, cold drinks, to know sharp contrasts. Long ago Murray Coombes had decided what a fishing-camp should be.

A camp should be as unobtrusive as possible because every jungle camp is an invasion into another world. It should be dry, pitched on higher ground than the river and the surrounding forest, but shaded against the fierce sun and free of undergrowth which brings the fear of snakes. It must be near running water. There must be no village, no other encampment for several hundred yards up river, preferably not for miles or not at all, but it is easier if there is a village or settlement not too far away where beaters for a shoot, boatmen, and perhaps milk and eggs and a chicken or two can be found. It is necessary to work and plan to make a camp to be inhabited by many people for several weeks seventy miles from the nearest railway in the heart of the forest. When the site has been chosen and the track made through the forest from the nearest road, the camp elephants clear the ground, pushing down small trees with the granite-hard base of the trunk below their foreheads, uprooting bushes and tree stumps and piling fallen tree trunks and branches into a rough stockade. It is incredible how quickly this can be done by two grey swaying mountains while the third is deep in the jungle on the endless quest for cane and grass, elephant fodder which must be brought back to the camp every day. When there are only a few large trees left standing for shade on a patch of bare earth well trodden down by the great circular feet, the elephants depart to make their own and their mahouts' camp near at hand behind the trees. A tarpaulin shelter is spread at the back of the camp for the car and the truck and the pile of petrol tins. The tents are pitched with canvas stretched wide and tight, tent-pegs driven deep into the ground and a trench dug to drain off possible rain. The airy sleeping huts, known as bashas, which many people prefer to tents, are built of bamboo and thatch cut from the forest and made weatherproof and pleasing to the eye with their gold grass roofs. The dining-hut, which is a wide-eaved roof set on strong bamboo posts, is made near the edge of the bank facing the river and the hills. The cook tent is important: the cook, at all costs, must be contented; the oven is a clay-lined trench covered by a sheet of iron pierced by round holes. The numbered packing cases of stores are arranged in their proper order and a low branched tree is chosen as a larder where new killed meat will hang. The servants' tents and the tents of the hunters are pitched so as to ensure privacy for everyone. A path is made to the river and steps cut in the bank to enable the water carrier to fill his tins. Then the latrines require thought and care. They must be sufficient for the needs of everyone in the camp and placed well apart in the fringes of the trees. Inside circular walls made of bamboo or of gunny stretched on poles, holes are dug and a pile of earth and a spade left beside them; when a hole is full it is filled in and another dug. This is simple and efficient and, if a large pit is also dug for rubbish near the

§ 8 §

cook tent, the camp will be as tidy and fresh as a camp should be. Not everyone enjoys a cold bath in the river. If the bathroom is a round roofless bamboo-walled hut with a narrow curving entrance and a platform of logs on which the canvas or tin tub can rest, it is very pleasant after a long hot day to sit in the warm soapy water that smells of woodsmoke and to look up at the evening sky and leafy branches. The mechanics of living, what to eat and drink, where to sleep, how to keep the body clean, are of importance everywhere, as the men who fought in the forests between India and Burma know. To many of these men it would seem incredible that anyone could pitch a tent again for pleasure, or find delight where they knew only fear and boredom and discomfort; but to make a shelter as far from the familiar and everyday as possible is a universal dream. Children build their first houses in the branches of a tree or deep in the grass of some orchard; holiday crowds streaming out of the cities with their picnic baskets make for the nearest forests; the hermit seeks a cave deep in the woods.

Now this particular camp was ready and waiting. The camp beds were in their places, rough tables and chairs had been put together of wood cut from the forest. The stores were unpacked. In the camp larder was a small deer that Murray had shot two days before and the six pound fish that he had caught that afternoon. The truck and the car had left for the station where they would arrive safely before dark to wait for the morning train. There was nothing more for him to do, except to pass the sixteen hours that remained to him before the others could arrive.

He was a small, thin, upright old man. He looked as light and as fragile as a bird does but, like a bird, he was wiry and tough and resistant to heat and cold and almost untirable. Under the shining silver hair his skin was reddened and darkened by years of exposure to the sun. His eyes were a fierce, pure blue.

Few people knew how old Murray was; this was a secret that he carefully hid. He had been born sixty-eight years before in a suburb of Manchester. At twenty-six, when he married, he was an earnest hard working young doctor with a large practice in the poorer districts of a North country town. After two years of marriage his wife had left him suddenly and without explanation for a man who had been his friend. For ten years he had wandered round the world as a ship's doctor, a silent, unfriendly small man. Stranded by his ship in Calcutta and out of work, he had found himself engaged by a great Managing Agency and sent to a group of tea-gardens in the then remote Province of Assam. He had been a tea-garden doctor for over thirty years. Anyone else would have been retired years before on a pension, but Dr Coombes was a recognised character, a privileged person, to be indulged in the matter of leave, whose eccentricities were to be ignored. He was a successful doctor, respected and liked by the tea-planters in spite of his reserved and often strange ways, revered by the doctor babus, compounders and dispensers who worked under him, and tolerated and trusted by the thirty thousand men and women and children of the tea-garden labour force who were in his care. He worked hard for them, working against malaria, and kal-a-azar, and hookworm and ignorance and greed, fighting for better sanitation, better housing, better hospitals for them, as if they were his chief interest in life.

His group of gardens, covering ten thousand acres of land beyond the river in the north of the Province, was surrounded by thick jungle. There the town-bred man taught himself to shoot and fish and to live. Every spare hour and every day of leave that came to him were spent in the jungle. In his neat, bare bungalow was little except guns and rifles and rods, books on hunting and natural history and, later, cameras, trip wires, all the apparatus of flashlight photography which before long was in its turn discarded. Slowly, through the years, with increasing absorption, he learnt the forest and a life different from his own. Patiently, leaf by leaf and feather by feather, he pieced it together until there was nowhere else in the world where he was at home.

He would disappear for weeks on end, alone except for his elephants and his hunters and trackers, and reappear again to work in his office and surgery, to visit his hospitals, to turn up at the district club where he would drink and play a game of billiards or take a hand at bridge, a carefully dressed fastidious, silent man, given to fits of bad temper, known for his sudden kindnesses and generosity.

Sometime between the two wars he made the first of his large fishing camps. What compelled him to do this he never clearly knew. Every year, early in February, he would obtain the necessary permits, rent a couple of blocks of forest from the Government, collect his elephants and his men, and ask to his camp a very diverse collection of people: planters, soldiers, business men, men from his own Agency (Philip Tallent was one of these), friends, and men that he scarcely knew. They would come and fish and shoot, bathe in the rivers, see all that he had to show them. Sometimes they came again, and the camps went on. As the years went by, perhaps to prove that his experiment, if it had been an experiment, had succeeded, four people came to the camps regularly: Philip and Alice Tallent, Eric Cathcart, and Kay Trench. Every year, until the war, he looked forward to their coming, but when they had gone he would strike camp, cover what traces he could and, leaving the rest to the jungle, move on somewhere else until it was time to go back to his work again. Of all the people who had been to his camps, of the four people who that evening were drawing nearer to this new camp and to all that was to happen there, perhaps only Alice Tallent suspected what it meant to him to make the camps at all.

From the day fourteen years ago when Philip Tallent had brought his wife to one of the by then well known camps, the old doctor and Alice Tallent had understood each other. By now they knew each other as teacher and disciple seldom do. It had often seemed extraordinary to Murray that she should know so effortlessly what it had taken him many years to learn. Alice had arrived almost before she had started at the point that he, in his old age, had reached. Not that they thought alike in everything. They had always shared an absorbing interest in animal and bird life but, while he could only admit the untamed and wild, Alice included all the tame animals she knew, her own and other people's children and, he had often thought, not a few men. In the early days, before cars and motor-cycles and jeeps had come to the tea-plantations, he had been forced to keep a horse but he had never owned a dog and never would. At that moment, as he sat looking at the hills, he was regretting that Eric, to whom, of course, nothing could be denied now, was bringing his old labrador to the camp again. It was seven years since he had seen Eric and in those seven years he had only seen Alice for short intervals and in a world where he was not at ease.

After that last camp in 1940 the war had closed over them all. Murray had worked for three years in the labour camps on the Burma road. For years he had watched the forest fall back before the aerodromes and gunsites and new roads that pushed it back far more quickly and efficiently than the tea-gardens and the small clearings of the Nepali settlers had done. The forest retreated but he had known that it was still there, more difficult of access, further off, but poised like a wave against the foothills and waiting its chance to flow back and cover all again, as it would cover this new fishing-camp as soon as they had done with it, as soon as their backs were turned.

Murray sat up in his chair and took his cigarette case out of his pocket, and slowly fitted a cigarette into a short amber holder. He had not meant to make another camp. He was old and tired. He had meant to creep quietly back to the forest, alone except for his elephants and Manoo and Sangla, the men who now were not servants or even friends but a part of himself, as his eyes and his hands were. Eric Cathcart had written to him first, but the other letters had soon followed. He did not want anyone here, but here he sat, having made yet another scar for them on the forest, waiting for them again.

For days his eyes had been busy with the small and necessary: with the pencilled plan, the list of stores, hammer and nail and saw, the bag of silver change for the village, his case of instruments and bottles and dressings, busy with the rise of a fish, a knot in a gut cast, the sights of his rifle, the movement behind a screen of leaves, the spoor slowly filling with water in the mud by the stream. Now he lifted his head and looked over miles of silent tree-tops, over water, earth, leaf, to the hills. On the other side of the river the trees began again. At night their massed heads made a wild black jungle pattern on the sky and in the day the foothills showed above them, pale blue and misty in the mornings and, at evening, as purple-blue and green and gold as a peacock's breast. Above the hills, at certain times of the year, if the weather were fine or after a storm, the distant range of great snow peaks would sometimes appear. This evening they gleamed faintly, higher even than he remembered them in the sky.

§ 13 §

The Peacock

The evening colours were retreating from the hills. As the day fell away the trees came closer. At his feet the river was running deep and black. He dropped his match onto the dark water and watched it spin round and disappear. His ever interested eye was caught and held. It was deep down there. Under the bank would be a shelf scoured out by the water where a great fish could lie. If such a one lived there it would show itself in the morning when the sun was up.

"I will watch for it first thing," he told himself, speaking aloud as old men sometimes do when they know that they are alone. "I must make sure that it is there, then I can show it to Alice before the others notice it."

He looked up from the dark water to the sky. Now the hills were dark and in the sky one star had appeared.

Their letters had all said much the same thing. "I need a rest . . . the sort of holiday that we used to have . . . I need to get right away." But Alice had written: "What has happened to the world, Murray? From here your jungles seem a Paradise. Can we get back?"

"Why not?" he asked himself, looking across the river at the dark hills. "If this is what they think they want, who am I to stop them? I'm no angel with a flaming sword barring the way."

Barua, the new Divisional Forest Officer, only that afternoon had said: "Dr Coombes, these friends of yours, for what are they coming here?" That, taken by itself, was an odd question for a strange, self-contained, rather cold young man to have asked, but it had been asked at the end of their talk, a long surprising talk beginning with questions about permits and ending with a discussion on game sanctuaries.

Murray had found this young Assamese impressive, if young he was, for his thin dark face, light eyes, close curling

§ 14 §

hair, and tall light body in the conventional khaki shirt and shorts, had an ageless look. This Barua, burning with zeal and energy, with a touch of righteousness and arrogance, was very different from his predecessor, the fat, pleasant, easy going Chatterjee who seldom left his bungalow, whose only interest was in his files and his sāl plantations. While he talked to him, Murray had felt cheered and more hopeful; Barua knew the forest and its inhabitants, although he talked as if he knew every beast and plant and tree in his wide district as, of course, no man could do. If only there were more like him the future would be safe, and the forests, the rich and wonderful forests of north India, would remain unspoiled and guarded under the hills. He had arrived in the camp, out of the blue, apparently, on his way back to Hokgaon from some tour of inspection accompanied by one of his forest rangers. At first he had been stiff and politely disapproving, although it was clear that he had heard of Dr Coombes, but, as they sat together in the shade above the river discussing the inroads that the Nepali settlers were making in the forest, the prevalence of poaching, the indiscriminate shooting of hinds by the local hunters and the movements of the big game of the district, he gradually unbent. They talked of the mukna, the tuskless male elephant, who had done much damage to villages beyond the Dipsiri plain and of the famous big tiger who, during the war in a shoot arranged by inexperienced men, subalterns on leave from Burma, had killed a beater and was now regarded with superstitious fear in the district. It became clear that Tarun Krishna, Barua and Murray Coombes had much in common, including a dream. Their voices had taken on the same enthusiastic note when they came to talk of the great game sanctuaries of South Africa and of their vision of another sanctuary, one even larger, richer, more beautiful and varied,

§ 15 §

which might one day stretch along the foothills of the Himalayas.

"Sportsmen!" Barua had said, "I tell you the time of such is past."

Murray, who agreed with him, but thinking perhaps of Eric, had pointed out that the sportsman at least must know his quarry, that it was the hunter who became the naturalist, enthusiast and lover, not the man who stayed at home.

"Perhaps, but if I could I would forbid this sort of thing," Barua had replied, waving his hand at the camp. "But you are here, you and your friends. I can't stop you, not while you keep the rules!"

As he stood up to leave a smile had taken the sternness from the dark face. "Goodbye," he had said. "Perhaps I shan't see you again, but I will not be far off. I'm always about." He had vanished into the trees as abruptly as he had come.

Now Murray looked round him, at the camp and the trees and the river, almost as if he expected to see some sign of that visitation. A question still seemed to hang on the air; but he knew the answer. They were coming to the camp, Alice and Eric, Philip and Kay, for the same reasons that they had come before: for pleasure, for refreshment, for a holiday. Once again, he would be glad to see them come, he would do his best for them, and he would be glad to see them go. This would be a camp like any other.

As he sat smoking in the growing darkness above the river, Murray was frowning. Could this be a camp like any other? It is never easy to find an overgrown road, one that has been lost for many years. The forest road, every year, after each rains, had to be reclaimed again from the jungle by gangs of men recruited from the villages, so rich and unseemly is a few months' rain growth, so insistent is the forest.

He thought of the large, blond Eric who would be lame and scarred for the rest of his life, of Kay, the quick and restless, two years in an Italian prison, and of Philip who had spent the war where he began it, working at his office desk, and who was now grey, overworked, unapproachable and silent.

"And Alice?" he said aloud, with his eyes on the pale star. "Nothing must touch her. I can't have her changed."

He stood up suddenly and faced the camp. Dusk was falling and the outlines of the trees were sinking back into the sky, but he could see the shapes of the three empty huts facing him: the large one for Philip and Alice, and the two smaller ones for Eric and Kay. He had been glad that no one else was coming to the camp that year. These four knew each other well; with no stranger among them they would be able to be themselves, at ease and natural. But now, standing with his back to the river and staring at the row of dark, waiting doorways, he asked himself if it would have been safer to have had one stranger among them, someone disinterested.

Lights were springing up in the servants' tents. The petrol lamp was lit in the dining-hut. The yellowed hands of Kancha, his Nepali servant, were spreading a cloth, and setting out fork, knife, glass. The two shadowy forms that stood together under the big trees were Manoo and Sangla waiting for their evening talk with him. Manoo was an old, bent, very dark man who came from South India; if anything, he knew even more of the jungle and its ways than Sangla did and was wise and cautious as well and a fine rifle shot. Sangla came from one of the tribes of the foothills. He was a great hunter and tracker, silent, gold-skinned, imperturbable and strong. They had both been with Murray for over twenty years and the sight of them standing there reassured him.

As he watched, a lantern was carried in and out of the

tree trunks and set on the floor of his tent by the tent pole showing his red blanket and the side of his mosquito net. Everything was as usual: the camp was preparing for the night, following the ritual that he had planned.

He began to walk up and down on the edge of the bank. His shadow, cast by the lamps, lay dim and huge over the river, reaching out to the darkness on the opposite bank. Soon, all round the camp, the night sounds would begin.

Manoo had declared that all the auguries were good. The weather could not have been better; there was not a cloud in the sky and in two weeks the full moon would shine down on the forest to delight them. There was plenty of water in the river for the time of the year, plenty of fish. Already news of tiger had come in, and the big village had promised sufficient beaters. The preparations had gone smoothly, almost too smoothly, but everything seemed as it had always been, everything was as usual. Except that this year there seemed an inordinate amount of peafowl about. He had never liked the noisy, troubling birds; they were over coloured, too insistent for the forest. Only that morning he had found a feather, a train feather with its great purple eye, almost in the camp. He had picked it up and stuck it into the woven wall of Alice's basha above the table that he had made for her. She liked feathers and all soft bright things, but some people thought that a peacock's feather was unlucky. Would she be pleased to see it there?

On his right as he turned and walked towards the lamp, was a pile of logs waiting at the edge of the bank where the camp fire was to be. Here they would sit in the evenings with the fire light on their faces and the darkness at their backs. Already chairs had been set out in a semi-circle; they should be taken in out of the dew: six empty chairs waiting for them.

§ 18 §

"Six?" Murray Coombes said aloud. "Why did I say six? We will be five of course."

In the darkness on the other side of the river, a peacock, disturbed perhaps in its roosting place, gave one high mewing scream.

CHAPTER III

AT half past five in the morning the railway station of Kishnagar was lapped in mist. Mist lay over the double tracks and over the cindery open space that served as a platform, over the low bushes and the iron fence of the stationmaster's garden; it covered with its fine wet cloud everything that was below four feet high. The two signal posts and the red corrugated iron roofs of the booking-office and the sheds were islands in a shallow white sea that stretched across the plain to the foothills. The hills were sharp and flat and grey; later in the day they would withdraw into the sky, leaving only the station and the plain.

Someone had lit a dung fire beside the tracks and smoke lay in blue wreaths on the mist. The biting, acrid smell drifted to the man standing by himself, looking in the direction that the train would come. He lifted his head and breathed deeply: if he woke after a sleep of a thousand years with that smell in his nostrils, he would know before he opened his eyes that he was in India.

Last night, for the first time for many months, he had slept the night through. He had lain on his camp bed on the veranda of the small shabby rest-house with his face turned towards the foothills and the invisible forest. His leg, which in plane and train and hotel had been almost unbearably painful, had not hurt him at all. His heart had beaten evenly and strongly, as if it knew that it now beat where, for a long time, it had wanted to be. The alien's desire for this dark hostile land seems strange and incomprehensible, but it can be an ache, a need in alien bones.

Eric Cathcart's father and grandfather and great-grandfather had been Indian Army officers as, until a year ago, when India had become independent, he had been. As a child living in the cantonments of Indian towns and later in schools and homes in an England which for a long time had been a strange country to him, he had never imagined that he could be anything else. He followed a tradition and a pattern that was once thought as good as a pattern could be but which is now seen as out of date and a little absurd. There was nothing about him at first sight to set him apart from any other Indian Army officer except his height and the extreme good looks which he accepted calmly, as his due. He was honest, conventional, narrow and proud, as his kind are supposed to be. He took himself and his work seriously and was as vain and careful of his regiment as he was of his magnificent body. Perhaps it was the vitality and restless strength of this body, as well as a carefully controlled fierceness in his character that sent him, before he had been many years in India, in search of his second preoccupation, his first love. The born soldier is first a born hunter. For years, as Murray Coombes had done, he had spent all his leave in the forest, first in the forests of Central India, and then after he came to know Murray, in the jungles of the foothills further East. Unlike Murray, his interest, instead of broadening, had narrowed until he was preoccupied with only one form of the life that he found in the forests, with tigers and all that had to do with them. Alice once said that he had even come to look like the great red and gold beasts; although he never admitted it, this pleased him very much. Perhaps of all the people who were to live together in the camp, he and Sangla had most in common.

The shock of his wounds, which he had received at the end of the war against the Japanese, after he had fought through the Burma campaigns, and from which no one had thought that he could recover, had been severe. He could not reconcile himself to his spoilt body. Other men could lose a leg below the knee, could be scarred down one side of the body from cheek to thigh with mauve and white puckered scars, but this could not have happened to Eric Cathcart. The shock of emerging from over two years of hospitals and convalescent homes in India and England to find his regiment disbanded, himself and his brother officers unwanted and his army, as he knew it, a thing of the past, was even greater. He was a soldier and nothing else, but even if he had not been disabled, there could be no other army for him. He refused to realise that he was luckier than most of his kind; he was unmarried and he had a house and land and an income of his own. For a time he tried to farm his land, but he could not settle down. The habits and affections of another country were strong in him. All that was restless and fierce in him came to the surface. He was contemptuous of his maimed body and drove it as hard as he could, and his friends found him bitter and complaining and full of self-pity. He was thirty-eight when the idea came to him of going back to India. As a soldier he was no longer wanted, but, for a few years at least, perhaps he would find other work to do in the country where he felt most at home. He knew that he must have a breathing-space first, a time to get on reasonable terms with himself again. Sitting by the fire in his room, looking out at his fields and woods, he had thought of Murray, and of the forests that he had known. "A short holiday," he had written, "a breathing-space." And directly the letter had gone he felt that he had made the only decision that he could have made. There was nothing else for him to do.

Now, here he was at the end of his journey. Below the hills, still hidden by the mist, was the forest. But first there was one unpleasant moment to be endured, the moment when Alice would see him as he now was. In that moment, for a second, the expression on her face would be unguarded.

He turned and limped back beside the rails which could now be seen shining through the mist. The sun had not yet risen and his pale hair and smooth, red, expressionless face seemed to have absorbed all the light that there was in the early morning and the checks on his tweed coat looked startlingly clear. He walked with his head well back, following the line of the hills with an absent gaze. Beside him the head of a large black dog was just visible in the thinning mist. Both man and dog, against the flat distant hills and the background of the station, looked outsize, incongruous, out of place.

As they passed the drinking fountain and a line of dripping bushes, a voice said, "Good morning, Major."

An old man wrapped to the ears in a cream woollen shawl stood in the shadow of a doorway. One small, brown, veined hand held the soft wool over the mouth and above it sharp old eyes looked up at him.

"Good morning, Babuji. Why, it's Das, you still here?"

"Still here, Major Cathcart. There are many changes in the country, many changes, they say, everywhere. But here you will find us much the same."

"That is what I had hoped."

"Dr Coombes was here a week ago waiting at the rest-house for his elephants to arrive. He gave me the news. He told me of your wound. I am sorry, it should not have happened to you."

"As you see, I still get about."

"And now you have come back. To shoot us some tigers again? There are many in this district since the war, too many, they are a pest to the villages."

"But surely, every year, there is less jungle?"

"Every year there are more men, and men must eat. But the jungle is still there, we have not got rid of it yet. As for your tigers, you will find their evil hearts unchanged."

"I will get rid of as many as possible for you."

"Be sure and kill the Dipsiri tiger, the big one. I am counting on you for that."

"The big tiger? There is always a big tiger."

"Very true, but this one killed two beaters. Not that it was his fault. Some ignorant and foolish countrymen of yours, but doubtless you will hear all this from Dr Coombes."

Eric smiled, looking down at the old brown face that he had known for many years. "I will do my best," he said. "Any messages for the camp?"

"Please tell the Doctor that the two packing cases came on last night's mail. They are in the truck and Puran Singh has the receipt."

The sun was coming up beyond the edge of the plain and now the mist was rising, uncurling, moving away. The sheeted forms that had lain on the ground all night waiting for the morning train in the shelter of the iron-roofed veranda now rose and discarded their shroudlike coverings to show themselves as men who moved out to the bare ground behind the sheds to relieve themselves, moved to the drinking fountain, collected their belongings and waited again. Behind the stationmaster's house a cock began to crow.

"The train is late?"

"Forty minutes, but the signal is down."

"Then I had better be moving. Goodbye, Mr Das. I am glad to have found you still here."

"Good holiday, Major. I will look out for you on your way back and then you can give me the news, just as you used to do."

Eric turned back. Behind him the rising sun shone on the rails which were now two converging silver lines vanishing into the East. The encounter had cheered him. The old man had always been interested in their comings and goings and helpful over forwarding supplies to their camps. At their last meeting Eric had given him a small jar of tiger fat and a few of the precious thick white whiskers; a present that caused much laughter; tiger fat is good for rheumatism but the whiskers are considered to be powerful aphrodisiacs. He felt unreasonably comforted and reassured by this welcome. Now he felt that he could face the coming meeting with Alice. How foolish he had been to try and evade it, or to put it off even by one day.

Until he read Murray's letter in Calcutta, Eric had not imagined that the others would be coming to the camp that year. He had thought of nothing except the forest. "You will of course stay with Philip and Alice," Murray had written, "they are expecting you and you can all travel up here together." It had been cowardly and rude of him to have sent one of the hotel servants to Alice with a note asking for his dog and saying that he thought it better to go ahead to the camp. What she must have thought of him he did not know; the dog had been returned without a word or a sign from her. And what good had it done him? Murray had asked him to wait at the rest-house until the whole party arrived, as petrol was too scarce for a double trip to the camp. Now the moment that he had tried to avoid was here.

As he limped back to the edge of the clearing where the low scrub began, he knew that, in spite of everything, he would be glad to see them again. Philip he had known and liked for many years. As for Alice, there could not be much to be dreaded in the company of a pretty woman with whom you once thought yourself in love, uncomfortably in love for a time, then lightly, easily, and with whom you are in love no longer. He had been cured of Alice many years ago. It would do him good to be with them all again, even with Kay Trench, that entertaining, aggravating small man whom Alice, for reasons of her own, encouraged. He had been alone too long. There was no reason why he should creep back to hide, as a wounded animal does.

An animal that is badly hurt creeps into a quiet hidden place and there is alone until it dies or until the skin grows over the wound, the broken bone in some fashion comes together and its new mis-shapenness becomes a part of itself. For a moment Eric stood still with his hand on the dog's head. He did not see the station buildings or the people in his path. He was looking down a long tunnel of grass and leaves at a tiger that he had wounded many years ago. He had glimpsed it once and then lost it again although, following its tracks, he had searched for days. Now he saw it with extraordinary vividness. Each stripe on the tawny hide, each drop of blood on the leaves shone down the years at him.

As he walked on again he said to himself, "We never found it, but there was so much blood it must have died. Somewhere, soon, it must have died."

On his right, beyond the railings, he saw the waiting truck and the car. Puran Singh, Murray's old Sikh driver, stood with folded arms beside the picnic basket, looking at him expectantly. Eric lifted his arm, which was the signal for the Primus to be lit under the tea-kettle.

§ 25 §

The roar of the approaching train was heard. Behind Eric the little station sprang into life. He stood as straight as he could with his hand clenched on the dog's collar.

CHAPTER IV

A great cloud of dust was rolling behind the car. The tarmac ended abruptly a few miles from the station and Dr Coombes' shabby Ford V8 swayed and bumped down the raised, uneven earth road that pointed at the hills. Below the hills was a thick, dark green line. This was the forest. It looked quite close but the hills were not to be trusted. The camp was over seventy miles away and it would be at least an hour before the car reached Hokgaon and turned on to the forest road.

On each side of the road the flat wide landscape might have been the same that they had seen all the day before from the train: the same small, bare, sad-coloured fields baked hard by the sun, clumps of trees marking villages scattered like islands on the plain, small figures moving behind yoked cattle, dark furrows growing in the fawn earth of the fields. It seemed incredible that later in the year this same expanse of earth would be one huge shallow lake alive with the parrot-green of young rice.

Philip Tallent was tired and his head was aching as, these days, it often did. The white road wavered before his eyes. He would have been wiser to let someone else drive, Kay, or Murray's second driver, there was plenty of room in the car; Kay and the rod and gun cases had the back seat to themselves. But when he suggested this at the station Alice had seemed so surprised that he had said nothing more. Of course, he always had driven out to the camp, as Eric had always gone in the truck with his dog and the drivers and the luggage, as they had always drunk an early morning cup of tea, standing round the picnic basket between the truck and the car before beginning the drive out to the camp. It was curious that they all seemed to find it necessary to do exactly as they had done before, as if they were following a safe, well-worn pattern, or a doctor's orders, a prescription for happiness.

He glanced at his wife. She was looking straight ahead through the windscreen and all that he could see of her was her profile and her hands folded on her knees. She had not spoken since the car left the station but he knew that she was far ahead, entering the trees, already approaching the camp.

At times it seemed to Philip that he knew his wife's mind as well as he knew her body or the inflections of her voice. At other times he was not so sure. He had seen her first when she was a child and he had married her directly she was eighteen. After fourteen years of uninterrupted married life there should not be much that he did not know about her. It was not that she was difficult or secretive; Alice had always been easy, pliable, open, as transparent as water, and as difficult to grasp. As a child she had a way of lifting her eyes in an open, shining, innocent look, and then of looking sideways and away under her lashes. At this moment he knew that she had worked herself up into a state of intense excitement as she easily did, that she still felt a little sick and giddy from the long train journey, and that she longed for a bath. He knew that for the time being she had put behind her her home, her friends, her animals, all thought of her children, the three small daughters who were in England with their grandparents. He knew that she had forgotten every-thing except that she was hurrying back to a world that she had not seen for seven years. But was there anything else in her mind, anything that she was carefully hiding? This trans-parency of hers was an illusion; she was as transparent as a deep pool that only gives back a reflection of the sky. He had never been sure of her, that was the trouble. For in-stance, there was the scene at the station; he thought that he knew why she had greeted Eric Cathcart as she had done, but he was not sure; he had never been sure.

Philip had often asked himself if a plain, dull, middle-aged man can ever be sure of an attractive woman eighteen years younger than himself. He had asked this question re-signedly, and sometimes near despair. Now, unwillingly, looking at the hills and trying to think only of the river and its quiet waiting pools, he could not stop himself from ask-ing it once again.

Kay Trench woke from an uneasy doze and lifted his chin from the collar of his camel-hair coat. For a moment he did not know where he was, and then he saw the familiar road and the back of Philip's and Alice's heads. The dust was thick on his hands and on the car cushions. He disliked dirt and discomfort as a cat does and he had always hated the drive out to the camp. He put his hands into his pockets and leant back against the car cushions and asked himself why he was sitting there. Why had he gone to these camps year after year? What pleasure or profit could there be for him in catch-ing unnecessary fish, shooting inoffensive tigers, sitting round camp fires like an overgrown boy scout? Kay Trench always knew the answers, and now he answered his own ques-tion promptly and clearly. He had always believed in con-trasts. Life in camp was a complete change for him; it re-invigorated him for the city life that he usually led. He had never been bored in camp, never for one moment; there had always been too much to do. Of course, he had extracted a double enjoyment from everything that happened there. One half of him was pleased and flattered that he, Kay Trench, was accepted by these people as one of themselves and that he could join in everything they did and excel them all at one of their own games; he was a gifted and stylish small game shot and no one could beat him when it came to the birds. His other half stood back and watched and noted. It amused him to watch himself and the others at their absurd, earnest pursuits, their posturing, poor khaki clad fools, against the huge background of the forest. Sometimes he would put out a finger, or say a word, that would set them all off in a new direction. The difficulty was not to get too involved himself. He liked them all and not for the world would he have forfeited their friendship. This year, more than ever, he must be careful not to go too far. As for the forest, it repelled and fascinated him. At times, when he had been depressed or overworked, it had seemed to him that he lived for the month each year that he passed within it. The knowledge that it was still there, huge, apart, indifferent, in the background, had sustained him all the war years.

Kay Trench was a small, black haired, black eyed man. Alice, during one of their many quarrels, had said that, in his favourite soft thick coat, he reminded her of some small expensive pet, an Italian greyhound, a marmoset, something with a nasty bite but not to be taken seriously. But there was nothing delicate or effeminate about him. He gave an impression of wiry strength and his small-featured face was brown with surprisingly deep hard lines round the eyes and mouth. His hands were as small and finely made and fastidious as the rest of him, and few people would have suspected that he had been born in one of the poorest parts of London of a hard-working Cockney father and an Italian mother, the daughter of a fruitseller who had once been a farmer in Lombardy. From this background and his elementary school Kay, with his exceptional brains and quick wits, by hard work and tremendous concentration had emerged from Oxford with a First in Law. None of his friends knew what had brought him to India. He was a clever lawyer and at thirty, in the year before the war, he was already Senior Assistant to a prosperous Calcutta firm of Solicitors. After a year of war in a tank regiment in North Africa and two years in an Italian prison, he had returned to his work apparently unchanged, unless it were that he had lost a little flesh from his small body and added a sharpness to his tongue. He had told Alice, who knew him as well as anyone did, a great deal about himself and his years in prison and his escape, but he had not told her everything.

As he sat in the car with the gun, that he had put together in the station, between his knees (there was always a chance of jungle fowl on the forest road), he was considering Alice, Alice and Philip. All that he could see of her was the top of her head, feathery brown hair above a blue scarf. The back of Philip's head was long and hard and ugly, and covered rather sparsely with dark brown hair, but the hands on the steering wheel were small for his height, well-kept, gentle hands. Kay liked Philip Tallent, perhaps better than anyone he knew. Alice had always delighted and exasperated him. It was Alice who had introduced him to Murray's camps. Now he was used to her, used to her ways and to her looks, although her smooth white skin would always fascinate him. Long ago he had almost decided that Alice did not realise the effect that she had on men, that she did not mean half of what she said and did, that she really was the delightful, unaffected, often childish creature that she seemed and not what he sometimes thought her. If he could have made up his mind about her once and for all, he would not have been thinking of her now.

That morning when they had climbed down from the close compartment that the three of them had shared through the night into the cool fresh misty air, there had not been time for them to pull themselves together before Eric was there, bearing down on them with his new strange lurching walk. The shock on their faces must have been plain for him to see. Luckily the train only waited for a few minutes on that lonely spot on the plain, and it had been all that Kay and Philip could do to get the rolls of bedding and suitcases and rods and guns out of the compartment in time. Alice, without a moment's pause, had opened her arms wide and run to meet him crying, "Eric, darling Eric! It's been such years. I am so happy, so glad." That was an odd thing to have said at that moment but what was there to say? Being Alice, she had of course overdone it; there was no need for her to have thrown her arms round Eric's neck. At the time Kay had been grateful to Alice. The dog who was old enough to know better had set up a mad scampering and barking, and when they could hear themselves speak again that difficult moment was safely over. His own greeting when it came had been natural enough. But later, he had begun to wonder. Sitting on the running-board of the car with a cup of tea in his hand, he had looked carefully at each of their faces in turn.

When Kay had looked at the grey hills standing up behind the truck and the iron roofs of the station buildings, it had seemed to him that they had never been away, or that it was again the first time that they sat there. Alice, standing over the picnic basket in her faded corduroy trousers and blue sweater, holding her cup in both hands, might have been the girl whom he had seen years ago standing on almost the same spot of ground. That morning he had tried to look at her critically, to tell himself that she was fourteen years older, that she was heavier, thicker through the waist, that even for Alice time did not stand still. In the sunlight her skin had the smooth pale gleam which he remembered so well; he could find little change in her. He had looked from her to Philip. Philip, leaning against the mudguard of the truck, had been watching his wife, but the long sallow face had worn its usual pleasant expression and there was nothing to show what he was thinking.

Kay stretched himself impatiently. The journey had gone on too long. He was beginning to be not only cross and uncomfortable but bored, bored. Already he was impatient with them all and with their troubles. Alice was Philip's business, no concern, thank God, of his. He thought for a moment of Eric sitting with his dog behind the old Sikh on the high back seat of the truck, looking out over the fields with that calm, superior look of his. Then he frowned and laid the gun on the seat beside him. Where was the forest? For the first time he peered impatiently ahead through the windscreen. There was nothing to be seen except the white empty road, low scrublike bushes, and the hills. The hills were no nearer; as the sun rose higher and the light brightened they seemed to retreat like a promise that is not going to be kept.

Alice touched Philip on the arm. "Can't we go a little faster?" she said. "At this rate we shall never get there."

"The road is very rough, Alice," Philip said. "We have all day, what's the hurry?"

"I want to be there. I can't wait to see and hear and smell it all again."

Philip turned his head and looked down at her. Her

face was turned up to him and he was touched to see how white and exhausted she looked. There were dark marks under her eyes. He put his hand for a moment over hers.

"It won't be long now," he said gently. "We will make better speed on the forest road," but he saw that she was not listening.

"Can't we hurry?" she said again, and to his surprise he saw that there were tears in her eyes.

"Why Alice," he said. "There is plenty of time. The camp isn't going to run away."

"You never know. It seems to me that there is no time to waste."

Philip took his hand away. He felt extraordinarily tired, too tired to worry over Alice's tears, or over anything else. The familiar depression, the flatness and staleness that were more than tiredness, was on him again. He thought with longing of the forest and his foot pressed more firmly on the accelerator. The sun was growing too bright. The dust was trying. It would be good to be driving in the shade of the trees. He thought of the river. He would like to find a deep green pool and to float there by himself for a long time.

CHAPTER V

THE trees pressed close on each side of the road and the car fled silently between the opposing ranks, hurrying towards the distant circle of colourless sky which shone far ahead at the end of the road, which never seemed to come any nearer. The trees laid their shadows on the road and from their stillness came the loud continuous humming of the

§ 33 §

cicadas. The car ran between the orderly ranks of the sāl plantations and the wild creeper-hung tangle of the evergreen forest. When it crossed a bridge of wooden planks set high above a slow dark stream or a jungle-filled ravine, the rattle of the loose wooden planks under the wheels was as loud and shocking as gunfire.

A dark speck far ahead on the road quickly became a plodding bullock cart. The car was not to be delayed; swinging off the deep ruts, brushing through the long grass and the ferns, it soon had the road to itself again. At the side of the road was a resting place for slower travellers, an encampment of low thatched shacks with black marks of old fires on the dung-littered ground. Wider clearings were marked by tree stumps and the slow blue smoke of charcoal burners' fires. Firelines at right angles to the road made artificial avenues where the sky looked down. But these were only brief interruptions in the continuity of the trees which stretched for mile upon mile, acres planted and regimented and planned, but for the most part bird-sown, self-sown, untouched forest, growing for itself alone, going back, layer upon layer of green, a sea of growth which at last broke and rose on the flanks of the foothills. The road was a rope, a lifeline, an almost imperceptible challenge to the trees, which opened a passage for the car and closed behind it again. The car sped on through this green and gold, striped, barred, and silent world.

Each stump and dead branch at the side of the road could be seen from a long way off. A distant log, brown and suggestive, might suddenly become the still head and shoulders of a deer, a black root the rump of a grazing pig, that patch of bright fern, a leopard. But the silence and the stillness continued. Each stump and twisted root was only a stump, a root, and nothing moved behind the screen of leaves. Was there no life under the trees beyond that of the cicadas who could be heard and the birds who are always where leaves are? There was no sign, nothing to show. The grey tree trunks, the veiled entrances, the hanging creepers, went back and back to the secret places. The great ferns waved. The grass hid nothing. The world was a silent, unending conspiracy of trees.

A sound, not to be described, because it was so unexpected, came out of the forest. The car slowed, and stopped at the side of the road. The sound came again, a sharp crack, followed by a high, shrill, trumpeting squeal. The screen of leaves hung as before; nothing moved; but now the deception was useless. A vast ripple of life was moving somewhere in the trees.

"Elephants. A herd is moving. Not so far off, either. Listen."

The trees along the road were as undisturbed as they had been before; not a leaf was moving. But behind the trees was a movement, not seen so much as felt, like the stirring under the surface of a pool. The sounds were louder: crack! crack! Now the far high branches of a tree were moving, were violently agitated against the sky.

"They are moving this way, feeding parallel to the road, a biggish herd by the sound of them."

"Listen, can you hear the young calves grumbling?"

"They are getting a bit close."

"Oh, let's wait until we can see them. They don't know that we are here, they won't worry about us."

"We don't want them between us and the camp. Come on, let's be moving."

The car slid cautiously down the road and, gathering speed, hurried away between the trees. Now the road was as it had been before, as were the curtains of leaves and the silence. But the air hummed with a new vibration. The car seemed to run more freely as if an invisible brake had been removed. Hearts were beating more quickly, blood ran richer, more freely than it had done before. The forest had declared itself and something in them had answered. The car fled on and behind it the trees closed in. The forest, miles upon miles of dark trees, was behind them. No one gave a thought to the way back.

Part Two

The Camp

The Camp

CHAPTER I

IT was early afternoon and a warm silence lay over the camp. Everyone was asleep or half asleep except for Murray who sat at a table in the shade of a tree soaking gut casts in a bowl and rubbing down fishing lines; every now and then the harsh whirr of a reel joined the continuous hum of the crickets that were making an unnoticed background of sound to the sunlight.

In a deck chair at the edge of the bank above the pool, Kay was asleep with a tin of cigarettes and an empty bottle of beer beside him. Philip's long legs could be seen through the doorway of his hut where he lay stretched out on his bed. No one else was in sight, but none of the camp's inhabitants was far away except for Sangla who had slipped off into the forest long before the car reached the camp.

On a blank day, such as the day of arrival always was, he would make a reconnaissance of the forest, circling the camp in widening circles, watching the ground, watching the trees and the sky, following the game tracks that ran through the forest and carrying nothing except a short stick and his curved knife slung with a skin pouch across his back. When he returned, slipping back between the trees well before sunset, to make his report to Murray, he would know where the tiger that he had heard down river the night before had crossed the sands and where the tigress, answering his call, had joined him. He would know where a small herd of mīthun, the Indian bison, that beautiful dark-coated white-socked beast which stands over sixteen hands high and has curved horns springing horizontally from a calm broad forehead, had passed the heat of the day. He would know that, for the time being, there was no large herd of elephant within several miles radius of the camp and he would have seen a herd of chital, the spotted deer, grazing in the forest across the river, and a sounder of pig which, unfortunately winding him, had gone crashing off, waking the drowsily indignant forest and setting the small brown monkeys chattering a warning from tree to tree. In the middle of the day he would rest. This was the time of day when everything in the forest might almost be said to declare a truce. It was the time to sleep off the heavy meal eaten in the night, or to drowse under the trees chewing the cud, to crouch in the long grass, letting go for a drowsy moment the eternal vigilance. At this moment Sangla was sitting with his back against a tree, his knees drawn up, his eyes closed to two gold-green slits and his mouth a little open. On the ground before him lay his small silver and brass pān box. A moment before he had taken one of the green heart-shaped betal leaves from inside the lid, folded it into a triangular envelope, filled it from the many small compartments of the box with a mixture of crushed areca nuts, lime, clove, cardamon, musk and acacia catechu, and placed it in his mouth. He chewed slowly and pleasurably and his lips and tongue were now stained with a red juice. He had passed the limit of his circlings and after a pause in this clearing among the trees, he would begin his roundabout return to the camp. He was feeling pleased. Eric Cathcart was back. The jungle was full of game. There would be much doing in the next few days. Meanwhile, hanging from his belt was a small plump monitor lizard, the great lizard that sometimes grows to five feet in length and that is armoured like a dragon. He had come across it as it lay in the sunlight on the stones of a dried-up stream and, throwing his stick at it, had caught it across the back of the head. This would give him the supper that he most preferred and the grey and white skin, well dried and cleaned with wood-ash and well softened, he meant to present to Alice.

Alice pulled a chair up to the table in the shade of the tree and sat down beside Murray.

"Where have you sprung from?" he said without looking up from the reel in his hands. "It's early. No one else is about."

Alice had bathed and changed into thin khaki trousers and a white shirt. Her bare arms and her throat and up-turned chin were dappled and tinged with the green of the leaves overhead. In her hand was a peacock's feather which she was using as a fan.

"Philip is in our hut. I asked Kancha to put my bed outside under the trees. Have you noticed that directly we get to the camp we all try to get as far away from each other as we can?"

"But here you are, sitting by me."

"You don't count. You are a part of it all. I'm rested enough and I haven't talked to you properly for years."

"You look less tired, better already. Let's hope that a

few hours' sleep will have as good an effect on the others. I was shocked when I saw Philip."

"He has changed a lot lately, hasn't he?" Alice said. "Murray, I have been very worried about Philip. I don't understand, I don't know what is the matter. It's no use, he won't say anything." She looked down at the feather, turning it from side to side. "I'm not going to worry anymore," she said. "Philip needs a holiday. A few days on the river will put him right. It always did."

Murray laid the reel down on the table and looked at her.

"You expect a lot of this place, don't you Alice?" he said. "Perhaps you expect too much."

"Can you expect too much of Paradise? That's what Philip and I thought the forest was once. Why shouldn't I try to get back? Why shouldn't we be where we were before?"

Murray did not answer and she laughed, stretching her arms above her head and looking round at the ring of trees.

"I feel quite different already," she said. "Even my eyes feel clearer and larger. Already they are beginning to see again."

"What do they see, Alice?"

"That the leaves on this tree are like small two-bladed propellers, that the colours in the river are the colours of mother-of-pearl, that there is a procession of black and red ants passing under your chair. What are you doing Murray? Is that a night-line?"

Murray lifted the tangle of line and barbed hooks. "I think that we might set it in the pool below the bank. It's our only hope of getting that old fish I showed you this morning."

"We will try for him with live bait and dead bait and anything else we can think of. Do you remember, there was always one special fish that you and I had in mind? We never caught him, did we?"

"Come and help me with this. I thought that we might all walk up the river for a bit after tea. I'm sure that Philip would like to put a rod together."

"It can't be tea time yet."

Murray felt in his pocket for the flat gold watch which he always carried there, fixed to the lining by a leather fob.

"Don't tell me the time," Alice said. "Tea will appear sooner or later. In its own good time the sun will go down. You always said that time is only good when it's forgotten."

"I said that? It depends who forgets it. Tea won't come of itself you know."

But Alice was not listening. He saw that she was busy pursuing some new thought of her own. He was not surprised when she pulled her chair nearer and said, "Listen, Murray. Talking of time, I was thinking that our time in camp is always divided into five distinct parts. The first day, perhaps the whole of the first week, is spent settling in. When Eric's dog got out of the truck he ran about sniffing and looking, lifting his leg, getting used to it all again. Well, like old Ebon, that's what we are doing."

Murray laughed. "We are? And what comes next?"

"The second part goes on quietly from day to day. Each of us will be busy doing what we want to do. Philip will fish. He will steep his soul in the river and get rid, I hope, of a few uncomfortable kinks in it. Kay will amuse himself quite happily without getting into any particular mischief. Eric and Sangla will vanish to wrestle with their striped demons. You and Manoo will go on as you always have done and keep an eye on us all."

"What will you do?"

§ 43 §

"I shall do nothing. I shall sit and look and let things happen."

"That would be the wisest thing you could do, Alice. Don't change your mind, don't try and help things to go the way you want them."

She looked quickly up at him, and then went on as if he had not spoken: "Next there will be a time when everything will suddenly be quick and exciting. Perhaps we will have one day when everything will seem to happen at once. Do you remember the day when Philip caught that fifty pounder, and we saw the two huge tuskers, and Eric and Kay were stung by those forest bees? That was a day if you like."

"There must be some eventful days in a jungle camp."

"That's what I'm saying. Then in the fourth part we drop back again, go on as we were before, at least I hope so. That is the dangerous time. Something usually goes a little wrong about then, a small accident, a disappointment, some little thing. But it will be nothing serious, Murray, nothing wrong, nothing to spoil it?"

Murray looked up from the line in his hand. Alice was sitting up in her chair, looking past him at the river where the trees were hazy in the sunlight on the opposite bank. In the green, strong light her eyes looked enormous, colourless and blank.

"Don't look like that Alice," he said. "Why should anything happen? Why should anything be spoilt? Here we are, five people who know our way about in the forest, who know and like each other, doing what we want to do in a place we all know and like. What more could we ask? Come, complete our programme for us. Tell me about the fifth part."

"That will be the end," Alice said slowly, looking down at the feather in her hand. "That's when we go back, but there's no need to think about that now."

§ 44 §

The Camp

Kay was not asleep. His chair had been carefully placed and from where he sat he could see the whole camp from behind his dark glasses. As usual, he had made himself as comfortable as possible, arranging a cushion behind his head and a stool under his feet in their leather sandals. The almost imperceptible breeze that came to him from the river played on his bare arms and touched the silky black hairs that grew there. His hands were folded on his stomach which was pleasantly full. His body was contented and at peace but his mind was busy, as busy and as restless as a squirrel in a cage.

To sit there above the river was pleasant and restful. Close at hand, for the taking, was nearly all that he had promised himself that he would never again be without: good food, drink, something to smoke, a soft place on which to rest his body, an attractive woman to look at. This sufficed for the present, but the free man does not need to live from moment to moment; he can look ahead. Would this suffice to-morrow? He moved uneasily in his chair as he asked himself if he had been wise to return to the forest. Would there be enough to occupy his mind and body? Bored he must not be, that would be asking for trouble. The flat, liverish word was enough to call up his old spectre, to send his mind running down endless stone corridors, past barred windows, twisting and turning away from that small square stone cell. He thought quickly of the farm. It was strange that he had never known a moment's boredom there. The farm had come naturally to him although the months that he had lived there, hidden at first among the sheaves in the barn, and then working in the fields, an Italian farm worker among the other workers, now seemed like a dream. He thought of Pia who was now only a part of that warm, golden dream. He had owed everything to her, his escape, his comfort, satisfaction, and, of course, his life. He had promised to go back, but was

§ 45 §

that a promise that he had ever meant to keep? Kay Trench married to a peasant girl, fathering a horde of children, committed to that narrow small life; it was, of course, ridiculous. He had not thought of the farm for months. Why did he think of it now?

He opened his eyes and saw the trees standing across the river and the dim blue line of the hills. Murray and Alice were sitting together in the shade on the other side of the camp. He could see Murray's white head shining under the dark spread of leaves and the white shape of Alice's face and arms. He wondered what they were talking about at that time of a warm sleepy afternoon. Alice was holding something in her hands which, even at this distance, gave out a flash of colour. From where he sat he could not see what it was. He thought of getting up and joining them, but a movement in the trees above the pool caught his eye. He leaned forward. There it was again, a movement in the leaves. It was a bird, he decided, a kingfisher, a blue-jay, not a game bird and of no interest to him, and then, as he sat back, he saw Eric standing at the edge of the pool.

Eric had lain all afternoon on the strip of sand beside the pool in the full blaze of the sun. As Kay looked at him he turned over, stretching himself, looking up into the sky, and then stood up, supporting himself on his crutch, to throw a stick for his dog. From where Kay sat the stump below the knee and the scarred side could not be seen. The pale hair shone in the sunlight. The naked Eric looked lean and red and splendid. Kay watched the arm go up, the stick turn in an arc far out across the water and the dog flash from the shade of the tall grass, then he frowned and turned his head back to the camp.

Philip was standing in the open doorway of his hut with a book under his arm. Kay could see every detail of the tall

§ 46 §

figure in the short-sleeved blue shirt and creased khaki trousers. Philip was looking at the river, his head raised and his eyes narrowed against the light. The long-nosed sallow face wore its calm and pleasant expression but the mouth with its heavy underlip was smiling as if Philip were seeing again a lost friend. Kay felt embarrassed and, for no reason that he knew, ashamed. He sat still in his chair until Philip turned and walked away. Then he told himself that he would take a gun up to the fireline that evening. The green pigeons would be fighting. After all these years he would be rusty and they would give him plenty to think about. He put his hand down to feel if the tin of cigarettes were still there and shut his eyes and fell asleep again.

Philip walked towards the group under the tree. The long sleep under the sweet-smelling thatch roof of his hut had banished his headache. After tea he would take a rod up the river and try a pool or two before the evening rise. Alice looked up and smiled at him.

He saw a very different face from the one that he had seen in the car; now she looked untroubled and extraordinarily young. He put his hand on the back of her chair, waiting for her to look up at him and perhaps to lift her hand to touch his. He saw the brown lashes lift and knew that in a moment they would fall again to cover that slanting sly-child look. As he moved away from her chair he saw the feather in her hand.

"Where did you find that?" he said, bending down to take it from her. "Let me see."

"Don't touch it," she said, holding it out of his reach. "No one must touch it. It's mine. Murray gave it to me. But you can take a good look at it. Have you ever seen such colours, such a great blue brilliant eye?"

She held the feather out, waving it from side to side. The

sunlight slanting through the leaves sent an arch of colour flashing between them.

"Look!" Alice cried. "All the colours in the world are here, the colour of the hills and the river and the sky, and it's soft, as soft and warm as silk." She lifted the feather to her lips and shut her eyes.

Murray smiled, but Philip said sharply, "Don't be silly, Alice. A peacock's feather is unlucky. I should leave it alone if I were you."

CHAPTER II

A few hundred yards above the camp the river flowed round a small thickly wooded island. Here the river bed was broad and open and an expanse of white sand lay on each side of the stream between the high tree-covered banks. Below the island was a long narrow pool that ended in a rapid. Clumps of tall silver-headed grass grew here, rising out of the sand at the edge of the water.

The sun was going down into a dark sea of trees and sand and sky were washed by the same pink flood. The little figures moving by the river under the huge sunset sky were slowly making their way back to the camp; the birds flapping home across the evening glow saw them there, strange and dark and sudden on the sand.

Kay and Sangla were hurrying across a clearing in the trees towards the river. In a few moments they would emerge on the bank above the pool where Alice was fishing. As she cast down stream below the island she was in sight of the camp and the blue smoke rising from the evening fire; Manoo sat on the stones behind her holding Philip's rod. Murray stood with his shotgun under his arm half way across the expanse of sand, waiting for the others to catch up with him. Eric and Philip, as they walked, examined the tracks on the sand where the delicate pointed tracery of the water-birds overlaid the impressions left by jackal, deer, otter and fishing-cat.

"Time that we were back," Murray said. "The sun will be down in a moment. Alice caught a baril, which she will call a snow trout, in the island pool. As usual, she put it back but now there's no stopping her. She means to cover every yard of water back to camp. She won't be able to see the line much longer."

"Did you see where a tiger crossed above the island, Murray?" Eric said. "The night before last, I should say."

"The island would be a good place for him to lie up in in the day," said Philip. "I suppose all these elephant tracks are made by our own elephants?"

"All except these large ones, a little larger than those made by Akbar. These were made by the old Ganesh who crosses the river almost at the same point nearly every night."

As they approached the dark line of trees that marked the river bend above the camp, the sun sent its last strong rays across the sky. Sky and sand flamed with colour and the hills took on a deep strong blue. The tide of colour spread before them across the sand, flooding pool and overhanging trees and the figures of Alice and Manoo in the same steady, unreal gold light. Alice had seen them coming towards her but, as she waved to them, there was a sudden commotion in the trees, a crackling and rustling of branches and disturbed leaves. They saw Manoo jump to his feet. Something rose with a loud discordant cry from the undergrowth into the air above the pool, streamed across the open space and plummeted into the trees again.

§ 49 §

The three men saw it go, a dark shape trailing a comet-like plume of colour, but their eyes were on the trees above the pool where the long grass was moving.

"Look out, Alice. Run!" Murray shouted, but she stood transfixed holding her rod with the line trailing in the slack water, looking up into the sky. As they ran to her, the grass and the hanging branches parted and Kay stood on the bank looking down at them, his gun in his hands, Sangla close behind him.

"What the hell are you doing there?" Murray shouted as they reached the pool. "Crashing about like a buffalo, frightening Alice out of her wits."

"Oh, Murray," Alice cried. "Did you see him? A huge peacock, he passed straight over my head."

As she reeled her line in she said, "What's the matter? I knew that it was Kay. We heard his shots some time ago and Manoo says that there's a path, a short-cut from the road to the camp, somewhere in there."

Kay slid down the bank and waded across the end of the pool towards them. His usually neat person was dishevelled; there was a tear across the shoulder of his khaki shirt and leaves and twigs clung to his hair. Behind him Sangla, carrying a heavy game bag and holding the black dog on a chain, was grinning broadly.

"That bird led me a dance," Kay said. "I spotted him as we started to the camp. Ebon and I had got three brace of greener, not bad considering how out of practice we both are, when there he was, skulking with his hens at the edge of the trees. He ran like a racehorse."

"You were going to shoot him, shoot that peacock? You horrible little man."

"The jungle is full of peacock, Alice," Kay said. "There's nothing to stop me shooting them if I like. They are very good

§ 50 §

eating, as we all know. But I was only trying to get a good look at this particular bird. Sangla says that it and its harem have been hanging round the outskirts of the camp for days."

"I don't believe you," Alice said. "I know that look in your eye."

"Kay knows that I won't have anything shot near the camp," Murray said. "And he knows that I would rather he didn't shoot a peacock at all. Apart from anything else, there are several Hindus in the camp and to them the bird is sacred. I don't want Manoo upset, you all know what he can be like."

"In some parts of India the peacock is as sacred as the cow," Eric said. "Near Muttra, for instance, you would be in serious trouble, Kay, if you even killed one by mistake. I have never seen any point myself in destroying anything so harmless and so easy."

"Easy!" Kay said. "I should like to see your tigers run as fast. Don't look at me like that, Alice. I'm not going to touch your precious bird."

"That's what he is," Alice said. "Precious and sacred. The jungle is full of other targets for you. Can't you leave anything alone, Kay?"

"While you try to inveigle him into the camp," Kay said. "I can see you laying a trail of dried peas to entice him away from his hens. Perhaps you would like to make him a neat silk collar and lead?"

"That's an idiotic thing to say, Kay," Eric said angrily. "Alice only means that from now on that bird will be something special, a mascot for us."

"A symbol surely?" Philip said. "No, the familiar of this place."

"I didn't mean anything," Alice said. "Only that it was too beautiful to die."

§ 51 §

"That will do," Murray said. "I don't want to stand here all night. From now on all peacock are taboo."

As they walked on, Philip said suddenly, "Look back at the hills. What an amazing colour they are, peacock blue, peacock colours. Alice is right, why should such colour die?"

But the colour was already fading from the hills and from the sky. Now the sand round them was grey and under the trees the pool was dark. The evening breeze came swiftly down the river.

"How cold it suddenly is," Alice said. "Fresh and cold and clean. What an evening! I forgive you Kay, I could forgive anyone almost anything on an evening like this. Look, the stars are coming out already. I'm cold without a coat, I'm freezing. Come on, let's run back to the camp, let's all run home."

Holding Kay's hand she held her other hand out to Eric and the three of them started across the sand, Eric hobbling grotesquely but keeping up with them.

Murray and Philip followed more slowly with Manoo and Sangla. They watched the dark figures disappearing across the sand, and heard their laughter and the dog's excited barking. Above the trees and the lights of the camp the new moon shone in a sky that was still faintly coloured by the sunset.

CHAPTER III

THE first supper in the camp was ready. The lamps were lit, the cloth was laid under the gold thatch of the dining-hut. From the camp fire where the flames were leaping, the waiting table looked as if it were on a stage, a small floodlit stage set high above the river and hung with the dark curtains of the night. To step from the warm flickering anonymous light and dark of the fire circle into the cold limits of Murray's two petrol lamps was like stepping suddenly behind footlights.

"Why must we have those lamps, Murray?" Alice said. "After the fire their light is so hard and white."

"I like to see what I'm eating. The bones in a mahseer are forked and sharp and very dangerous."

"I believe that you are more frightened of a fish bone in the throat than of anything else in the jungle."

"Murray is quite right," Eric said. "We all know that even a minor accident is awkward in camp, so far from anywhere. You needn't mind a bright light, Alice."

"But Murray is a doctor even if he tries to forget it while he's here."

"Do you remember the camp on the Baumuti where Kay fell out of a machan and broke his arm?" Philip said. "Murray was so furious that he could hardly bring himself to set it."

"I remember only too well," Kay said. "And yet he will spend hours cleaning out an elephant's abscess, a nasty dangerous job if you like."

"There's a doctor babu or, rather, a compounder, at Hokgaon," said Murray. "I warn you, any accident or illness in this camp will be dealt with by him."

"If we chanced to fall couldn't you include us poor human beings with your sparrows, Murray?"

Kay laughed, and Murray said, "Sit down, sit down, all of you. Kancha is waiting with the soup, sit here, by me, Alice."

The chairs were set in a semi-circle round three sides of the table so that no one sat with his back to the river. As they took their places Philip said, "There's one chair too many."

Murray looked round the table suspiciously. "What, again?" he said. "Kancha must have forgotten how to count. Put it outside, Philip. We mustn't sit down with an empty chair."

"Poor chair, outside by itself in the cold," said Alice. "Put it with the others by the fire. It won't be noticed there."

"What will you say next, Alice?"

"Anything that comes into my head, however foolish, Kay. I'm sorry for anyone who isn't sitting here with us to-night. Think of them all, poor things, outside the forest. They don't even know what it's like to be here."

"The whole point of this place is that no one else is here."

"There's plenty of room for everyone in the forest."

"There would soon be no forest," Murray said. "Kay is right. Perhaps we are too many as it is. We must be careful."

"Careful? What of? What should we do?"

"Make as little disturbance as possible."

"Perhaps you would like us to disguise ourselves with leaves?"

"Why not put out those lamps for a start?" Alice said. "They must be telling everything for miles that we are here."

"You had better put them out, Murray," said Kay. "We will get no peace until you do."

"Very well, Alice, we will compromise. Let me finish this fish and then Kancha can change these for the hanging oil lamp. But now that we are here and have staked our claim, even if it's a temporary one, it's just as well to let the forest know exactly where we are. The forest doesn't want trouble any more than we do. There's an elephant who keeps a nightly eye on our doings. This camp is built across an old elephant path, and we don't want him or any of his relations to assert their old right of way."

§ 54 §

The Camp

"Why build the camp just here?" asked Kay. "Every camp that I have ever heard of seems to be built across an elephant path. It seems odd to me."

Murray smiled. "True enough," he said. "But these paths run along the banks of most rivers here. It's impossible to avoid them. This one hasn't been used for years."

"Have you seen this elephant?" Alice asked.

"I saw him the first evening that I came here and I have heard him several times. I don't suppose that you will get a glimpse of him but, if you do, give him a wide berth. He's a solitary old bull and his temper is probably uncertain. There are many tall stories told about him and some of them are true."

"Tell them to us, Murray."

The tablecloth was white checked with blue that in the soft lamplight looked grey. The light fell from the gold ceiling, spilling over heads and shoulders onto the cloth, leaving deep and sudden shadows. Murray sat at the centre of the table facing the river. His white head shone as if it wore a halo. He lifted his hand as if to focus their attention.

Philip Tallent was leaning back in his chair at the end of the table watching the semi-circle of faces. He was thinking that the group sitting in the lamplight would make a fine picture. He held up, as he often did, an imaginary frame, setting it over what he saw, shifting it a little from side to side over the subject until he saw what he wanted to see. It was a long time since the day when he had realised that he would never be painter, that, work as he might, his hand would never make what his eyes saw so clearly. At once he had left his schools and studio to return to his father's dark, comfortable, London house, to the city office of old-established tea-merchants, to his golf and fishing at week ends. He almost forgot his brief rebellion, as he took up the life that

§ 55 §

he knew he was fitted for contentedly enough. He was glad when, a few years later, he went out to the Calcutta office of his firm; in another country there were new combinations of colour, deeper shadows, another light. His secret frame went with him everywhere. He would bring it out, hold it up, and there was the perfect picture, the complete painting living for him in the medium that at the time seemed most suitable. He would tell himself that he had the best of it; the satisfaction without the struggle, birth at the moment of conception, and no chance at all of a failure, nothing unhappily imperfect left to confront him. No one suspected his secret satisfaction. He was a busy, prosperous, middle-aged business man. No one, not even Alice, knew what he was at when he sat back in his chair, half closing his eyes, smiling his quiet, polite smile. This time he saw a dark painting, a rich dark oil in a gold frame, a First Supper. There it was: the long line of the table and the hanging cloth disappearing into blue shadow, the sharp details of glass and bowl and fruit and bottle, the line of seated figures. Murray's crimson scarf was balanced by the yellow of Eric's hair. His own dark green coat gave warmth and colour to the greys and browns. Kay's head was a needed note of black, and Alice's face repeated the white of the tablecloth in an interesting three-cornered shape. But there was something wrong about this picture. The composition was pyramidical, two figures on each side of the central figure that was Murray. Perhaps it was too even, too rigid. Something was missing. Perhaps a critical eye, watching from the surrounding darkness, far enough away to see the balance of light and shade, the lines reaching in from the gold frame over head and shoulder to the focus point of Murray's uplifted hand, would feel the need to add another shape, another figure, perhaps here, between Alice and himself.

The Camp

Philip moved his picture frame uneasily, enclosing his wife's head, separating it until it was complete in itself, a detail taken from the larger picture. Here was a portrait of a brown-haired woman with a white face, rather too short for beauty, turned a little away from him to show the shadow in the slightly hollowed cheek. It was an elusive face, and indefinable. He tried to draw an outline round it, a strong gold line that would fix it once and for all in the frame for him. Here was Alice Margaret Tallent, the only daughter of one of his father's friends, whom he had watched growing up in the quiet, old-fashioned country house. She had been an enchanting child and before she was fifteen he had made up his mind, quietly, purposefully, and secretly, as he did everything, that he would marry her. He had waited until she was eighteen but perhaps it would have been wiser to wait a little longer. A young tree that is carefully pruned and watched and cherished, shapes and flowers and fruits in a satisfactory manner but sometimes puts out sudden unexpected shoots and deep roots underground. Philip found it impossible to draw a line round Alice; her face wavered and changed as he looked at it and now he could not see it at all. It is a mistake to look too long and closely at one point in a picture; the way to see it clearly is to stand some way off. But now Murray lowered his hand, heads were turned, the lamp swung, and the shadows shifted on the cloth. Kancha was beside him holding out a dish. Philip picked up his knife and fork and heard their voices again.

Alice was saying, "Look at us, tents, huts, tablecloths, glasses, sherry. It's absurd, all wrong here, unnatural. We would enjoy it even more without all this paraphernalia."

"There's no sense in being uncomfortable if you needn't be," Kay said. "We are not here because we have to be here. Contrast is everything, hot after cold, soft after hard, beer in a desert."

"Our being here at all is unnatural," Murray said. "This is not our country, for that matter the jungle is no man's country. We are an invasion, unwanted and unnecessary to the forest. If we meant to stay as the Santals and the Nepali settlers try to do the fight would be on, no compromise would be possible, it would have to be the forest or us. As it is we are visitors, doubly strangers here. As long as we behave ourselves and break no rules it doesn't matter what we do. A little more or less makes no difference. We might as well have our hot baths and our baggage, I my sherry, Kay his beer. We are here on sufferance anyway."

Eric looked up as if he would protest but Alice said, "On sufferance? I don't like the sound of that."

Now the small lit space under the gold roof was more like a stage than a picture. On it they moved self-consciously. Their voices sounded shrill and their laughter unconvincing. This was not surprising considering the size of the auditorium before them. The lights could be seen from a long way off, from the darkness in the woods on the other side of the river.

"I feel exposed sitting up here under the lamp," Alice said uneasily. "I feel as if I were on show."

"That's only fair," Kay said. "We came here to stare at the animals, to spy on them and their ways and habits. It's only right that they should do the same to us. It's always unnerving to be seen and not to see."

"Why should we be fascinated by the thought of something wild and different from ourselves roaming about out there?" Philip asked.

"If you were not sophisticated civilised people, if you were at the opposite end of the human pole, say a member

§ 58 §

of one of these jungle tribes, you would not be fascinated," Murray said, "you would be terrified or hungry or indifferent."

"All human beings like to look at animals," Eric said. "Think of the way the town dwellers flock to the zoos. Why do they press their faces against the bars? Is it to feel the thrill of an old fear?"

"Perhaps they are envious of something that they have lost," Philip said slowly.

"Lost?" Eric said.

"If you come to think of it," Murray said, "there's no mention of the animals leaving Eden. Man went alone."

"This is too deep for me," Kay said. "Eric is looking puzzled and Alice isn't listening to us. What's the matter Alice?"

From the dining-hut nothing of the outside world could be seen. The lamplight was a gold film between them and the darkness which, as the thin moon disappeared, grew more profound round the camp. Alice lifted her head and peered uneasily across the table.

"I'm sure that there's something watching us," she said. "Can't you feel it? There is something out there."

"It's the forest that you feel there, Alice," Murray said. "You always said that at night the trees come closer. Most probably there is nothing moving in miles, but that old elephant may be somewhere about."

"I hope that he doesn't choose tonight to look at us more closely," Eric said. "I have never been so sleepy."

"That's the fresh air," Alice said seriously. "It's blowing straight at us from the hills. I'm sure that I can smell the snows."

"*Smell* the snows! What does a snow peak smell of, Alice?"

§ 59 §

The Peacock

"A great pile of frozen lilies, I should think, with a touch of something sharp and clean, menthol, perhaps."

Murray laughed. "It's no use Kay. Alice always has an answer. You should know her by now."

Kay looked down the table. Until that moment the group gathered there had been a united one, bathed in the same gold light and joined by the same carefree sense of escape, as children are, sitting in the compartment of the train that is taking them further and further away from school. Now a new and less innocent air stirred among them. Murray, looking at Kay, sensed it and held up his hand.

But Kay looked blandly from face to face and said, "Do I know Alice? Seven years is a long time. How do I know what she has been up to all these years?"

Alice looked at him. "I wonder what you think you mean by that," she said. "You always were a mischievous monkey, a trouble-maker. The years haven't changed you, whatever they have done to the rest of us."

Murray said, "Gently, Alice. Kay doesn't mean anything."

"Perhaps you had better explain yourself, Kay," Eric said from his end of the table.

"Do any of us know each other?" Kay said, tilting his chair back and looking up at the straw roof. "Do we know what each of us is capable of doing in an emergency or if pressed too hard? I only picked on Alice because she is a woman and so even more incalculable. I wouldn't trust her a yard myself."

Alice leaned forward, her hands on the table, and her face in the strong light of the lamp. "Why are you staring at me like that, Kay?" she said. "Now you are all staring at me. Philip, are you going to sit calmly there and not say a word?"

Philip only smiled, looking down at the glass in his hand.

After a moment Eric said loudly, "You mean to be offensive Kay. Leave Alice out of this, do you hear?" He pushed his chair back.

Murray's face was red with anger under his white comb of hair. "Be quiet, all of you," he said. "I won't have an ugly clamour here. Leave each other alone. Why can't you give yourselves a chance?"

They turned surprised faces towards him and he said more gently: "Talk, talk, the world resounds with talking. It's dangerous, it leads to trouble. The human voice has become formidable, something to be dreaded. You can drive that great rattling truck of mine through the forest and the deer hardly bother to move off the road, but say a few words, just loud enough to be heard, and they are off so fast that you can't see them go. There's something wrong about that, something sad."

For a moment no one spoke and the sound of the river came loudly to them from the darkness. Then Alice said, "We won't do it again. We won't spoil it. Oh, Murray, we will be good."

But if clamour there had been it was soon caught and muffled by the trees. From the borders of the camp or across the river the voices could not be heard. Not a leaf was moved or a grass disturbed. A close circle held the group of human beings. Only the dog, lying like a black shadow under the table, moved restlessly and, rising to his feet, touched Eric on the knee. No dog is free; he lives uneasily within the fringes of the circle.

§ 61 §

Supper was over. The circle was broken. It moved and formed again round the fire. The light went out in the dining-hut and the firelight shone alone. The fire dominated the camp.

CHAPTER IV

THAT night the flames were magnificent. They flew far into the black sky from their burning nest of logs and branches and were reflected in the black water of the pool.

The breeze blew down the river and the smoke went with it, veering a little but streaming away from the camp and the half circle of chairs. The heat was intense; it reached far out beyond the fire's smouldering fringe of white wood ash. The chairs were moved back from the fire and moved again, but the flickering heat and the strong, uncertain red flame light followed them and discovered a hand, a lifted face, a glass. The shadows moved too, wavering largely over the dim grass roofs of the huts, over the trees, and settling low down on the ground. It was difficult in the exchange of light and shade to recognise anyone. Murray's head shone on the right where he sat talking over the plans for the next day in a low voice with Manoo, Sangla, and the mahouts, but the others for the moment were indistinguishable, seen only as shapes and shadows, an outstretched hand, a gleam of firelight on a shoe, a gleam of colour, and no one could have said for certain how many sat there. Five, six, seven? It was impossible to say. The wind changed slightly, the smoke shifted, the shadows moved, and for a second Alice's face was seen, dyed gold by the firelight but distinct on the darkness.

Whoever it was who sat beside her at the edge of the circle was lost in shadows. It might have been Eric, it might have been anyone; it might even have been an empty chair.

Through the sound of the fire, the hissing and singing of the flames, remoter sounds were now heard. From the darkness a voice was calling.

"What is that?"

"Only an owl. We shall hear them all night. They sound like lost souls calling."

"Listen, that's a deer, yes, a barking-deer calling down the river. Did you hear that sambhur? He sounded like a bell ringing at sea."

"It's beginning."

"Yes. There go the jackals, but we may hear nothing much else tonight."

"I should like to hear a tiger."

"Murray heard a tiger a few nights ago, Alice, quite close in the forest across the river."

"We saw his tracks this afternoon."

"We may hear him again, sooner or later. This has always been a great place for tigers and the villagers say that there have never been so many about."

"I want to hear one now, this minute. Then I should know that we really were here."

Of all the sounds heard in the jungle the tiger's shattering roar echoing across the intervening miles of dark trees is the wildest, the fiercest, most the jungle's own. Made in anger or more often in love, it affirms the remoteness of the forest. Then the stars begin their fierce cold dance in the black depths of the sky and the branches take on fantastic shapes. Fear runs swiftly through the forest as somewhere, perhaps by the starlit sands of the river, death waits. But that night, if a tiger spoke it was too far off to be heard in the camp. Towards morning Sangla, rousing from his light sleep, was to think that he heard the slow sawing sound that only a leopard makes, but the sounds were not repeated and he soon fell asleep again. The owls were to call all night from tree to tree and an otter to splash in the river, but these familiar sounds would disturb nobody.

Murray pulled his chair closer to the fire while behind him the mahouts, wrapping their blankets round their shoulders, disappeared into the darkness and Manoo and Sangla returned together to their tent.

"Well, that's settled," he said. "Everything is all set for to-morrow."

He looked round the half circle of chairs and held his hands out to the red warmth. "Last night a peacock shrieked on the other side of the river after dark. I have never heard one call so late. I wonder if it was that big cock that we saw this afternoon."

"I expect so," Alice said. "Yes, it must have been. I'm too sleepy to hear anything more tonight. It's time we went to bed."

But no one wanted to move from the circle of light and heat. The cold darkness pressed against the back of their chairs; they could feel it there, waiting, and they turned up the collars of their coats and sank lower in their chairs. No one spoke and anyone watching from the darkness might have thought that they slept where they were. The flames sank lower. The dog lay relaxed and at ease in the warm fringe of ash. Quiet fell with the night dew over the camp. Now it might have seemed that the different shapes and shadows had lost their identity, had become one, had at last escaped, and that no one sat there. But a log, burnt through, fell with a crash. The gold sparks soared upwards, and with them the separate and secret thoughts went twisting and turning.

From the centre of the fire, from some secret core of wood, a new tall flame shot up, a gaseous flame of blue and green that burnt with a sharp sound. For a moment it was there before their eyes and when it went it was as if a spell that had kept them sitting there were broken.

"Time to make a move," said Murray. "The dew is soaking."

Philip was the last to leave. He and Murray stood with their backs to the river, looking down at the smouldering fire. The river sounded loudly behind them and the lights in the huts went out one by one until there was only one light showing. Murray looked at Philip. The long face was reddened by the firelight and made unfamiliar by heavy shifting shadows.

"Well, Philip?" he said.

Philip looked up. "Here we all are once again, Murray. Seems extraordinary, doesn't it, after all that has happened?"

"You look as if a quiet time would do you good. Anything specially wrong?"

"Who isn't worried these days? Nothing is easy for anyone. It's difficult to know what to do for the best, difficult to see anything clearly."

"Does that apply to personal problems too?"

"I suppose so. You know, Murray, the only way to see anything clearly, as it is, in proper proportion, is to stand well away from it. I had forgotten that there was anywhere left in the world so far from everything."

"A quiet time in the forest? Pity that every problem can't be settled so easily. You all seem to have great confidence in this place, to be counting on too much. That seems to me to be dangerous, it might lead to trouble."

Philip smiled. "But we are not trying to found a new Utopia, Murray. We are only here on holiday. We only ask to escape for a few weeks. Surely we might manage that safely?"

"Why not?" Murray said at once. "Here we are, five people with the best intentions, and here is the forest, exactly as it has always been. Why not, indeed?"

"Give me a few days on the river. That's all I need."

"A few days?" Murray said. "We have a month. Plenty of time. Time to catch all the fish we want, time to see all that is here to be seen. We will make a good start to-morrow. Now what you need is a good night's rest, my friend. Say goodnight to Alice for me. She slipped away so quietly that I didn't see her go."

He watched Philip walk away to the light in the big hut. Then he bent down and kicked the sprawling logs together until the sparks flew, and half seized, half dragged a dead tree trunk from the waiting pile and heaved it on to the heart of the fire. The flames rose sullenly and, in their light, he walked up and down at the edge of the pool with his hands in his pockets and his head bent. His lips moved as if he were still asking a question.

There was no sound from the camp where a single lantern burned palely before the dark huts. As the flames sank down he stood still, looking first at the black steadily rushing river and then up at the sky.

The sky above the crouching black line of the trees was a fan, a spread of deep wild blue, eyed gorgeously with stars.

Part Three

The Forest

The Forest

CHAPTER I

In a forest camp it is not only the exciting moments
that are important. Such moments are rare. It is possible to
live for days and weeks, even for months, in the jungle as
monotonously and peacefully as in any country village. The
huge emptiness of the forest is soon felt and accepted. Behind the façade of trees across the river are trees and trees
again, the same dense tangle of creeper and root, leaf and
grass, repeated indefinitely. The forest holds a small, pulsat-
ing, humming life that is always there, but to expect to see
any particular and desired shape in this immensity would
be like searching for a needle in a hayfield. Perhaps in the
whole month that they were to spend in the forest, no one
in the camp would see any animal larger than a monkey, or
fiercer than a squirrel or a bird. If long monotonous hours
on the back of one of the camp elephants, or of patient
watching from a platform in a tree, or following on foot the

course of a river bed, were rewarded by a glimpse of something moving or a recognised flash of colour, the first feeling would be one of incredulity. The forest was always there, listening and waiting, and from it anything could emerge. Meanwhile, here was the camp with its minutes and hours of every day. Perhaps it was the huge indifference of the surrounding forest that made every moment spent in the camp seem precious and important, and set apart from the moments of other days.

The first days passed slowly and evenly for everyone.

Murray woke every morning to see the sunlight shining through the canvas of his tent. He would turn over in bed to look at the watch on the box beside him, and then, putting the mosquito net up, lie a little longer, listening to the river. The day was only a step away through the open tent flaps and, as he lay, he would hear the birds calling in the trees across the river and the camp stirring as the day began.

His tent was neat, with everything in its own place. It is impossible for an untidy person to live comfortably in a tent but, for those who know how to set about it, there is no better place in which to live. A tent is intimate as no room can be, almost like a second skin, and, like a skin, sensitive and appreciative of every breath of the outside world. It shelters and ensures privacy, keeps the body warm and dry, but does not encroach as a house does and, in a tent, belongings must be few and simple. Murray's spare sweaters, socks and shirts, hung from a cord that went from tent pole to tent pole well above his head. His books and papers were stowed away in pockets in the inner walls of the tent. His thick coat served as a second pillow, and his shaving and washing things were kept in his enamel basin that had a leather travelling cover. In this tent was a camp bed, a small camp chair, a box that served as a table, Murray's small medicine chest, his gun cases and cartridge bags. On the floor a rug was stretched over a thin layer of straw. Some people think that straw brings snakes into a camp, but Murray enjoyed the fresh straw smell and had little fear of snakes.

The sleeping huts had a fresh grass smell of their own. Their woven matting walls made them cooler than a tent could be and from their open doorways, over which a curtain could be drawn, a wide view of the river and the hills could be seen. Alice had arranged her side of the big hut with care. Her travelling mirror stood on the wooden shelf that Murray had made for her, above her jars of powder and face creams. On the folding table beside her bed were her flashlight, a candlestick and a box of matches, a book, her travelling clock with a luminous dial, and a tube of anti-mosquito cream. Alice knew that it is of the first importance that a camp bed should be as comfortable as possible, with as many blankets under you as on top. She never used sheets in camp where it is difficult to keep them clean but slept between soft cotton quilts. Like Murray, she had hung Philip's and her own spare clothing on strings stretched from wall to wall under the straw ceiling but, unlike Murray, she never left her shoes to stand on the ground but arranged them carefully on top of the suitcase under her bed. Once, in her first camp, she had found a snake curled up in her shoe; it was a harmless grass snake, as Philip had pointed out, but, fourteen years later, Alice still carefully shook each shoe before putting it on.

Insects had no terrors for Alice, which was lucky, because there are insects in every camp. At night moths fly into the candle, and by day spiders haunt the matting walls and ants pass and repass across the floors and invade every open tin and glass. More exotic creatures may be found in unexpected places: praying mantis, centipedes, even scorpions.

§ 71 §

Insects must be taken for granted in a jungle camp, and pre-
cautions against flies and mosquitoes cannot be relaxed for
a day. When evening comes, long sleeves and mosquito boots
should be worn, and at night the white film of the mosquito
net shrouds every camp bed. Every camp has its moments of
discomfort, and there will be times when the food seems
dull, the drinks warm, the beds hard; there will be moments
of heat, and dust and even of boredom when, while they last,
it will seem foolish to be there.

Every morning, when the business of getting up and
dressing was over, they would stand together round the still
smouldering camp fire, waiting for Kancha to tell them that
breakfast was ready. Alice thought this one of the best moments of the day. The morning would be cold and fresh,
making them shiver a little and hold their hands out to the
warmth. A thin mist rose from the river and drifted away
between the trees. A strong smell of coffee and woodsmoke
pervaded the camp, and the hills above the trees were a deep
and shining blue.

On most mornings after breakfast, Alice made a loaf of
soda bread and baked it in a covered saucepan placed deep
in the hot ash of the camp fire and covered with red-hot
wood embers. No other bread tasted as good as this did. For
that matter, any food eaten in camp has a flavour of its own,
often, it must be admitted, tinged with woodsmoke, but
acceptable and recognised. Murray's old cook, Kristo Samal,
was a good camp cook; which is to say that, with a frying
pan and a few handleless saucepans, his precious sheet of
iron and a woodfire made in a hole in the ground, and his
wooden box in which he kept a strange collection of condi-
ments, spices and old spoons and bits of wire, he could pro-
duce a hot and eatable meal under any conditions. He knew

the way to take the bones out of a mahseer, the way to cook barking-deer or wild-pig chops, and all there was to know about the cooking of game-birds. The making of puddings he despised, and Alice knew better than to advise him. Even Murray left him to organise the cook tent as he thought best, to order the other servants about, and to obtain eggs and fresh milk for the camp by means known only to himself.

In the evening they returned to the camp from the river or the forest, hot and tired, wet or dusty, to fling themselves down in the chairs on the bank above the river, but the hours between breakfast and evening did not concern the camp. For a short time in the morning the bedding was aired in the sunlight, Kancha moved from hut to hut, shaking a duster, the sweeper, a thin legged boy in a khaki shirt, raised a cloud of dust with his brush, and the water carrier moved between the river and the camp with his tins. The pots and saucepans were carried down onto the stones and scrubbed with sand. Perhaps Kancha and Jetha, naked to the waist, their khaki coats discarded, would squat together at the edge of the water, washing out a pile of socks, while the smoke from their cigarettes rose into the air, and the river carried the soapsuds away. But these activities would soon be over and the camp would drowse under the mid-day sun as the smell of cooking curry rose into the warm air. Then the old, heavy fish, who lived below the bank, rose slowly to the surface and moved out to sun himself in the shallows. Soon the afternoon peace would settle over the camp.

Alice sometimes spent the whole day in the camp, sitting alone on the bank above the river, or lying on her bed under the trees, or mooning about at the edge of the river by herself. She would bend down to pick a coloured stone out of the water, or she would stand still to watch the trees on the opposite bank for minutes on end. No one asked her what she did by herself in the camp and, if they had, she could not have told them, but these days, during the first part of their time in the camp, were necessary to her.

The raking and re-lighting of the camp fire was the signal that the evening had come. Perhaps one of the camp elephants would walk heavily through the camp, carrying a tree trunk which would form the base of the piled logs and branches. The blue smoke eddied round the camp until, with the evening, the gorge breeze blew steadily, and the sound of Kancha setting out the tea cups, and the sound of the water carrier filling the baths was heard.

The time between the lighting of the fire and sunset was perhaps the busiest time of the day. Then the fish caught that day were weighed and noted in Murray's game book, the shot deer was skinned and dismembered behind the cook tent, the evening fires were lit, and wet shoes and clothes hung out to dry before the night dew fell. This was the time when rifles and shot guns were cleaned and oiled, rods wiped and laid horizontally under the eaves of the dining-hut, casts carefully coiled and put away between damp flannel in the cast boxes. Perhaps a late tea would be drunk and eaten round the fire and, if the day had been long, Murray would take out his silver flask and add a little rum to everyone's cup. It was pleasant to lie back in a chair, with muddied and wet legs stretched out to the fire, to hold a hot steaming cup, while, in the camp, the first lamps were lit and in the sky above the trees and the river the evening star appeared.

After baths were safely accomplished in the circular bathroom where, perhaps, a damp smoking torch had been left to drive the sandflies away, and clean clothes had been put on by the dim light of a lantern in tent and hut, came the

culminating moment of the day when they met again round
the fire to drink their first drink before supper was ready,
under a sky now thick with all the stars.

At night the camp slept peacefully between its black
trees, the light of the fire shone in the river and was seen
from a long way off. Alice liked to wake once in the night to
listen to the river running close to the hut door, perhaps to
hear an owl call, to realise for a glad moment where she was,
before she fell asleep again.

The days and the nights passed, and the camp settled
into the forest.

CHAPTER II

IT was the fourteenth dawn of their time in the camp
and still dark when Murray's two elephants swung one behind the other down the forest road. They moved like two
great ships through the darkness and their passengers, still
half asleep, might easily have thought themselves to be in a
boat breasting the black swells of the sea.

Above their heads, following the course of the road, a
narrow ribbon of stars was unwinding. It was pleasant to
travel through the night down the smooth road whose disturbed dust rose to their nostrils, piloted by the stars, their
bodies swinging and rising, swinging and rising. There was
nothing to be seen in the darkness except the black passing
branches against the stars and the faint shapes of the mahouts
who sat directly on the creased grey necks, their feet in rope
stirrups, their knees under the huge waving ears, their
hands, holding the hooked steel goads, resting on the grey

domed skulls. The four passengers, two to each elephant, might each have been making the journey alone through the darkness, borne silently along by the great shapes under them. This progress through the night could not have been called riding; it was too impersonal, too remote a contact. Under them they could feel nothing except the cushion, the ropes, and the rough sacking of the pad, and there was only that lift and fall, that sense of something enormous and powerful thrusting beneath them, to tell them they were carried by a living thing.

The beam of a flashlight picked out the suddenly grey trunk of a tree and swung across the road onto a shining snake-like coil of creepers. The circle of light fell onto close thick leaves, and moved to show the black mouth of a tunnel through the trees and the shine of black water. There was the sound of splashing. The passengers on the second elephant saw human heads silhouetted against a circle of light, and a huge lurching shape which was suddenly below them. Then it was their turn. They clutched at the ropes of the pad. It was like riding a landslide when the elephant slid its front legs down the steep bank into the stream.

The elephants were turning off the road into the jungle. The direct route to the plains of the game reserve was through the thick forest. This was a difficult journey in the dark but necessary, as the time to see the great sanctuary was at dawn when the animals were still moving on the open plain before the rising sun sent them back to the shelter of the trees.

In the camp, grey early morning light spread slowly from the sky to the river where wreaths of mist were rising, and penetrated the trees, flowing past the tents and the row of quiet huts. Philip woke for the second time and for a moment he did not know why Alice's bed was empty. He found himself standing at the door of their hut, shivering in the grey air, before he remembered that she had gone long before dawn with Murray and the two elephants to the game reserve. At this moment, as the sun was about to rise, the two elephants would be completing their journey through the forest, moving one behind the other, across the grassy dew-wet plain. Murray and Jetha the Nepali boy, Kancha's nephew, would be on Akbar and Alice and Manoo on Sitara. Sangla that day was to go with Eric and Kay to the big village down the road to arrange for beaters for the next day's shoot.

Philip had lain watching Alice as she dressed quickly by the light of her electric torch. He knew that she was shaking with excitement although she had seen the reserve at dawn many times. For a moment he had wished that he were going with her to the great sanctuary whose grassy plains, divided by walls of forest, lay between two rivers close under the foothills. Perhaps it would have been worth-while to give up one day on the river, even the day which he had planned to start at the junction pool, fishing down to unknown water beyond, to sit close behind Alice on the pad, as he had often done, to feel her warm excited hand clutching his knee, to see her expression as she turned her head to signal: "Look, look! There by the clump of thatch grass, there by the thorn tree." When she stood up to pull her sweater on over her head, her shadow had run across his bed and over the wall of the hut. For a moment, more than half asleep, he had dreamed that she was bending over him to ask him to come with her but, when he opened his eyes again, she was tiptoeing to the doorway holding the torch in front of her, and she had not looked back.

The camp looked as if it had been on the bank above the river for a long time. Philip thought that it had a settled

§ 77 §

air, as if they had all lived there for months instead of for two weeks. It was raw no longer but comfortably fixed in the forest. A well-worn path led down to the water and the thatch on the roofs had already mellowed, a row of socks dripped dew from the washing line, the fringe of ash round the still smouldering fire was deep and broad, fishing-rods protruded from the eaves of the dining-hut and someone had left a book face down on the table under the trees. Philip saw Eric's dog emerge from the doorway of the furthest hut, and lift his leg against a favourite chair, and stroll to the edge of the bank where he stood lifting his nose towards the river scents.

"Come for a bathe," Philip said to him, and pulled off his pyjamas and dropped them at the top of the steps that led down to the water. He and the dog plunged in together. The water seized him with an icy grasp. He felt the dog's seal-like body against his; then he was swept away by the current towards the bank and out again. As he struck out diagonally across the pool, freeing his legs from the downward pull of the water, he saw the dog's black head going before him and the sun coming up behind the trees.

Murray and Alice were often to remember that ride through the forest. Years later they were to wake in their beds and see, not the pale shapes of windows across the room or the pale shine of some dressing-table mirror, but ghostly trunks of trees emerging from the darkness as the light grew stronger through the leaves. As the thick forest surrounded them, they were borne along in close leafy darkness. Thorns caught at their feet, leaves brushed their faces, a shower of dew fell onto their heads and shoulders. When a tangle of creeper barred their way, the leading elephant, in answer to a low command from the mahout, checked and swayed. In the thinning darkness the mahout's arm was seen slashing at the branches with his knife while, beneath them, the great feet stamped and pressed. The sound of a knife on wood and the crashing and tearing of branches was heard through the forest, until a path was cleared through the obstruction and on they went, but for the greater part of the journey they moved silently, passing like shadows among the other shadows. The flashlights grew paler as the dawn light grew steadily. Now, all round them, were trunks of large trees and below them bushes crouched like dark sleeping animals on the ground. Avenues of greyness led away down vistas of trees. As the light increased, the silence seemed to grow more profound. There was no sound except the faint sounds of their progress, a faint rustling of disturbed leaves, the almost imperceptible creaking of the pad. Now the ferns growing along the grey branches above their heads were visible. Flowers, still colourless, but wet and sweet, hung at a level with their faces. A wave of sweetness ran through the forest. Did it come from the trees or from the ground?

The trees were thinning against a colourless sky. Manoo touched Alice's foot and pointed, not moving his hand, pointing with his chin. There was nothing to be seen except the dim tangle of undergrowth, the coils of a creeper that hung from the trees onto the ground, and the dark shape of the other elephant disappearing between the trees. Nothing moved, nothing detached itself from the shadows. Alice shook her head but now the mahout, too, had seen it. Something was there under the trees.

A grey shape stood among the grey bushes below them. The line of the neck was seen against a background of lighter leaves. A pointed ear moved once, and now the half-seen shape was clear.

§ 79 §

"Harrin," Manoo breathed. They were looking at a deer.

The deer shape, unconscious of the eyes on it, flicked a tail to show a paler gleam, moved its swan-like neck, stood with its dark slender legs in the dark grass. Manoo and Alice had seen deer countless times, deer alone and deer in herds, but this grey shape seen in the grey quietness of what might have been the first dawn in the forest had no affinity with any other deer. It stood alone at the head of a long vista which stretched back into the dimness where strange shapes moved down grey tunnels into primeval darkness and the arching leaves were shaped like spears.

Manoo touched Alice's foot again. Now they were crossing a more open glade and ahead, beyond the low thorn trees, was only the sky. The two elephants were moving parallel to each other, perhaps fifty yards apart. In the knee-deep grass between them deer were grazing, a small herd of whom the first solitary one might have been an outpost. Anyone leaning down from the elephants might almost have touched the antlered heads as the deer moved unconcernedly away, taking the elephants to be as wild as themselves. They drew together to watch the great swinging grey legs go past, noticing nothing of the silent human load carried above them.

Murray looked down on the grey-brown backs, each about the height of a pony, and counted seven antlered heads, a bachelor party, seven sambhur stags grazing alone together where the long grass of the plain began. He looked across the clearing at the white intent shape of Alice's face under her felt hat. As she turned her head to watch the deer vanish into the tall clumps of grass, he knew that she was thinking that this was a good beginning to the day. A group of young stags is often seen together, but these, lifting their crowned heads in the pearly dawn light, had a fabulous air. They might have been seven young princes of some fairy tale standing proudly together.

The grass was taking on its green and the sky above the heavy forest behind them was a pale fresh blue. Murray turned his head and there was the plain, the great sanctuary, miles upon miles of high waving grass and clumps of trees divided by its streams, bound on three sides by the forest and on the other stretching away to the foothills.

Far out on the plain a herd was moving, a dark herd so far away that he could not see what it was. The boy on the pad behind him was thrusting a pair of binoculars into his hand. For a moment he did not lift them to his eyes. He had seen this sanctuary at sunrise many times but once again the colours of the great plain were rising, were springing up before him, fresh, untouched, new and shining, as they had been at the beginning of the world.

As the elephants, one behind the other, moved through the high grass, the sun came up above the rim of the plain.

CHAPTER III

THE big village ten miles down the road below the camp was stirring before the sun rose. The blue smoke of early fires was escaping under the thatch of the huts and the cattle, herded by small naked boys, were already on their way to graze in the forest. Only three young bullocks and a white goat were left behind. They were destined to be tie-ups, tiger bait, and now, tied to a post in the headman's yard, awaited Sangla's approval. The sun's first rays reddened the beaten earth of the courtyard, touched the still closed flowers on the hibiscus bushes, shone on a brass pot and turned the silver bangles of the headman's wife to gold.

Later in the day, Eric and Kay were to sit on wooden stools in the courtyard, to be offered a drink of warm buffalo milk from the brass pot, to hear the bangles clinking in the shadow of a doorway and to see the wide-open scarlet flowers, while the villagers crowded around them. All round the village were small fields that had been carved out of the jungle. The forest road ran between the houses and into the jungle again. A path led from the centre of the village to the bathing place and the place where the women filled their water pots. The village was beset on all sides by the forest, and why it was there no one seemed to know. Every year when the rice and maize were harvested and threshed and stacked, it was raided by wild elephant intent on the grain store. Every year it lost cattle to tigers. The Dipsiri tiger, known as the big one, was famous in the whole district although, being strictly a game-killer, he was rarely seen, but the village's own tiger, an old and indolent beast who long ago had made this village the centre of his beat, habitually lived on cattle. The villagers grumbled but they did not grudge him his food; for the most part he destroyed the sick and old cattle which their adopted religion forbade them to do. By now he was regarded with tolerance and respect if not with affection. He was a part of their lives, and his effigy, crudely cut in wood and crudely coloured, was displayed on all feast days. Every year he grew bolder, and soon he was to go too far. The rising sun that morning shone on one of the five village ponies, a bay-coloured, shaggy coated animal who, tightly hobbled as it was, grazed on the stubble of the fields too close to the trees. This was its last sunrise. That evening it was to be seized in sight of the village and dragged into the bamboo-filled ravine below the bridge, where it was soon to be revenged by Eric. But now the sun rose, the shining pots and the earthenware pots were carried to the river, and the pony grazed, sounding the bell tied to the blue beads round its neck, while, ten miles away, Eric sat on his bed drinking his morning tea, and Sangla, squatting on the ground, took the heavy rifle from its case and touched the dull barrels lovingly. On one of his red-brown thighs below the khaki shorts was a deep bluish scar. Unlike Eric, his feeling for the striped beasts was simple and plain. At that moment he was thinking, a little anxiously but also with anticipation and pleasure that had in it no question or pain, of the village and of the promised beaters and the arrangements that he hoped to make. It was a long time since there had been a beat within miles of the village, not since that disastrous occasion when a beater had been killed.

That morning Eric had woken from a night of uneasy dreams. His leg, or the place where his leg had been, was paining him. He ran his hand over the red and white stuff of his pyjamas, feeling his thigh which was stiff and tense in every muscle, and wondered if, that day, he would be able to stand the weight of the artificial leg. All the last week he had been unusually careful not to hurry himself, or to try himself too far. Sangla had done all the hard work, the tracking, the tying-up of the bullocks, the building of the machans, the platforms in the trees from which the hunter shoots, and Sangla, unobtrusively and tactfully, had seen that the machans were as roomy and as comfortable as possible for him, who once had shot from the ground, or a hide, or the fork of a tree as he thought fit. All these two last weeks he had had no luck. Was it a question of luck or had he lost his skill and nerve? After nights of sitting up

§ 83 §

over natural kills, or over tie-ups, all he had accounted for was a small leopard. He and Sangla had come across the tracks of the big tiger. Once they had found his kill but, do what they might, they had never come within shot of him, never even glimpsed him. Sangla declared that this tiger was educated, having encountered men several times. He would seldom return to a kill, never glance at a tied-up bullock, and in a beat, he would only turn back on the beaters as he had done before. "When it is his fate to die, he will die," Sangla had said at last. "There are other tigers." But was there now any other tiger for Eric?

He put his cup down on the tin tray that Kancha had placed on a box beside his bed. He usually shaved himself while he sat comfortably on his bed, but today he adjusted the straps of his leg and stood up. As he hung his mirror on a nail high on the tent pole, he saw the river and the waiting forest. He bent down to take the folded towel off the jug of hot water and a stab of pain went through his thigh.

The day before, Sangla had tied three bullock in the forest across the river from the big village. This, of course, was the old village tiger's country but a large tigress had lately been seen here, and where a tigress is several tigers may gather. This was good country for a beat and if a bullock were taken a beat there would be. It was time that his luck changed, time that he ceased to look ridiculous. After an early breakfast he would drive down to the village and not wait for news of a kill to come to him.

The face in the mirror stared back at him. The eyes above the lather were a blank pale blue and, that morning, a little bloodshot and glassy, and a little stupid in their determination. As he passed the razor carefully round the angle of his jaw, he was thinking that it was unfortunate that his leg, as if it knew how much depended on it, had chosen that day to give trouble. It was also unfortunate that he would have Kay Trench with him all morning. Those sharp black eyes would miss nothing, no wince of pain or change of step. Perhaps it was not unfortunate after all. With Sangla there was no need to pretend, Sangla knew, but Kay's presence behind him would act like a goad. To-day, or the next, would be his testing time. He felt it in his bones. If all went well, Alice would be there. He would show her, show the whole camp, show the whole village, that he was Eric Cathcart still.

The trees across the river were shining under the newly risen sun. The sky was a clear strong blue. He stood for a moment with his hands on his narrow hips in the doorway of the hut looking out and breathing in the wild bright air. The morning was a promise.

Kay had been awake for some time. The sounds of the elephant's departure for the reserve had woken him; he was a light sleeper and he had not slept again. Now he lay, looking out through the doorway of his hut and saw the sun coming up behind the trees and heard the splash that Philip made as he met the water and the sound of the dog's glad bark. He was wondering why he had decided to go with Eric in the truck to the village. It might mean a chance at jungle-fowl on the forest road, but the drive would be short and, if he knew his Eric, the day would be long and arduous. He wished that he had gone with Murray and Alice. One or two hours on an elephant were usually more than enough for him, but the sanctuary was always worth seeing and it might have been entertaining to sit behind Alice on the pad; Alice being enthusiastic amused him. He lit a cigarette from the tin on the camp stool beside him and, putting his dressing gown over his shoulders, got up and went out onto the bank. The early mist was disappearing from the river, rising with the sun which now had cleared the trees.

Kay could see the two heads, one black, one brown, crossing the pool above the rapid. As he waved and called out to them, his voice was snatched away and sent back in high raucous calls, like a huge cat's miouing from the trees.

"There goes that damn bird again," he said, staring at the trees as if he would force them to give up the trailing feathers and the flaunting imperial crest.

"Do you hear him?" he said to Sangla, who only nodded impassively as he laid the rifle back in its felt-lined nest.

"Mor," he said. "Peacock," and, as if he thought that Kay did not understand, he spread his arms out, making the shape of a great fan.

CHAPTER IV

WHEN the sun rose, the peacock was crossing a clearing in the trees above the camp. He walked on his large muscular grey legs with their long-spurred hind claw, picking his way slowly across the wet ground. The naked patches of skin behind his eyes looked startlingly white and his eye, which was black and shining and large for his small, poised head, sparkled like a diamond in the sunlight. The sun shone directly onto him and the glade was resplendent with colour. Blue fire streamed from his neck and breast, but there was no one to see him or to watch the four-foot-long eyed train, held a few inches off the ground, emerge from the trees and disappear into the trees again. While he was there no lesser male of his own kind dared to show its colours and his five

brownish wives, each carrying a crest to show that they were
the consorts of a king, kept to the shadows. The small intrud-
ing lizard, rashly exposing itself on a stone, was still unconscious of him.

The peacock must have known that the camp was near;
its sounds and smells penetrated as far as his glade, but for
the time being he ignored it. The forest was his and he was
the forest's Sacred One. Did not the crest that he wore on
his head proclaim him to be the god Indra's favourite bird?
The blue snake-neck darted towards the ground. The inter-
loping lizard disappeared.

CHAPTER V

DIRECTLY he had finished his breakfast, Philip set out.
He had decided that he would not fish down from the
junction pool that day. Below the junction the river was
deep and overhung with thick jungle. Here mahseer of
enormous size were found; he had once caught a fifty-
pounder in the junction pool. The rapids were long and
fierce and it was impossible to cross the river without the
help of a boat or an elephant. It would be wise to use strong
tackle, wire traces, a heavy rod. The true mahseer fisher
covers a great deal of water in one day. He makes a few
casts to each run and rapid and over the likely spots in each
pool, such as under the bank, a rock or a dead tree trunk,
and on he goes; if a taking mahseer is in a pool he will often
take at the first few casts. A strenuous exciting day was not
what Philip needed. To-day he would fish their own more
gentle river, working slowly up-stream, pausing as long as

he liked beside each pool. He would take only a light rod and use a fly-spoon, and perhaps, if fish were rising under the cliff below the island, he would try a fly. Pior, who was to go with him, would carry his 12. bore shotgun and a few lethals. On the right bank the jungle soon thinned and gave way to grass and scattered woodland but on the left it continued solidly and deep in the huge marshy triangle that joined the two rivers to the hills. They all had seen elephant and tiger and leopard tracks on the sand; he must be back near the camp well before sunset, well before the time that Alice, with her fondness for anything highly coloured and for anything that promised excitement, liked to call tiger time. He was not asking for excitement and it was unlikely that he would see anything more formidable all day than a monkey or a deer.

As he waded through the first shallows above the camp with Pior following a few yards behind him, Philip thought for a moment of a smaller river, a slow Hampshire chalk stream that he knew well. There the day would pass evenly and peacefully with no chance of excitement beyond that of rising a good fish. The mid-day sun would not scorch the skin or send sweat trickling and running. There would be midges, but no stinging flies, no dam-dims, those dreaded blister flies, no leeches, and no inch-long thorns or dangerous currents. He looked at the wild blue hills and the thick humming forest. Here there was no possible chance of meeting another human angler, unless it were a naked poacher busy with the red bark that can poison every fish in a pool. Here there were no gamekeepers, no notices warning trespassers away, no sound of distant traffic. Here, as nowhere else, he could be alone to let his thoughts range and flow while his eye and his hand, his whole body, were already at peace, intent only on the water and the end of his line. The day was before him. He meant to take it easily, as it came; to let the hours flow past him as the river was doing, green and gold and clear, with hardly a sound.

To fish, to spend all day beside the water, watching the glassy current, seeing the reflected colours break and flow, is of all pleasures the most pure and serene. There are many kinds of river fishermen who fish for pleasure, from the salmon fisher by his quick green water and the dry-fly expert moving his gossamer cast nearer and nearer to that one dimple on the stream, to the man who sits all day under a tree beside one slow pool. But the urchin playing truant, hurrying to the river in the early morning with his stick and string and glass jar for minnows, knows what they know. To go fishing is to escape, for a while to be for oneself alone.

There is, of course, excitement in fishing, a thrill as fine and strong as a tapered line, but it is not this or the skill of eye and hand or the fighting silver bodies that is the secret. Perhaps the solitary angler, lying all day in the grass above the pool with his rod and lazily bobbing float and his packet of sandwiches, is the true fisherman. The hours flow over him slow and undisturbed, as hours rarely flow.

Philip drew a yard or two of silk line from his reel and, holding it in his left hand, made his cast. The line flowed, shot out, straightened, and checked above the surface and, at the end of the shining gut trace, the half-inch mother-of-pearl fly-spoon fell with a gentle plonk where it was meant to fall. Under the fallen tree below the bank the water ran deep and brown. Here was the home of the stout fighting boka, that black-backed cousin of the true mahseer, Barbus Tor, the long-headed king of Indian fish. Another cast and another, and the line jerked sharply, was pulled twice with a deep slow tug that was unmistakable. Away went the fish across the pool to the remembered shelter of a hidden snag.

As Philip checked the first rush and the battle began, he remembered another and smaller pool on the headwaters of the river that he was fishing now. It was fourteen years since he and Alice, whom he had married two weeks before, had stood beside that pool. It was their third evening in camp and they had wandered down the river with the idea of his giving her a first fishing lesson. He had been astonished when, in that shallow, sunny pool, he had hooked a fish. Alice had been wildly excited. For some reason that fish, and no other, had been suddenly important to her. She had waded in with his landing net and when at last, disregarding his shouted instructions, scooping at the water, hitting his line, she had managed to net the fish, she splashed back across the pool to him flushed and laughing.

Together they had knelt on the stones with the still hooked fish between them, a small fish it had been, weighing not much more than a pound. "It's ours," Alice had said, and then, putting her small wet hand on his: "Put it back." Together they had watched it slip into the water, pause a moment uncertainly, and then flash away with a last swerve and flick of its tail.

Why did he remember that now? This was not the moment to think of anything except the fish at the end of his line. He let the line run for a second and lifted the point of his rod. He could see Alice's bent head and the crossed straps of her blue dungarees as clearly as if she knelt beside him now. A rosy light was on that scene. He had been happy then as he had never been since, but even then he had been quiet, plain, dull and too old for the girl that he had married. The next day Eric and Kay had arrived at the camp, as he had known that they would, Murray had stopped

§ 90 §

effacing himself, and never again, not for a day, not for an hour, had he been free of his carefully hidden, foolish unreasoning jealousy.

Philip brought his attention sharply back to the present. It was unheard of that any emotion or remembrance, certainly not the thought of a wife of fourteen years standing, should come between a fisherman and a fighting fish. He smiled, a little grimly, but now the battle was familiar and comforting. The reel sang its song through the forest, the rod was a quivering arc. This was a good fish and if it reached the snag, it would twist the gut round the black downed branches and the line would come limply back across the pool. The fish made its last short rush; was drawn towards the bank, and turned on its side to expose its white belly. Pior was waiting, thigh deep in the water, and now the fish was in the net.

Kneeling on the stones, Pior held the fish up by the gills. "Three and a half seers?" he said, looking up at Philip.

"Three pounds, more likely, one and a half seers, as you very well know."

Philip stood looking down at the fish. It lay across the white stones, still firm and shining and relaxed. It was, he saw, a cock fish and heavy for its length, a perfect small fish from the round open mouth to the deeply cleft tail. The colour on the scales shone up at him. Dark green, silver, rose and blue, the colours glistened in the sunlight. What a perfect small still-life it made with the smooth blue-shadowed stones as a background. The round eye was still as clear as the water it had come from. The single drop of blood oozing from the gill was exactly what was needed to emphasize the staring eye. Philip sighed, and felt the pang, the momentary regret that he always felt as he saw that the colours were already fading from the once bright scales.

§ 91 §

He sat down on the sloping beach of stones and lit a cigarette while Pior squatted acquiescingly a few yards away. The stones, rounded and polished by the swollen waters of many rainy seasons, shimmered in the sunlight and beyond them was a line of silver sand. The trees on the opposite bank were shaking and bending to the passage of a party of monkeys who leapt and swung from branch to branch. Philip saw that they were the big, long-tailed, cream-coloured langoors who are tipped and marked with dark brown like a Siamese cat. He counted five quick swinging bodies before they were gone, disappearing into the trees, leaving a ripple of disturbed leaves on the forest. He turned his head. Pior, too, had seen the monkeys.

Nine years before, Pior had materialised out of the jungle. One day he was not and the next he was there in the camp, as shy as a deer is but meaning to stay. He was then a red-skinned, lean stripling, naked except for a rag round his loins and a strip of red cloth round his head. He was a member of one of the aboriginal tribes of the foothills which, perhaps because of the depredations of some other tribe, had descended with the rivers to the plains and become a tribe of boatmen, expert in river lore, shooting rapids in their narrow canoe-like dugouts, and fishermen who, if they had been more numerous, would have denuded even those great rivers with their nets and traps and poison bark. This year Pior had turned up again, wearing a khaki shirt that Murray had once given him to show that he was a recognised if independent member of Dr Coombe's retinue.

Philip preferred Pior as a fishing companion to anyone else in the camp. Sangla was too ambitious, wanting to hurry from pool to pool intent on big catches, while Murray was a surprisingly clumsy fisherman who always knew exactly where a fish would lie and, using heavy old-fashioned tackle and casting clumsily, always caught more fish than the expert Philip could do. Pior sauntered along, a part of the day, his hunter's eye noting every mark on the ground and every spoor. He would stand as immobile as a red-wood image at the correct distance from the pool watching every sign on the river, as alert as a fishing-cat. When the spoon or the hook of a fly fouled a snag or an overhanging branch, he would instantly drop his shirt on the bank and flash into the water, slanting across the current, where no one else could have lived, diving and turning like an otter, disappearing in a smother of foam between the boulders to re-appear triumphantly with the spoon in his hand.

A day on the river with Pior was seldom dull. For him tiger tracks seemed to multiply on the sand, fish to swim in greater numbers in the pools. With him to round a bend in the river was to see a sambhur doe and fawn picking their way across the shallows or a wild boar drinking at the edge of a pool, or a great hornbill displaying its black and white plumage and bony naked bill on a dead branch above the water. With him Philip had once seen a pack of red dog running silently across the sands on the scent of a stag who, a few seconds before, had dashed out of the trees across the open beach and into the trees again with terror visible in every line of its leaping body. With Pior as a companion anything could happen, and his wild dark beauty matched the beauty of the forest. For Philip the sight of his crimson headcloth showing boldly against the leaves was a guarantee, set like a seal on the margin of the day.

Pior sat on his heels staring at the river, and Philip wondered what he was thinking of, if he were thinking of anything. Was he watching the dim shadow-shape of a fish making its way up-stream below the surface, or was he waiting for a movement to be repeated in the leaves? Perhaps he was thinking of the meal that he would eat in the evening, apart in his own smokey branch-roofed shelter; like many wild creatures, he ate largely only once in the day. Or perhaps he was thinking of his village, of a house built on stilts at the edge of the water, of children playing like brown young otters in and out of the river, of a woman moving in the shadows of the wide-thatched eaves. Did Pior, the untamed and solitary possess a wife or wives? Or did he mate as casually as an animal does, sowing his seed through the forest? The border tribes are bound by mysterious marriage customs and old taboos. Many are strictly monogamous. It was impossible to think of Pior as a family man bound to the bed, the hearth, the home, but a wife he most probably had, a wife whom he kept in her proper place in his scheme of things. Pior was lucky. Only civilised man with his complicated emotions, dreams and uncertainties, strange tenderness and uneasy acceptance, confuses and elaborates the relationship between man and woman. For Pior life was simple and direct. Among many of the border tribes, for instance, the murderer goes free while adultery is rewarded with a prompt and double death.

Philip was startled. Such a savage thought could only have come from the wild strong life round him. It was not his thought, it was too highly coloured, too outsize for him. Was he not a civilised man, always doubting his own reactions and given to seeing two sides to every question? He stood up abruptly and saw with astonishment that his hand was clenched round a stone.

He dropped the stone and brushed his hands distastefully together. Even if he had actual proof of what he had never for a moment believed, such a direct gesture was not for him. His, when it came, would, he suspected, be a very different gesture, something irrelevant and futile.

§ 94 §

The Forest

As he walked blindly across the stones to the river he
asked himself why he could not be spared these thoughts
even for one day, even in this place. "Not here. Not to-day,"
he said and did not know that he had spoken aloud until he
saw Pior's head turn questioningly towards him.

"We go on?" Pior said hopefully.

"Of course," Philip said. "What else should we do?"
and bent down to pick up his rod.

CHAPTER VI

IF the fish in the pools saw Philip and Pior it was as
huge shapes darkening their green sky. To the fishing-eagle,
circling high above the forest, they were two specks beside
the pale loop of the river and of no significance.

The eagle looked down on the camp and on the village
ten miles away where, two hours before, Eric and Kay had
descended from the truck into the dust of the village street.
It saw the vultures dropping suddenly one after the other
like stones into the sea of trees. As they had done, it marked
the kill, half hidden in the grass where the trees were cut
by the white of a dead river bed. It saw far over the changing
greens of the forest to the brown-green spread of the reserve.
Its fierce eyes encompassed horizons and at the same time
marked the fish in the shallows. It watched the dark herds
moving across the plain and the slow progress of the two
elephants, pin-spots of grey on the thatch grass but, by the
eagle, known at once for what they were.

The eagle swung higher in widening circles, as if it
hoped to reach the sun, its tawny wings spread against the

sky, its gold eyes turned to the slanting world beneath it.
Now the camp had disappeared, and the river was a thread.

CHAPTER VII

THE two elephants halted close together in the shade
of a clump of teak trees. It was nine o'clock, five hours since
they had left the camp.

Akbar, Murray's big tusker, who was two feet taller
than the small cow elephant, Sitara, knelt obediently but
taking his time, kneeling on his hind legs, as human beings
kneel, and with his forelegs stretched out in front of him on
the ground. After a few grunted protests, Sitara copied him
and Manoo slid down her tail, stepped off one of her great
oval hind feet, and hurried to help Alice to dismount.

Where the big-leafed trees cast their dappled shade,
Jetha, the Nepali boy, who was a cheerful, broad youth
dressed in the usual khaki shirt and shorts but with a striped
woollen scarf tied round his head, beat the long grass flat
with the back of his khukri and spread a rug. The two elephants withdrew into the deeper shade and stood there, swaying gently, slapping at their sides to keep the flies away with
bunches of leaves held in their trunks. Their mahouts, still
mounted, rested their arms on their reversed goads and
dozed where they sat. Manoo and Jetha sat smoking silently
together; the smoke from their biris, the strong smelling
country cigarettes, rose into the still air, and behind them
the two rifles and the shotgun were carefully propped against
a tree. A green wall of undergrowth filled the spaces between the tree trunks and tall clumps of elephant grass

closed in on the scene, but straight ahead, beyond the limits of the blue lacy shade, lay the yellow shining plain.

Murray took off his hat and sat down, crossing his legs under him in his favourite position. He reached for the thermos flask of coffee and the packet of sandwiches, and looked up, a little anxiously, as Alice joined him. She had not spoken when he had given the order to halt and, when he had warned her not to wander more than a few yards into the trees as, that morning, there seemed to be an unusual amount of game about, she had only nodded. Five hours on an elephant is a long time; the peculiar motion, the lift and fall and sway, although gentle, is trying to unaccustomed muscles, and it would be several hours more before they were back in camp.

Alice lay flat on her back on the rug with her arms crossed behind her head and shut her eyes.

"I'm horribly stiff," she said. "My back's broken."

"Have you had enough? We had better go straight back to the camp."

"Oh, no, please Murray. Give me some coffee and I will go on for hours."

"It has been a good morning, hasn't it? Although we have seen more on other days."

"I can remember days when we saw nothing at all except the plain and the hills. We have done very well—sambhur, mithun, a buffalo."

"The buffalo was far off. We saw nothing close today except the stags."

"I liked the stags best, and don't forget those two foxes streaking away across the plain."

"Do you remember the day, it must be eight years ago, when you and Philip and I saw that wounded elephant on the other side of the Reserve? Of course you remember, you must realise how lucky we were. In all my years in the forest I never saw such a thing before and never will again."

On that never to be forgotten day, they had seen a tusker standing knee deep in a pool. The forest made a dark background behind him and even from a distance they had seen that something was wrong. He did not move as they drew nearer, but allowed them to come within a few yards of the pool without making any demonstration, only lifting his head towards them and curling his trunk. Akbar had shown none of his usual nervousness as the elephant faced them, slowly and painfully wheeling to show the tusk marks on his side. From the stump, that was all that was left of his tail, blood had dripped to stain the water of the pool.

"I'm glad that we didn't see him to-day," Alice said. "This is a happy golden day. Do you think that he lived, Murray?"

"Probably not. He had lost a lot of blood. Elephants fight terrible battles between themselves, Alice. He must have been badly hurt before he turned and ran. That was when his tail was twisted off. Manoo says that the bulls sometimes treat their reluctant females in the same way."

"I won't think about it now, although it was nothing to do with us. I mean that no human had a hand in that tragedy anyway. It was the forest's affair."

"You know very well that the forest can be cruel to its own, almost as cruel as men can be."

"Perhaps, but men should know better. Don't talk about it any more, the sanctuary has never seemed so beautiful and peaceful as it does today. Was that really a rhinoceros that we saw? Manoo said that it was but it was so far away that even with the glasses I wasn't sure."

"I think so. That's why we turned back. Akbar doesn't like rhinoceros."

"Manoo wanted to go nearer. I thought for a moment that he was almost excited. I should have known better. Do you know what he's doing now? He's sitting there reading in a little book. I saw him take it out of his pocket. Think of reading here."

"This is all in the day's work for Manoo," Murray said. "He is probably doing his accounts and adding up his savings. If you want dash and enthusiasm Sangla is the man."

"I didn't know that he wore glasses, gold-rimmed ones too."

"Who? Manoo? Yes, he and I took to them together. We both can see as far as ever but the printed page is another matter. I took him down to Calcutta while you and Philip were in England last year and we both were fitted up together. He and I are growing old."

"You will never be old," Alice said.

"The day will come when I will be too old for this life, too blind and deaf and slow for the forest. What shall I do then, Alice?"

Alice raised herself on her elbow and looked at him. "It will never happen," she said. "You will fade away into the forest one fine day, cease to be Murray Coombes and take on the form of something else, let's say a young grey heron beginning all over again."

"Thank you, Alice. You mean that I mustn't talk about being old on a morning like this?"

"The morning isn't finished. We shall see more on our way back."

"The sun is getting higher. They will be moving back into the cover of the trees. We won't see much more."

"It doesn't matter. Just to be here is enough. This plain is like nowhere else. I have seen it again and again and it's always new. It's a revelation."

§ 99 §

"A revelation?"

"There's something Biblical about it. This morning, when we came out of the trees and saw the miles of lonely grass rolling away to the hills and the little broken streams, I thought of the first day of Creation. 'And God created the Heaven and the Earth and every living thing according to its shape.' I always liked that part. When I was a child I used to think of all the different shapes, the tall and the broad and the beautiful and the odd, unheard of shapes appearing suddenly in the grass. Do you know, Murray, I believe that Eden was not a garden at all but a great grassy sanctuary like this."

Murray laughed. "And where are your Adam and your Eve? None of us qualify."

"They are sure to be somewhere about. It wouldn't surprise me at all if we came suddenly upon them sitting side by side under a tree. But perhaps this is Eden after they were turned out and the animals were left to go on by themselves. I like it better that way. We shall probably find Adam and Eve somewhere close outside."

"And the serpent? Where is he?"

"Gone out into the world too. There are no serpents here, only gentle snakes."

"Like that python whose track we saw, I suppose. You said that pythons have cold eyes and that his track on the sand was like the ugly track of a huge motor tyre."

"Don't you try and pin me down like Kay always does. You know what I mean, you always do. It's a nice change to be understood."

Murray looked down at her, but she had turned her face away from him. She lay very still as if she were waiting to see what he made of that remark. He hesitated, not knowing if he were meant to withdraw or advance. After a moment he said:

"What is it, Alice? Something is worrying you, I know." He hesitated again and said, "Are you missing your children? They are too far away?"

"I don't miss them here. I hardly think of them here." She sat up suddenly and turned to look directly at him.

"Murray," she said, "I'm a good mother, everyone says so. I love and cherish my dull dear little girls. They each look alike. Something is missing. Why are they so colourless? One of them, at least, was conceived in our forest. She should be different."

"My dear Alice!"

"Don't be silly, Murray. I can say anything to you, I always have." She looked past him at the bright plain and said, "I always wanted a son."

"Why not? You are young, there's plenty of time."

"Is there? Unfortunately it takes two to make one, a one of any kind, let alone a brilliant special one."

"You say the most extraordinary things, Alice. You don't mean them. Are you trying to tell me that you and Philip are not happy together? I had always thought that you two, at least, were a success. It has comforted me. Now you upset me very much. What's wrong?"

"Nothing's wrong. Philip, I suppose, is everything a husband should be, kind and generous and unexacting. We began well, but we have lost it. Perhaps it was my fault but almost at once there was a space between us and every year, especially these last years, he has gone further and further away from me. I hoped that I should find him here again and that we would go back, but he is further away than ever. Where does he go to, Murray?"

Before Murray could speak, Alice stood up, and pulled her hat down over her ruffled hair. "Why must I talk like this?" she said. "We came back to the forest to get away from ourselves didn't we? From our horrid little human needs and wants and dreams. Why can't we be just two pairs of eyes for one morning, just see and take in and nothing else?"

"I thought that you, at least, were happy here."

"I am happy, perfectly happy. Don't you dare to think anything else. Murray, look at the elephants. They have winded something. Look at Akbar!"

The elephants' trunks were raised like two grey interrogation marks and turned towards the trees.

"What they have scented is still a good way off," Murray said as he bent down to pick up the rug. But now the waving trunks, turning this way and that, seemed to hesitate as if the upper air no longer carried what they sought. Slowly they uncurled, hung for a few minutes, moved hesitatingly and together slowly lifted again and were held straight out a few feet from the ground.

"Time we were off," Murray said. "There must be something on the other side of this wood. Wild elephant, most likely. Manoo tells me that there is a big mukna in the district who has been making a nuisance of himself to the Nepali villagers near the border. They chased him off, peppered him with those old blunderbusses of theirs and from all accounts he was last seen making for the reserve. He will be an angry elephant and one of these big tuskless males who has left the herd can be unpleasant to meet."

"Manoo isn't here," Alice whispered. "He must have gone to have a look round." But Manoo was returning through the trees. He nodded and held up three fingers. "Two females," he said, as he came up to them, "and another big one. They are in the high cane behind the trees. He might be the one, or they might be part of the herd."

"We had better make a quiet departure," Murray said.

Akbar knelt placidly, still fanning the flies away with

his bunch of grass, his huge ears, which in his old age had grown ragged and turned over at the edges, gently moving. Sitara refused to kneel. She was a temperamental young female, very different from the third elephant old Moti who, at that moment, was returning to the camp from the jungle under a great load of cane and grass, part of the day's fodder for the three. Sitara was Murray's favourite; he liked to scratch the ridged skin of her trunk, the tip of which was lined with pink and had a touch as light and delicate as a girl's hand, and to put sugar cane and parcels of cooked rice done up in banana leaves into the rather small pink mouth which she held open for him.

"Kneel daughter of Satan, kneel!" Her mahout hit her on the skull with the flat of the goad and dug his hard toes into the soft flesh behind her ears, but she only backed away, rolling her eyes hysterically, shivering and swaying.

"She needs a good beating," Murray said. "She's staunch to tiger and rhino, afraid of nothing in the jungle except fire. That's why I put up with this sort of thing."

"You spoil her," said Alice. "She's only showing off."

"He will get her down sooner or later," Murray said, "but she will be up again at once and you will have to make a quick jump for it. Come with me on Akbar and we will leave her to Manoo."

Akbar straightened his front legs. His back sloped like a roof which slowly levelled as the hind legs unfolded. As he clutched at the ropes of the pad, Murray watched Manoo and Jetha climb like agile brown monkeys up Sitara's tail. The moment that they were firmly seated on the pad, she stood quietly and then, taking her place behind Akbar, she broke off a leafy branch and walked along, using it nonchalantly as a fan.

An elephant is a mass of contradictions. He is powerful

and huge but as gentle and as timid as a dove, fierce and mild, easily captured and tamed, hard-working and faithful, treacherous and unmanageable when roused or when mūsth, a state of nerves which comes periodically to bull elephants, making them often temporarily mad and sending oil pouring from the oil glands above their eyes. Female elephants are of all creatures the most mild, tractable and sweet-tempered unless they are accompanied by calves, but even they are unaccountable. Murray watched Sitara carefully.

"I admire Sitara," Alice whispered. "She always gets her own way. Look at her smug expression. She doesn't care if a whole herd of her relations is near."

"Akbar won't be happy if we suddenly find ourselves among them," Murray said. "If you want to see what is making him uneasy you had better not talk."

The two elephants swung silently along at the edge of the trees. The sun, now high above the forest, filled the green spaces between the trees with confusing shadows. Even the huge pink and grey shape of an elephant standing between the grey tree trunks in the dapple of light and shade would be invisible until it moved. It is possible to approach to within a few feet of a feeding elephant without seeing it and, if the wind is right and no stick breaks under the approaching feet, without it knowing that anyone is near. It is easy to believe anything of elephants, even that they dance together in the moonlight on vast trampled ballrooms in the forest, and that they follow secret paths to the same bone-whitened valley when, perhaps after as much as a hundred and fifty years, their time comes to die; but the truth of them is strange and interesting enough without the added legends. The elephant is an astonishing, although by now familiar, sight: an unwieldy mass which can travel silently through the forest, floating between the trees like a grey cloud: patchy, loose, grey wrinkled skin, with here and there a few black hairs sticking up: naked muscular tail ending in a small fan of stiff black bristles: noble double-domed skull, small wise cunning eyes, strange lumbering earthbound gait. The udders of the cow elephant are between her forelegs. The period of gestation in elephants is twenty-two months. Their act of love is rumoured to be long and awe-inspiring.

There is no difference to be seen between tamed and wild elephant except, perhaps, a faint difference in colour because the tamed elephant is frequently washed and scrubbed while the wild is often caked with mud and dust, but anything wild carries with it its own strangeness which sets it apart. Alice had been close to the two elephants all day but now, from her place on the pad behind Murray, she whispered: "We must see them. Suppose we miss them? Do you think that the whole herd will be there?"

They had reached the limits of the wood and on their right was a sea of high elephant-grass. Through this green and yellow sea three shapes were moving, three grey curving backs showing as whales show above the water. A trunk waved against the sky; the grass parted and closed behind them again.

"There they go," said Murray. "The big one is a tusker. Look, beyond them. There is the herd."

Some distance away, crossing the shorter grass, a herd was moving, between thirty and forty grey shapes in the grass, the females and the calves in advance and the males straggling behind. The herd was led by a tall and bony female, a watchful beldame who wheeled suspiciously, lifting her trunk in their direction, before making off at a quicker pace across the plain.

"Listen to the calves," Alice said, kneeling up on the

pad to see better. "What a squeaking and grumbling. Can't we go after them and see them closer?"

Murray shook his head and touched the mahout on the shoulder. Between them and the herd the big tusker had halted. They could see the ridge of his back above the tall grass and a gleam of tusks. He looked menacing, but there is no knowing what an elephant, tame or wild, will do. Of all the inhabitants of the forest the elephant is the best known and liked by men but is often misrepresented. "An elephant never forgets," "As wise as an elephant," are well-worn sayings, but Murray, for instance, knew that if they could now remove themselves from the sight and scent of this tusker, they would probably be gone from his mind. The elephant, compared with the fox or the monkey, is not particularly intelligent. It is the great dignity of the elephant and his size that have made him lord of the forest where, in his long and peaceful life, he has nothing to fear except men. Akbar gave no sign that he knew that the tusker was there. He moved calmly and slowly away, followed closely by Sitara. When Murray looked back the herd had disappeared; only a light cloud of dust showed where it had been.

Now the cane grass was all about them. They swayed along with their faces on a level with the grass whose sharp blades, if unwisely touched, could cut like a knife. A howdah would have been an advantage in this open country; from its box-like elevation they would have been able to see far out across the plain. But a howdah would have been impossible in the thick jungle through which they had come. The air was full of the scent of crushed stems and the sun, now above their heads, was unpleasantly hot.

The two elephants were approaching the dark green wall of forest. Now the tall grass was left behind. The hills were retreating into the haze. The sun, mounting higher, seemed to be drawing all life from the plain, leaving a sea of colourless grass, a vast empty shimmering space.

CHAPTER VIII

As Philip was playing his second fish in a pool far above the island, and the two elephants, leaving the plain behind them, slipped into the green depths of the forest shade, Eric and Kay with Sangla and the two men from the village were crossing the dead river bed. They walked silently, taking care not to dislodge the stones under their feet. Eric was leading, followed closely by Sangla. They, too, had seen the vultures.

Two hours before, they had arrived at the village. As they descended from the truck they were met by the news that a Nepali wood-cutter, following a path through the jungle on his way to work, had come upon the place where a tiger had killed. As he was examining the tracks on the ground and the threshed blood-covered grass, he heard a tiger's low, throaty, warning cough. He hurried to the village which, as everyone for miles around knew, was in touch with the camp.

"Where did this happen?" Eric asked, and the Headman, stepping out of the crowd, answered that if they drove back down the road and turned at right angles up the first side road, following a fire line, they would reach a dead river bed which was within a short walking distance of the place.

"The man comes from the wood-cutter's camp near

the Dipsiri clearing," Sangla said. "He says that it is the big tiger again."

Eric frowned. He had made his plans. On the road a mile from the village they had met the Santal tracker whom he employed to act as a link between the village and the camp. The man was on his way to report that a tie-up, a bullock, had been taken in the jungle across the river and that the tracks showed that this was the work of a tigress and a full grown tiger hunting together. The place, Eric knew, was suitable for a beat on a large scale, a spectacular beat, well organised, such as he had determined on. And now, to tantalise him, to distract his attention, to make a fool of him once again, the big tiger had re-appeared. He hesitated, trying to make up his mind, knowing that Kay was watching him.

"In any case we couldn't beat before tomorrow," he said slowly. "We shall need the elephants. I could sit up to-night but a beat is what I want. It's time that the village was shown something for its trouble."

"Only the village? It's time that we all had a spot of excitement."

"This other will probably turn out to be quite a different tiger or even a leopard, but we had better go and see."

"Now?"

"We will settle part of our business here first, it won't take long. I want to make sure of beaters for tomorrow. We can come back later for the rest."

"Two tigers in hand are worth one in a bush," Kay said. "Why have a long hot walk for nothing? That wood-cutter probably imagined the whole thing."

Eric took no notice. Sangla was looking steadily at him. The flat gold face was expressionless but he knew that Sangla felt the same stirring of excitement that he felt, a

premonition, an instinct, faint but sure, that was as com-
pelling to them as a fresh scent is to a hunting dog.

"Come on," he said. "Let's get this over," and, followed
by an attentive crowd, he led the way down the village street.

In the courtyard of the headman's house in the shade
of a fig tree, Kay sat on a wooden stool and surveyed the
scene. Eric sat beside him with his dog at his feet and Sangla,
dressed as Kay was in khaki shirt and shorts but with his
knife in a curved leather scabbard at his belt, stood near
them. The villagers sat on their heels in a semi-circle on
the flat beaten earth and behind them women watched
from the dark doorways. The buffalo calf, the bullocks and
the old goat chewed placidly at a pile of leaves and the
wood-cutter had been joined by two other Nepalis, two
carters who, seeing the truck standing in the road, had hurried to join the crowd. These three stood apart together
wearing the skull cap and sash and loose jodhpurs of their
race, looking down on the villagers. The villagers were settlers too, but Santals, aborigines, black-skinned eaters of
lizards, hunters and trackers before they were husbandmen,
who still carried bows and arrows.

Philip would have seen the dark skins shine as the sun
touched them through the leaves, the white and terra-cotta
walls under the thatch, the red flowers that hung like slow
drops of blood, the green leaf reflections on the white goat's
hide. But Kay's eyes, interested and alert, picked out details that caught his fancy and saw nothing else. He saw
that the goat had lost the tip of one horn, and that the Headman's long grizzled hair was tied back with an old boot-
lace. He marked on a bare brown chest an amulet of
red and silver beads and a tiger's claw. The women
leant from the doorways showing their wide flat bracelets
and anklets of silver; they wore white cloths wound round

their bodies, leaving their legs bare. Naked children played round their feet and babies, naked and wise-eyed, like young monkeys, sat astride their mother's hips. He turned his eyes away from them and from the old crone who, bent double, grey wisps of hair flying, was sweeping the ground between the houses, to watch a frieze of five young women coming from the river one behind the other with their water pots balanced on their heads. They paused to stare on the raised mud path behind the seated men, their arms still raised, and then walked on, thin-shanked, their wet clothes outlining their black protuberant behinds, their young high, bobbing breasts. When they had gone Kay yawned and stretched himself. The smell of warm bodies and cow's urine was growing stronger. The sound of raised voices, Eric's questions and the headman's chattering answers, and Sangla's deep boom went on and on, as did the barking of the village curs who were maddened by the sight of Ebon lying massive and indifferent at his master's feet. Kay looked round restlessly and saw a cock surrounded by his hens scratching the ground beneath the tree. He was a fine bird, small but magnificent in his reds and golds and black-greens, cousin to the jungle-cock that Kay had shot that morning. It had been a difficult shot as the bird whirled up from the road in front of the truck and into the trees. "Beautiful, Kay!" Eric had cried as the bird fell like a coloured stone between his brown flying hens and the dog dashed from the truck into the undergrowth. At the remembrance Kay felt pleased with himself again. He smiled at the small boy who, completely naked except for a string round his loins, was standing in front of him, his thumb in his mouth, his small pot-belly protruding. Kay liked all children and he held out his hand. The child retreated, rolling his eyes uneasily until Kay showed him an anna;

then he advanced cautiously, snatched at the coin and fled. Kay laughed and the crowd, diverted and pleased, laughed with him.

Eric stood up and the headman rose too, to show that the meeting was over. A youth offered six eggs in a twist of grass, a present to the camp, which Eric gravely took in his large, well-shaped hand. Kay watched as Eric stood looking over the heads of the crowd to the river. He was at least eight inches taller than anyone else there and his pale head, light eyes and dark red skin looked startlingly foreign among them. Kay wondered if they found his calm blond superiority annoying, but of course to them he was only something large and highly coloured to look at, a timely and efficient slayer of their enemies, and a source of gold for the village.

"What are you going to do with these wretched animals?" Kay said, pointing to the bullocks.

"We will use them eventually," Eric said. "They can stay here until we need them." As they walked down the dusty path to the truck, they passed an open shed in which, among spare wheels for bullock carts, rolls of matting, stood a roughly made and crudely painted wooden tiger mounted on wheels. Eric pointed to it as they passed. "That's the reason why these people are not particularly keen on a beat near the village," he said. "A beat further off towards the Dipsiri clearing they are all for, but not so near home. They are not sure that they want an old enemy destroyed, it seems."

"Perhaps on the principle that the devil they know is the best devil?" Kay suggested. "More sophisticated people have thought that."

The truck turned off the forest road into the long grassy ride. Eric sat on the high seat behind the driver with his dog between his knees and looked out over the forest. He felt the familiar tingling excitement. Once again it was beginning, the chase, the quest, that would lead to one end, to the tawny desired colours in the sights of his rifle. He lifted his head, drawing the forest air, the scent of leaves and dry grass and indefinable rank smells and the scent of flowers, into his nostrils. He was content as he had not been for years.

"How are we going to set about this?" Kay said beside him.

"The wood-cutter will take us to the place. Then we will track the tiger up, try to find the kill."

"It may be lying up somewhere close."

"Very likely."

Eric turned his head and looked down at Kay. They had known each other for a long time and had spent many days alone together. To-day he felt nothing for him except approval, remembering the perfect style, the swing and decision of that morning's shot, but as he met the look in the dark eyes, the old antagonism flared up between them. He wondered why such an exceptionally fine shot was not more use with a rifle, and he said, "You are not interested in the big stuff, are you? A quail is more in your line than the one we are after." As he said it he wished again that he and Sangla, who understood each other, were alone.

"You can always stay in the truck, you know," he said.

Kay smiled. "You will have to go carefully," he said. "You won't be able to take the chances you used to. It won't be quite the same. You may need me yet."

For a moment they stared at each other, but the truck had reached the end of their ride. The white of the sun-hot stones shone between the trees. Puran Singh switched the engine off and the silent forest surrounded them.

Eric bent down to tie the dog securely to a ring under the seat. As they climbed down from the truck he said in a low voice, "Puran Singh, you stay here too. Don't follow us or try to see what's happening."

The old man smiled. Eric knew, as well as he did, that the moment they were gone he would climb into the back of the truck beside the dog, pull the cushions down from the seat, and fall asleep until they returned or the sound of shots roused him. Not for anything, not even for Dr Coombes, would he have followed them, but he would sleep as soundly alone in the forest as he did in his bed.

A few moments later the party of five came out of the trees above the stones. It was then that they saw the vultures come down.

"That means that he has left the kill," Eric whispered. "We shall hear him if he comes back to see the vultures off."

"He had better be quick," Sangla murmured, "or the evil birds will leave nothing for him."

They moved off in a single file, the Santal tracker searching the ground.

There were many tracks on the sand between the stones: the sharp pointed delicate deer tracks, deeply cloven, varying from those of the barking-deer that were small, light, fairy-like, to the deep strong impressions left by the sambhur. They saw the round pad marks of a jackal, the diamond pattern left by the jungle cat. They found the track of the wood-cutter, the prints of a man's bare foot that are very similar to those made by the bear, only longer and narrower, following a faint path between the stones. Then, skirting the grass, they came upon the huge square pug marks of a tiger.

Sangla bent down and measured the great starred rosettes with his hand. "It could be he, the big one," he whispered.

"When were they made?"

"Last night or very early this morning."

The Santal nodded, and on they went, heads turned to the ground, following the wide spaced marks.

The impressions were deep and clear in the sand. Eric could not take his eyes off them. He saw the deceptively slow swinging stride, the shoulder muscles moving with inimitable grace, the huge paw descending as silently and lightly as a feather but with the enormous deliberation of six hundred pounds of weight behind it. He lifted his head to stare at the jungle above him, a wall of green whose leaves hung without a movement. Were narrow-pupilled, cold eyes watching every move he made?

The tracks ceased suddenly, vanishing into the grass beside the path. There were marks on the ground where a great body might have crouched. A few yards ahead the sand was disturbed, turned and trodden and heaped, as if a whirlwind had turned there. The grass on the sloping bank was beaten flat and, at the edge of the stones, were marks of dried blood. Sangla pointed, and they saw another line of tracks, deep, cleft, circular saucers that advanced towards them across the sand between the stones from the direction of the trees.

The tracks were not those of a cow, which they a little resembled, but of a small female mithun who, sometime towards the dawn, had crossed the stones to graze on the cool starlit grass. She had been seized from the rear and probably hamstrung, the severance of the great tendons at the back of the hocks, and brought to the ground unable to rise again. The horns of even a small mithun are formidable to any tiger. From the state of the ground it was clear that, even when on her knees, her eyes and muzzle caked with sand, she had fought back, making wide sweeps of the head, the pointed horns tearing up the grass and futilely scattering the sand.

In the torn undergrowth the path that killer and slain had taken together was plain. The mouth of the leafy tunnel stared back at them. No tiger could have carried or dragged such a weight far. Kay looked at Eric, but Eric had no intention of entering that tunnel. He would follow the river bed further, watching the ground for tracks. The tiger had very likely left the kill in the peninsula of trees and crossed the stones to lie up for the day in the thick and cooler forest beyond.

They followed the curve of the river bed. The stones shimmered under the sun and, in the distance, a heat haze danced. It was difficult to see where the stones ended and the jungle began. The deer tracks crossed and criss-crossed on the sand. From the trees came the continuous whirring hum of the crickets and the faint bird calls.

Two large boulders rose in their path and, skirting them, they came suddenly on a pool of shallow, brackish, dark water, a pool left behind in a depression in the rocks by rain or flood, or fed from some subterranean spring or river running underground, and surrounded by a wide rim of drying clay. The now familiar wide-spaced tracks stared up at them. The great pugs, pressed deep, led from the trees on their left, vanished into the water, and returned to the trees again. They all saw that under the fierce sun the impressions were still dark and damp.

Swiftly they retreated until the rocks were hidden.

Eric halted and gestured to them to wait where they were. Kay sat down on a rock and wiped his hot face. His hand was trembling. He would have given a great deal for a cigarette. He looked angrily at Eric and at Sangla, whose usually imperturbable face was split by a wide grin. They were enjoying themselves. This was for them a well-spent morning, but it was not in his line at all. What was he doing there? He had been a fool to come. He looked over his shoulder and saw the wood-cutter retreating rapidly towards the point where they had left the truck, but the Santal tracker, unmoved, squatted on the ground. Eric was leaning against a boulder, his hat tilted over his eyes, his head turned expectantly towards the trees. He held up his hand. From the trees came a sudden loud crashing, followed by a short coughing roar.

As they all turned to face the forest, they saw the vultures flapping up between the branches on their huge slow wings. A few of the birds, too gorged to move further, remained perched high in the trees in full view of the river bed, but the rest departed, winging slowly and heavily across the forest.

Eric's eyes were shining. He bent forward and whispered in Kay's ear. "He went down to that pool for a drink or a bathe. Tigers like to lie in water on a hot day. Now he is dragging the carcass deeper into the trees, perhaps covering it with grass, as he should have done before. Listen!"

The crashing and rustling grew fainter, and then ceased. Complete silence descended on the forest. They stayed where they were for what seemed to them all to be a long time.

"Isn't that enough?" Kay whispered at last. "You know that the tiger is there. The kill is near those tall trees, isn't it? What more do you want? Let's get out of this."

"He has moved off down the river. Didn't you hear those monkeys giving the alarm? I want to see how much those birds have left. I want to have a look round. You stay here."

"I'll wait in the shade over there," Kay said crossly. "You're a damned fool, Eric, with that leg."

The Forest

"I know what I'm doing. Come on, Sangla."

Kay retreated to the shade of the trees on the opposite bank and sat down at the edge of the stones with his back against a rock. He watched the two khaki clad figures walk slowly up river, examining the undergrowth, and then disappear into the green wall. Nothing would have made Kay follow them, and he watched them with the unwilling admiration, the contempt and envy that he so often felt when he watched Eric. He had never been able to make up his mind if this contempt was for Eric or for himself. The Santal, crouching beside him, took a box from the roll of cloth round his waist, and made himself a pan-supari and popped the folded leaf into his mouth. Kay watched the dark jaws chewing and wondered if he should risk a cigarette.

Even in the shade it was hot in the airless stony depression between the opposing trees. The heat was visible, lying like a gauze scarf over the stones. The wall of trees, the still, waiting leaves, were shimmering, and the crickets had begun their high shrilling again. Kay strained to listen, his rifle between his knees, but all that he could hear was a barbet calling, "Kotur-kotur-kotur" over and over again. The loud metallic call echoed through the forest and was answered by another bird further off. Kay, listening to the familiar sounds, slowly relaxed his tensed muscles and leant back against the rock. He looked at his watch. It was well past eleven.

The Santal tracker touched his foot and, starting up, he saw Eric and Sangla emerging from the forest between him and the place where the truck was hidden. They waited on the stones until he caught up with them.

Eric was smiling to himself, a pre-occupied and strangely gentle smile, but Sangla's face was impassive again. "Seen all you want to?" Kay whispered, surprised to find that he was shaking with anger and that he could hardly trust himself to speak. "For God's sake, let's get back to the truck and have a drink."

Eric glanced at him and led the way back without a word. When they reached the truck he said, "Why did you come? There was no need," as if he really wanted to know the answer.

"Perhaps I wanted to see how much of a fool you could be. Well, what do we do now?"

"Build machans across that neck of land above the stones. It's a perfect place for a beat, a silent beat with elephants. The forest narrows suddenly there, with open plain beyond and the river bed this side. There's a trickle of a stream running towards the plain and then more open ground with trees just right for machans. I couldn't ask better."

"But will he still be lying up here to-morrow? Why not sit up over the kill to-night?"

"Because there's no suitable tree near the kill for one thing, and he would never come back if I did—I know that beast by now. This is a chance worth taking. Our elephants will move him out without his knowing it. He has everything here, thick cover, a good meal, water. He will stay put this time, I tell you."

"He probably heard us down there."

"If he did, he would think nothing of it. Wood-cutters often use that path."

"I think we would do better to stick to your original plan and go back to the village."

"We can beat the jungle beyond the village anytime. This is too good a chance to miss."

"Have it your own way. We won't have any peace until you get that brute. Now I want some food and drink and a bathe. After all, we left the camp at eight o'clock. Let's drive the truck to the river. You can drop Sangla and these men by the road to collect wood for the machans. We can pick them up again and get back here soon after midday, plenty of time."

Eric hesitated, looking over his shoulder at the shimmering stones and the distant wall of jungle. "Very well," he said at last. Sangla and I have had our fun. Lead on, little man."

The sun sent its rays vertically between the leaves. It was noon, the hour when life withdraws into the forest, seeking the thickest shade. The two elephants had almost completed their circle back to the camp. They swung along, brushing at the flies, while their human load dozed and nodded on their backs. Philip reeled in his line and sat down on the stones in the shade of the bank, tilted his hat over his eyes, and undid his packet of sandwiches. Pior tied the three fish that he carried by a string through their gills to an overhanging branch above the river and let them swing lifelessly in the shallows to keep them fresh; lying down on the sand, he curled himself round like a dog and at once fell asleep. The eagle was still abroad, making his tireless circles. He saw the fish, but the sleeping Pior, a dark heap on the sand, was too near.

"Can't you keep still, Kay?" Eric said. "I thought that you wanted a rest."

After leaving the truck where the forest road ran close to the river, they had bathed in a pool between the rocks, eaten their food and drunk the beer that they had put to cool at the edge of the water. Now Kay lay naked on the flat rocks above the pool where the breeze kept the worst of the flies away, and Eric, naked to the waist, lay face down with his head on his arms and his dog sprawled beside him. Kay had set an empty bottle up on the shingle below them and was throwing pebbles at it.

"Must you make such a noise?" Eric asked. "Be quiet, can't you?"

"Not until I have hit the damn thing."

At the next throw the shingle was starred with broken glass.

"You can never leave anything alone, can you?" Eric said.

Kay lay back, looking up at the sky. "I wonder what the others are doing," he said.

"The elephants will have been back in camp some time."

"Not they. Alice will wheedle Murray into staying out hours longer than he meant to. She never knows when she has had enough."

"They left soon after four. Eight hours on an elephant is long enough for anyone. Alice will be too tired to enjoy the beat tomorrow, and too stiff to sit still in the machan."

"How pleasant it must be to have such a single-track mind. But you miss a lot, you know."

Eric turned over, leaning his head on his arm, and looked down at Kay. "Do I?" he said. "Don't be too sure of that. I haven't missed seeing that you are making a pest of yourself to Alice. How do you know that she always wants you hanging around?"

Kay laughed. "I thought that we should get round to this sooner or later," he said. "Quite like old times, isn't it? You and I glaring at each other, like two dogs circling round a bone."

"I don't know what you mean."

"Of course you do. You did your level best, and so did I. No one could have blamed us. Alice had us all on a string, including that old romantic, Murray. It took us time to grasp what she was up to, or rather, that she was up to nothing, that she was just being Alice. We got no change out of her then and I certainly won't now."

"Then what do you think you are doing?"

"It's an amusing way of passing the time. Alice is still Alice, and I like trying to get a rise out of old Philip."

"What a little swine you are."

"A jealous husband asks for trouble."

"Philip jealous? What nonsense! It always seemed to me that he was far too sure of himself, too bloody pleasant and calm and sure. He took too much for granted, if you ask me. Philip won't say it to you, but I will. Leave Alice alone."

"As you have done?"

"As you very well know I have done. Philip has never had any reason and never will. I know Alice."

"I wonder if any of us know her," Kay said. "I have often wondered. Philip must be a dull old stick for any woman. Don't look at me like that. I only meant that a warm-blooded, generous, attractive creature like Alice needs something more, whether she knows it or not, something exciting, highly coloured, extra, at least once in her life. Life is short. Perhaps it has already occurred to Alice that she isn't getting younger."

"And you hope to provide this excitement?"

"Oh, no, I'm only something to pat and tease. You, my superior one, would have more chance. As a matter of fact, now that I come to think of it, I have other fish to fry. Would you like to hear about her?"

"I would not. I'm not interested," Eric said, sitting

up and reaching for his shirt. "Apart from anything else, what woman would look at me now?"

"What a fool you are," Kay said. "What couldn't I have done if I had had your chances!"

"I have had enough of this," Eric said violently. Kay looked at him with surprise. The usually expressionless face was flushed a darker red. As Kay watched, the colour went, leaving Eric very pale.

"I've had enough of this," Eric said again. "This kind of talk is all wrong here. It's vulgar, out of place. It means a lot to me to be here again. I'm too busy here to worry about my friends' morals."

"No one is too busy for that," Kay said cheerfully. "All right, forget it. But you are wrong you know. This is the sort of highly coloured place where anything can happen. Look at it, nature rampant all round us, colour gone wild. It's enough to make any woman clothe the most ordinary goose in incredible feathers. I warn you, Paradise was always a dangerous place!"

Eric was limping back across the rocks to the road, with the dog at his heels.

Kay pulled on his clothes slowly and watched him go. "Why did I say that?" he said aloud, apparently to the forest. "Why can't I keep my mouth shut. Why start that particular hare?"

CHAPTER IX

As the two elephants left the park-like country with its open grassland and clumps of trees and turned into the thick forest immediately above the river and the camp, they came suddenly on a small clearing in the fringe of the trees.

Although he had been through this part of the forest many times, Murray had never come across the clearing before, or seen the turned earth, the bed of tobacco plants, or the hut under the wild banana trees. Round the cleared ground was a fence of thorned branches and a ditch dug wide and deep enough to keep out deer and pig, but perhaps it was its smallness and insignificance that had preserved this patch of sown ground in the forest so far.

"What is it doing here?" Alice asked as the elephants paused. She sat up on the pad, her tiredness apparently forgotten, and looked down eagerly over the fence. "It's miles from anywhere, among all those trees. It looks so careful and so brave."

"The forest road isn't far off," Murray said. "Look, there's a path going in that direction, but it's certainly all on its own. These people are not Nepalis or Santals. They look like Assamese."

Within the fence, a man was turning the earth over with a wooden hand-plough. He was naked except for a pink cloth tied round his waist, and his gold skin shone with sweat. The sunlight of mid-morning filled the clearing, ripening the hanging branches of fruit, opening the yellow flowers of the gourd-vine on the thatched roof. A young woman sat in front of the hut in the broad-striped shade of the plantain leaves, winnowing a pile of grain. She lifted her head to stare back at them, holding her flat, fan-shaped basket off the ground, making no move to cover her bare breast. The man straightened himself and looked up, shading his eyes with his hand and then, as if what he saw beyond the fence, however strange and unexpected, did not concern him, he bent to his work again.

"They are not here on sufferance," Alice said. "They are a part of this place, here for good."

"They are here for as long as the forest lets them stay," Murray said. "That ditch wouldn't be much use against wild elephant. An elephant can't take all four feet off the ground at once and his stride is less than seven feet. A seven-foot ditch is the only thing. I wonder that they haven't been raided before, with all that grain and fruit."

"Perhaps they were, and those two managed to drive the elephants off with torches and shouts. They must have overcome a great deal to be here at all."

"They are too near the camp for my liking. Why couldn't they have kept to the road or joined the other settlements? Until they came, there was nothing north of the camp except trees and water and earth and the life that belongs to the forest, nothing between the camp and the hills."

Alice slipped her hand under his arm. "Don't be cross with them," she said. "They have more right to be here than we have."

"We are not attempting to stay," Murray said. "If these two succeed this forest will never be the same again. Come back in a year or two and see what they will have done to it."

"Those two look as if they belonged here," Alice said softly. "They are beautiful, Murray."

Murray pulled his arm away from her hand. "The sight of them seems to please you more than anything else we have seen today," he said.

"They are more of a surprise, that's all. Our eyes were expecting almost any animal but these."

"What has come over you, Alice?" Murray said angrily. "You used to think as I do. I tell you I hate to see them here. Animals? These are not animals. They are that dangerous something more. Can't there be one place in the world still free of them?"

"We are here," Alice said obstinately. "Don't we count? We are the same kind, like it or not. You are not fair, Murray. The animals are perfect. They go on from day to day running along the rails laid down for them, doing only what they have to do. It's easy to be unconsciously perfect. We poor human beings have lost our rails, we can go anywhere and do anything and be anything, from a pig to a God. No wonder that it's difficult."

Murray shrugged his shoulders. "That alters nothing," he said. "I only know that I hate to see this clearing here. Let them go somewhere else and lead their lives where I can't see them. If you have gazed enough at this two-legged and very common species, shall we go on?"

As the elephants moved away, slowly circling the fence, Alice cried: "Murray, of course! Here are our Adam and our Eve, just as I said, beginning again outside the garden."

Murray, for once, did not respond to her. "I would rather that they were not here at all," he said. "We are almost back in camp. We shall see nothing else now to take their tame taste away."

But he was wrong. The elephants, making their way through the forest, were approaching the river. As the sound of the still invisible rapid was heard behind the trees, something brilliantly coloured, that shone and glowed in the sunlight, streaked across the bright ground of a small, open glade.

"What was it?" Alice asked, looking over Murray's shoulder into the trees.

"A peacock," Murray said. "What else in the world could it have been?"

CHAPTER X

I⊤ was late afternoon and Philip and Pior had reached the limits of the heavy forest. Here the river made a loop across the grassy parkland and was lost in the thick swampy jungle below the foothills where, without elephant, they could not hope to go.

The pools here were surprisingly large and deep. At some point behind them part of the river must run underground, as rivers in that region often do. Here there should be fish larger than any that they had seen that day, and Philip wished that he had brought a heavier rod with him. He looked from the water to the sky. The sun had begun its slant towards the trees. They had already gone further than they had meant to do, and it was time that they began their walk back to the camp, but what fisherman could resist a pool like this? It was long, narrow at its head, and broadened to a deep shelf above a rapid. Halfway down its length, beyond a spit of sand, it was joined by a small, slow-oozing jungle stream. A breath of wind, coming from the open grass land, crept across the surface.

"I will fish this one pool," Philip said to Pior, as he changed his cast for the thickest that he could find in his cast box, and the spoon for a three-quarter inch one of silver. "A few casts, and then we will walk straight back to the camp."

The fish, that he knew was waiting for him, took the spoon near the spit of sand. Its first rush almost tore the rod from his hands and took the twenty-five yards of silk line and most of the hundred yards of backing from the reel. Downstream it went, down the rapid to the next pool, and Philip and Pior went with it, leaping from rock to rock, running down the open bank, with the rod dancing and bowing in front of them.

When the fish at last checked, and dived steeply to the bottom of the pool, Philip was soaked through and out of breath. Pior, running backwards and forwards on the bank behind him, seized a stone and flung it into the pool, starting the fish into wild activity again. Philip retrieved a few yards of line and immediately lost them as the fish went off across the pool in yet another of its fierce rushes. He knew that if he were to land this fish on his light rod and tackle, this fish which he now so much desired, he would need all the skill and craft and patience that he had learned in the full, slow days that stretched in a long if broken procession behind him to his boyhood, back to the urchin setting out with his rod for the river in that far off, golden, early morning. He did not know how long he played that fish. Play is a strange word to use for that battle of wit and muscle. Perhaps it was not for as long as he thought, for when, at last, he drew the spent and feebly threshing shape towards the sloping shelf of sand, when Pior, creeping up at the edge of the water, fell upon it, seized it in his arms, his fingers in behind the gills, and carried it up the bank in one fierce rush, the sun was still high above the trees.

The brass amulet on Pior's chest was moving up and down, his narrow black eyes were shining as he looked down at the ten pound stream-lined bar of silver that was marked with dark greens.

"This is a good fish," he said. "A true fish."

"Then we will give him a quick death," Philip said.

§ 127 §

The Peacock

His hand shook as he forced the hook from the gristle-tough, gasping lips. Pior brought the back of his khukri down across the great narrow fighting head that took up a quarter of the length of the whole mahseer. A trickle of bright blood ran on the stones, and it was finished.

"It was its day to die," Pior said cheerfully, and wiped a few shining scales from his hands.

In the camp Puran Singh was tucking the truck up for the night, covering the bonnet with a tarpaulin and covering the cushions. Sangla, waiting outside Murray's tent for their evening talk, sharpened his curved knife on a stone, as he always did when he had a few minutes to spare; the sun, now slanting horizontally between the trees, caught the blade, and sent light flashing across the camp. The cook woke in the cook tent and, contemplating his oven, blew on the cinders and thought of the evening meal. Murray was dressing in his tent after his evening bath and watching the river between the tent flaps. Eric and Kay, who had taken a roundabout way back to the camp, driving down the criss-crossing forest rides but without seeing anything except a sounder of pig, sat on the bank above the river, drinking a late tea. Alice sat on the ground beside them with her legs in their flannel trousers and mosquito boots dangling over the water. The setting sun turned her brown hair to a bright honey-gold. She was holding a rod with the line trailing in the water and beside her was a pail.

"What *do* you think you are doing, Alice?" Kay asked. "Worrying that unfortunate fish again? I wonder that he doesn't clear out of this pool. You and Murray give him no peace at all."

Alice smiled and wound the line in and carefully examined the hook.

§ 128 §

"What are you trying him with this time?" Eric said. "It was grasshoppers yesterday."

"This is a kind of water snail. Manoo found them for me," Alice said. "But I have some dead-bait in this bucket."

"That fish must know us all intimately by now," Kay said. "But why sit there, where he can see everything you do? He is probably gazing up at your legs at this moment and laughing up his sleeve."

"You don't understand this fish," Eric said. "When he makes up his mind to oblige Alice by taking one of the tit-bits she offers him, it will be because he knows her so well that he can't bear to disappoint her any longer."

"Or because he would do anything to be left in peace."

"You two drink your tea and leave this fish and me alone," Alice said. "You are spoiling our evening session."

She dipped her hand in the bucket and brought out a small dead fish. As she impaled it on a long steel pin and arranged the treble hooks at its tail and belly, tying pin and fish together with a piece of gut, Kay said:

"Don't do that, Alice. Leave it to Manoo or Sangla. Your hands will smell of fish all evening."

"They will wash," Alice said.

"Let me do it," Kay said, and knelt down beside her holding out his hand.

"No. I must do it myself. This is between Murray and the fish and me, don't spoil it."

She pushed Kay's hand away and looked up at Eric appealingly.

"I hate to watch your fingers messing about with blood and scales," Kay said.

Eric put his cup down and, half rising in his chair, said loudly, "Why watch her then? Haven't you anything else to do?"

Alice looked from one angry face to the other, and laughed.

Philip and Pior walked down river towards the camp, taking the shortest way across the sands, their backs turned to the dark blue hills. Pior was carrying the heavy string of fish round his neck while Philip carried rod and gun. They had made good time and the island and the wooded bend that hid the camp were in sight.

Sky and forest were taking on the colours of evening. To Philip it seemed that the whole world swam in the same gold light. The day that he had asked for was nearly over. He was drenched through with fresh air and light and sun, and at peace with all the world. He saw the massed trees, the reflections in the deep water and the pearly gleam of the shallows, the mauve shadows lying in each sharp deer track on the sands, with a new distinctness, as if he were seeing them for the first time. His thoughts, unconfused, went before him to the camp. He looked forward to his first drink and his bath, and to the moment when Alice would look up and smile at him, as she always did when he came back. He knew now that the camp held a warm familiar happiness that was not to be risked for a dream. He walked on more quickly, only wanting to be home.

There was no need to hurry. The sun was still visible. He could take his time going back through the evening, savouring the last gold dregs of the day. He saw himself walking home across the sands: a middle-aged, plain, quiet man, an unremarkable, perhaps even faintly ridiculous figure with his rod and gun and string of fish. He no longer cared what he seemed. He knew and accepted himself as he was. He would take and be content with what he had, and cease to ask for the moon.

On his left a short-cut led through the trees from the river to the camp. Behind him the sun was sinking into the forest. After a moment's hesitation, a last look at the river, Philip turned into the wood.

The path was a narrow, scarcely perceptible line through the undergrowth and overhung and deep in shadow, but the sun's last rays shone into an open glade, gilding the tree trunks and turning the green to gold. In the centre of the glade, raised from the ground on an anthill below the invisible roosting hens, the peacock confronted him.

If the sharp eyes of the peacock saw the two men standing in the shadow, it gave no sign. It stood, poised, fan spread, for the moment unmoving, displaying its colours and its myriad shining eyes. Philip's eye was entranced. He felt only delight.

The peacock slowly moved the great fan, furling and unfurling it again in the last sunlight, as if it were reluctant to deprive the forest of its glory and to hasten the coming of night. As the train sank down for the last time, the bird turned its head, arching the supple blue neck. Philip saw the whole bird shape, he saw the look of arrogant male pride, the strong ruthless legs, the bright uncomprehending eye, the small-brained head carrying the starry crest. It seemed to him that the peacock looked directly at him and that the look was a challenge. He stared back and saw all that he had never had and all that he had dreamed. While the light persisted in the glade he saw the troubling beauty of the world, the always receding vision, the beckoning light behind the leaves.

He took a step forward, and the peacock, stepping high, descended from its perch, strutted a few paces, only a bird again now that the sun had gone. Swinging its train behind it, it passed across the glade and into the trees, disappearing like a dream.

Pior coughed gently, and Philip walked on. His new peace had vanished. His doubts and fears and his desires were thick about him again, drawing in with the darkness under the trees. He put his hand up to his head, as if he were brushing something away, and stood still on the path.

"Pior, is there anything here, under the trees?" he said.

For the last hour Pior had been thinking only of his evening meal. He looked over Philip's shoulder and turned his head to look into the trees.

"There is nothing here," he said. "There was a peacock, but he, too, has gone."

CHAPTER XI

THE full moon shone on the sleeping camp, making a pale mockery of the lantern and turning the still smouldering fire to a heap of ash. The trees were black against the sky, the silvered river ran silently, and the owls called softly from tree to tree.

In his tent Murray lay on his side, sleeping his trigger-light sleep. His flashlight and his heavy stick were on the box beside his bed and his rifle lay across a chair. On the other side of the camp, Eric slept uneasily, turning from side to side. Even in his sleep his leg was paining him. He had walked too far that day but his sleeping face was serene; he had done what he had set out to do, and proved that his old skill had not deserted him. In his sleep he was among the close leaves and the warm dry grasses, creeping nearer and nearer to the rank, strong smell, feeling in every nerve and upstanding hair of his body that his enemy, who was also his love and his obsession, was near. The dog, chained by a heavy chain to the head of the bed, out of reach of possible leopards, slept uneasily too, moving when the bed creaked above him, whimpering in his sleep, never wholly unconscious of the wild night beyond the thin walls. Kay, as he always did, had read a detective novel far into the night, turning the pages in the light of his own battery-fed electric lamp, until he fell into the sleep he always slept until dawn. All the camp was asleep: the three elephants swayed at their pickets, the cook tent was carpeted with slumbering bodies, Sangla lay in the doorway of his tent, wrapped in his blanket, his face turned away from the moon. The moonlight fell through the open door of the hut and through the mosquito-net onto Alice's bed. The light on her face did not disturb her. She slept as if resolutely, one hand under her cheek, frowning a little.

In all the camp only Philip was awake. He had slept for a short time and dreamt one disturbing dream. Now, wide awake, too troubled to think of sleep, he stood at the edge of the bank in the shadow of the trees, invisible in his dark dressing-gown, smoking cigarette after cigarette to keep the mosquitoes away.

Philip's body, after its long day, asked nothing better than to lie down again and to forget itself in sleep, but his uneasy mind kept it erect and prowling between the hut and the river, or standing still with bent head, looking down at the water until the mosquitoes forced him to move again. He did not know why he was standing on the bank above the river, alone in the night. A conversation over supper in the dining-hut, a quarrel with Alice, if it could be called a quarrel, and a foolish dream were surely not enough to keep him there? He turned away from the river. The moon-light fell on the chairs left by the fire and picked out an empty glass left forgotten on the ground. As Murray had done, he idly counted the vacant chairs and found them only five. But moonlight is strangely deceiving. On a moonlight night anything seems possible. Moonlight dazzles and distorts and yet makes crystal clear. Philip pulled a chair to the edge of the bank and sat down, leaning his head on his hands.

That evening, at supper in the dining-hut, they had all been a little above themselves, elated by their long day in the sun. They sat talking round the table long after the last dish was cleared away. Even Eric, rousing from the preoccupation that had kept him aloof from them, talked freely and easily. The sound of their laughter floated out across the river. The dog, touched by their excitement and unable to lie still, went from one to the other, laying his black head on their laps, and looking up into their faces.

Who first mentioned the peacock, Philip did not know. Perhaps he had done so himself; describing the bird to them as he had seen it that evening, poised on its anthill, fan outspread to the setting sun. It seemed to him that at the sound of the bird's name, the faces under the swinging lamp had changed and brightened. From that moment something was among them that had not been there before.

They all had seen the peacock that day. Eric and Kay had glimpsed it that afternoon near the forest road above the camp as it dodged away between the trees.

"I nearly had a shot at it," Kay said, looking at Alice. "It was asking for trouble, showing itself like that."

"You might as well shoot one of us," Alice said. "That bird seems a part of the camp by now."

"A special guest, or an extra host?" Kay asked, and Alice, her head on one side, paused to think, as if his question deserved careful consideration.

"I'm not sure," she said. "What do you think, Murray?"

But Murray only smiled, and settled himself in his chair and lifted his hand as he always did when he wanted their attention. Unusually silent, the need to talk, to hold forth at length upon a given subject, sometimes came over him, as it did then. He wanted to talk to them about peacock, not the peacock as it is, but the legendary bird who for so long has stirred human imagination, and talk he would until he had nothing more to say.

Philip listened half unwillingly as Murray told of Juno and her bird train, of the mediaeval legends of tapestries bright with the peacock colours, stories of ill-luck and super-stition to point men's centuries old pre-occupation with this bird. As the saga of the peacock was unfolded, Philip, listen-ing, saw the peacock walking under cold northern skies far from its forest home, trailing its feathers across a snowy lawn under yews cut and shaped to its own likeness. He looked beyond the lit circle and the over-hanging eaves of the hut and saw the wild bird colours repeated in the sky above the river. Murray was telling of the peacock feathers sent as a royal gift to the great Solomon, of the jewelled thrones of dead eastern kings. The peacock, it seemed, had returned from the West, circling back to the East where it belonged.

"To tell even the little I know of the peacock's place in Hindu iconography would take too long for one evening," Murray said. "It is a royal bird, the companion of kings. It is supposed to have many vices and virtues. It is a vehicle of the Gods, the charioteer of Kartikeya who is the com-mander-in-chief of the heavenly hosts, and you see pictures of him riding on its back." He smiled, "They call it, 'a belli-cose bird.' In some parts of India it is associated with Krishna; it's one of Krishna's favourite creatures and gave him the plumes for his headdress. But most of all it is the favourite bird of Indra, god of the firmament. The thunderbolt is one of Indra's weapons and the peacock is supposed to dance when the thunder is heard."

"Peacocks dance before a storm, that's true enough," Eric said. "I have seen them. I suppose it's the change in the atmosphere."

Murray waved this interruption away. "There is one legend that I have always liked," he said. "Indra so admired one of the dancers at the court of heaven that he found his one pair of eyes were not enough to look at her beauty. Being a god, he put on a thousand pair of eyes and, when he had done with them, he transferred them to the plumage of the peacock, his own bird."

"Very pretty," said Kay. "But you have forgotten one attribute of the peacock, Murray. In Hindu mythology, surely it is prized by amorous ladies? I seem to have heard that a peacock's feather will make a woman seductive, that its possession betrays the courtesan?"

Murray glanced at Alice and said quickly, "You are thinking of the legend that the peacock's plumage is useful in directing the arrows of the Hindu god of love, Madan, the Greek Eros."

"That's another legend," said Kay. "Yes, and there's another that a breeze from a peacock feather fan will promote love in a reluctant lover. Have you heard that before, Alice?"

Alice looked across the table at Kay. "You know everything, don't you?" she said. "What a clever little one you are."

She turned to Murray and said, "I shall keep your feather, Murray, in spite of Kay, but don't tell us any more. The peacock doesn't need all these legends that men have hung on it, all this dressing up, all this *talk*. It's itself, a rare and beautiful bird, that's good enough for me."

"But Alice," Murray said gently. "Don't you see? In all these tales the bird is only a symbol. That is the interesting part. Men have always made symbols for themselves and always will."

Eric, following his own thoughts said, "Not rare, Alice. Peacocks are everywhere."

Now Philip stood up, turning his back on the moonlit river, and walked to the door of his hut and stood looking down at his sleeping wife. That night, as they were getting ready for bed, Alice had gone to the doorway and, standing there in the striped pyjamas that she always wore at night in camp, looking a small, odd figure against the bright moonlight, had said: "Philip, look at the moon. Listen to the river. This is as it used to be. How right we were to come back here."

Coming to him where he stood between their beds, she had taken his hand, saying a little breathlessly, looking up at him: "Philip. Everything is all right, isn't it? We are the same—can't we be together, here, like we used to be?"

He had pulled his hand away, gently and decisively, without a word.

Philip moved restlessly back to the river, unable to face the thought of the bamboo-walled space enclosing them both, although, hours before, uneasily, sore at heart and conscience-stricken, he had slept there soundly enough until he had woken from his dream. He sat down again on the chair above the river. He did not know why he had turned away from warmth and safety, from all that he most needed. The ways of the human mind are dark and strange.

He leant his head on his hands and remembered his dream. Surely no one can be held responsible for what they dream? Dreams come from without, called up by stray associations and words that we have forgotten we ever heard. Our dreams appal us. They have nothing to do with our waking selves. "How absurd, how horrible!" we say, and push our dreams away from us. Sometimes we even manage to laugh at them.

In his dream Philip stood in the glade where he had seen the peacock, but now the glade was white with moonlight and striped and barred with black shadows. In the full blaze of the moon a white shape was kneeling above a shimmering pile of colour that burnt in the moonlight like a heap of jewels, like a white-hot fire. He drew nearer and saw, with awe and wonder, Alice kneeling naked in the moonlight with the peacock's crested head between her breasts. In his dream he turned away, as from something that he had no right to see, and left them shining there.

A dream until its colours fade can drown reason and humour and leave nothing in the mind but its own peculiar brightness. If Philip had woken from such a dream to the sane light of day, he would have tried to remember its details, smiled, puzzled over it a little, and would then have forgotten it. But he had woken to the moonlight, the troubling deceiving moonlight in which nothing is seen as it really is. He sat on where he was, lighting another cigarette, looking down at the river.

The river was running at his feet, deep and steadily, with its murmuring, soothing sound. In spite of himself he listened to its dark flow. "What does it matter?" the river said. "What does anything matter? Soon it will all be long ago."

Philip lifted his head and saw the white still beauty of the night. As he sat there in the full light of the moon, dazzled and shaken by the white steady light, he saw himself and his human thoughts as a dark blot, a stain, on the brightness of the night. He asked himself what he was doing there. None of them should be there. He saw the camp and all in it as a dark wedge driven into the forest, a spearhead that drew behind it a train of destruction leaving a desolate landscape that was as bare and stony as the cold earth of the moon.

He stood up and shrank into the shadows of the trees, away from the dangerous light. "What can we do?" he whispered, half to himself, half to the accusing forest. "We are here. We can't help it." Nothing in the night answered him. He stood there alone, apart from all the world.

As he peered out of the shadows at the aloof silver night, this cold and terrible sense of loneliness left him. His heart began to beat normally again. He was not alone; something else was abroad in the moonlight. Across the pool at the edge of the trees stood a large, calm, grey shape. It stood there for what seemed to Philip a long time, regarding the camp without moving, accepting what it saw, passing no judgment. The light gleamed whitely on a single tusk and he saw that it was withdrawing, as it had come, into the trees.

When it had gone, leaving no sign or ripple on the forest, Philip crept back to bed.

Part Four

The Beat

The Beat

ALL days in the forest are not eventful, highly coloured and set apart from other days as they, remembered, seem. Long stretches of time pass when nothing much happens, when life passes evenly and smoothly and imperceptibly. There is always something to be seen in the forest, but even there the colours can seem flat and muted, the jungle drained of life, and all the birds flown. But there are days that from the first hint of their dawn stand out as red-letter days, destined to be outsize, over-coloured, and long remembered even among other forest days. The day of Eric's tiger beat was one of these.

It began when the three elephants left the camp as the first light showed, moving silently through a dim dew-wet world for the meeting place north of the big village. Murray, lying awake in his tent, heard them go. He had slept little that night and now lay staring at the greying triangle in the open flies of his tent. Beats were always a worry to him; he dreaded the noise and excitement and the disturbance to his forest. In a beat there was danger for the beaters and for his elephants, and too many chances of disappointment, missed shots, bad temper. He turned over in his bed and, half asleep, was with the beaters advancing with their mongrel dogs through the high grass, keeping in touch with the next man as best they could, using their long sticks on every bush, thicket and tuft of grass, beating their empty tins and drums, shouting, bursting into wild catcalls. He was with the guns in the machans, peering down through the screen of leaves, feeling again the excitement and almost painful expectation, knowing the held breath, the tensed muscles and the quickly beating heart. He knew it all, and now he was in the narrowing strip of cover between the advancing beaters and the instinctively dreaded open space that lay before the shelter of those strangely silent trees, a space, either natural, or that had been cleared in the jungle so that the fleeing animals should be exposed for a moment to the guns above. Here the deer trembled at the edge of the undergrowth, peering out with dazzled eyes while the startled birds rocketed overhead.

"I don't like it," he said in his half-sleep. "There are other ways." If Eric still found it necessary to continue his pursuit, as it was plain that he did, let him wait for his striped quarry to come to him. Let it be a silent battle of wits, decently shrouded by the night, a long cold vigil over the kill or above the trap of the live tied-up bait. Yes, better death in the night after a few moments of sharp terror to one small cold lonely bullock or buffalo than this rude disturbance to the whole forest. But if Eric and Sangla were right and it was the big tiger that they had to deal with this day, a noisy beat would be useless; he would only break back through the beaters. Other tactics would be necessary: a silent beat perhaps. In a silent beat a few men advance confidently through the forest, occasionally tapping a tree with the back of their knives or talking in low voices, as if they were indeed a party of wood-cutters about their lawful business, or when the camp elephants advance quietly through the trees, as wild elephants might do, even a tiger gives way to an elephant and moves out of his path. Yes, a silent beat might bring the big tiger out without trouble. There must be no trouble, no trouble for anyone. Murray shut his eyes again and fell into the light, brief, before dawn sleep of old age. When he woke the waiting day was bright.

That morning the sun rose in a red-gold sky prophetically barred and striped in the east by a few dark clouds.

In the camp the fires were lit as usual, water carried up from the river, and preparations begun for the first meal. When Murray stood outside his tent in the cool fresh morning air, he knew that the day was going to be warm. Already, in mid-February, a hint of the hot weather days to come was in the air. The forest was thinning and drying; still green, still blue and rich, it was touched with the pale and tawny colours to come. Among the evergreen trees bare branches were showing which, almost at once, would be covered with the yellow-green leaves of the Indian spring. Already the open plains were turning brown and soon the scarlet flowers of the simul tree would burn through the jungle, as many small forest fires would when the dry, crackling tangle of undergrowth was fired by the herdsmen. Soon the forest would be scarred with black patches, a heavy scent of smoke would hang on the air, and then the new, bright, young grass would appear.

To Murray, looking down the line of huts at the orderly bustle of everyday, the coming and going round the cook tent, the sun-paled smoke rising from the camp fires, it seemed that the camp was untouched by this new stirring in the air. It presented a peaceful early morning scene to the watchful trees across the river. It pleased him to know that its inhabitants, men and beasts, had settled down well together, mellowing as the gold straw roofs had done. He was certain of the temper of his elephants, sure of his own men; as for the others, it seemed to him that they were quieter, content and busy with their own affairs, and that they were losing a little of their dangerous awareness of each other. Given time, given long enough here, they would become as healthily indifferent to each other as a party of grazing deer. He hoped that this day would not upset them again. The trouble with a beat was that it was so often a failure. After all the suspense and excitement, all Eric and Sangla's hard work and care, it was very likely that no tiger, nothing would appear.

"Nothing again, Murray," Alice said behind him. She held out the night-line roughly coiled in her hands. "Look, the bait has been taken, nibbled off the hooks. Can it be those otters again?"

As he took the line from her, Murray looked searchingly at her. Alice was ready for the day, dressed in the khaki which did not become her, in spite of the green-blue scarf under her chin. He saw that she had taken more trouble with her hair than she usually did; she looked spruced and ready for some special occasion, but she was very pale and there were tell-tale blue circles under her eyes. She met his look, lifting her chin warningly, and he only said, "Nothing? Is that an omen for to-day?"

"Of course not. You and I are only amusing ourselves with this line, playing our own game. What would we do if we caught this fish, Murray? We know very well that we will never catch it. But for Eric this day is serious. It matters to him if he gets this tiger or not, this particular tiger and no other. I feel sick with anxiety and excitement already."

"I thought that you disliked these beats as much as I do. I wish that Eric had chosen some other way."

"To-day a beat is the best way," Alice said. "It's important that Eric kills this tiger in front of us all, in as sensational a way as possible. And to be honest, when I'm there, in the machan, waiting, I have no heart or brain. I'm only two eyes waiting for the moment when the tiger will be there."

"To-day if it comes, what will you wish? That in spite of everything it will get away?"

"No. Not to-day. I'll wish that it will die quickly and splendidly."

"That doesn't sound like you, Alice."

Alice put her hand under his arm, standing so close to him that all he could see of her was the top of her head. "I'm worried about Eric," she said. "He has set his silly obstinate heart on this beast. If he doesn't get it, if it comes to one of the other machans, if he misses, anything can happen. I believe that he sees this beat as a kind of duel. Childish, isn't it? Four rifles, each safely up a tree and one soft-skinned gold thing on the ground. But today it's more than that, it's serious."

"Eric won't see only a tiger. Is that what you are trying to say?"

"He will see a mountain blocking his path. If he can get past it there will be only an easy valley and he will go on from there. Murray, it's important that today goes well. Where is Eric? I got up early to wish him luck."

"He and Sangla and the dog left two hours ago in the truck."

"That's too early. It's no use beating too early, is it?"

"Eric has to decide what to do to-day. Tigers seldom return to their kill more than once, two meals, one hot, one cold, and they leave the rest to the jackals and start on their hunting again. But with luck we shall find the big tiger still lying up near the place where he was yesterday."

"And if he has left the river bed?"

"Then Eric will give him up for the time being and beat the jungle across the river where that pair killed yesterday. Or there may be news of a fresh kill. Is Philip ready? I promised Eric that we would be at the crossroads above the village soon after nine o'clock. Kay has started his breakfast."

Alice did not answer and Murray, standing away from her, looked down at her face.

"What is the matter, Alice?"

"Nothing."

"You know that you can't hide anything from me. Where is Philip?"

"Still dressing, I suppose. Come on, Murray, let's eat our breakfast and get on with the day. To-day is going to be important, a landmark, in more ways than you think."

Murray caught her hand and turned her towards him.

"Look at me, Alice," he said, and obediently she lifted her face to him. Her eyes were at their most large and innocent and limpid. As he looked into them their lashes dropped and she turned her head away.

"You are up to something," he said. "Be careful, Alice. You said that you wouldn't lift a finger. Better to leave things as they are than to start something you can't stop."

She smiled at him and pulled her hand away. "Don't look so solemn," she said. "This is a special day, don't spoil it. I feel in my bones that this is Eric's day."

Standing at the edge of the bank above the river, she lifted her head towards the forest.

"This is a different morning," she said. "Don't you feel it? Can't you smell it? There's tiger in the air."

CHAPTER II

THE car, with Pior standing on the running-board, left the forest road and turned down the track which led to the dead river bed. Philip had hoped, until the moment when at the crossroads Pior signalled to them to stop, that the big tiger would have left the place and that the beat that day would be a beat like any other. But now there was no turning back, no evading what was to happen.

Philip had seen many beats. He was prepared for the long cramped wait in the machans, for the fresh stirring of interest as the beaters were heard in the distance and from the screen of trees and undergrowth the first living things fled across the open space, first the birds and then the deer, perhaps a porcupine rattling through the forest like a small quick train, or a troop of outraged and chattering monkeys, perhaps a leopard bounding across the open sunlight, or a lumbering sloth bear. He was prepared for disappointment, to see nothing except a line of crestfallen beaters emerge from the forest. He was prepared for the sudden hush that falls, or seems to fall when the tiger is there, standing in the open with lashing tail and head raised to listen, seeming larger than life and unbelievably bright. Philip had also taken part in silent beats before and he knew what to expect.

There was no reason why he should feel this unwillingness for what was to come, a foreboding. He looked at Murray who was driving with Alice beside him, and at Kay. All three were silent, but they looked much as usual. No one seemed perturbed or uneasy, as he was.

Alice was looking up at Murray as if she were asking him a question. Her profile was clear and sharp against the background of the forest. Philip wanted to touch her, to make her look round at him so that he could tell her that last night he had not been himself, to ask her to forgive him. He had been trying to tell her this ever since he had woken after his broken night to see her already dressed and slipping out of the hut. He knew that she had heard him call her back. She had been evading him all morning and he had not found himself alone with her for one moment. He leant forward. It was suddenly and desperately important that he should speak to her. Only now, at this inappropriate moment, did he realise that he should tell her, before them all if necessary, before it was too late, exactly what she meant to him. He knew now that he should have told her this years ago and repeated it again and again. And now it was too late. The car was approaching the end of the track. Ahead, through the trees, shone the white stones of the dead river bed. Eric was waiting under the trees. As the car stopped, he came forward.

Eric's face gave none of his excitement away. He opened the car door and bent his head to speak quietly to Murray.

"Better leave the car here behind the truck," he said. "I'm afraid that you will have rather a long walk, but it's safer to take no chances, the quieter we all are, the better."

"Then he's still there?" Murray asked.

"The new tracks are confusing and Sangla says that

there are the tracks of a small tigress going away down the river bed but, as far as we can tell, he must have gone in again. With luck we have him at last."

"It is the big tiger?"

"Not much doubt about that."

Now they were all out of the car and standing in a close group, talking in low voices. Pior stood behind Philip, listening uncomprehendingly, moving impatiently from one foot to the other. In the background Puran Singh, holding the dog on a strong chain, leaned against the truck.

"A quiet beat with elephants," Eric was saying. "They will go in half way between here and the Dipsiri clearing at half past ten. Sangla and Manoo are with them. The elephant will move him out, he will make way for them and think nothing of it. It's only a quarter past nine now. We will have a long wait, but I beg you all to be still the whole time in the machans. This is a different tiger."

"They say that if he is suspicious he looks up and searches the trees in front of him," Kay said. "Surely only a very sophisticated beast does that?"

"Who is with you?" Murray asked.

"The headman insisted on coming. I will send him back to the truck. The Santal tracker and Jetha and Pior will act as stops. Murray, I hoped that Sangla and I would be able to deal with him by ourselves on foot, I would have liked it that way, but the jungle here, even at its narrowest, is too broad. One rifle would never cover it, there are too many ways that he might come."

"Oh, no!" Alice said. "That's much too dangerous. And I want to see what happens. Let me go with you, Eric."

"No one knows where the tiger will come out, Alice," Eric said looking down at her. "It might be to any of the machans. I had thought of Murray on the left beyond the stream, then Philip and you, then myself, and Kay on the right."

"He will come straight to you. I know that he will."

"The ground is fairly open. You should get a good view of him from any machan."

Alice looked up at him and said, "Don't you see, Eric? I want to be with you."

There was a moment's silence, then Kay said, "Can't we get on with this? I hate this hanging about. This is no time for you to put yourself forward, Alice. We are far too busy to worry about you now. Wait until this is over."

Murray smiled, but Eric said, "Alice shall do what she likes."

The path led through the trees. Silently they followed it, walking in single file, Eric leading with Philip and Pior in the rear. They skirted the bank and, when they came out onto the stones above the long wooded peninsula that lay between the river bed and the open plain, Eric turned his head and looked back at them and lifted his hand warningly.

Murray, walking carefully over the stones behind Alice, looked over her head at Eric's face which was smoothly red and hard under the soft hat, and at the pale expressionless eyes. He knew that Eric had forgotten Alice, that he had forgotten everything except the need for silence and the waiting forest. Years ago he, too, had experienced this cold excitement. He had been filled with the same implacable, steady, soft-moving purpose. He knew that, for the time being, Eric was not only Eric but the hunter, the personification of the cold and ruthless instinct to kill which has been a part of men since the first man set out through the forest with his bow and sling, that is seen every day in the innocent cruel eyes of the boy with his catapult. Murray remembered what he had said two weeks ago on his first evening in the

camp to his visitor, the Forest Officer, Barua. It is the hunter
who knows his quarry, he knows the life of the forest and
its ways. The instinct to kill is often accompanied by knowledge and a strange affection, the greater the hunter the
greater the affection, the terrible affection of the hunter for
for the hunted. Like twins, dark and fair, killer and lover
walk hand in hand through the forest.

But now they had left the bed of warm stones and the
trees were round them again. Here a form rose silently from
the ground to meet them. It was Jetha, solemn for once, who
reported to Eric by signs and whispers, that the two other
stops were already in place, each high in a tree and com-
manding a view on one side of the stony river and on the
other of the open plain. He whispered that all was quiet and
that nothing had passed that way.

And here were the trunks of well spaced trees, and an
open glade, green and peaceful in the sunlight. Beyond the
heavy forest continued. This was the place.

The dark tree trunks rose from the low undergrowth.
Shining ferns caught the sunlight that filtered through the
leaves and sunlight lay in pools on the ground. The only
sound was made by the stream: the clear thread of water
trickled over its bed of drowned leaves and stones and the
small deceiving sound it made seemed to say that here was
only green coolness and peace, cool leaves, sun-warmed grass,
deep shade.

The minutes passed. A leaf fell slowly through the
heavy air, spiralling down to sound in the stillness like a
footfall. A cricket began its drowsy shrilling. The sunlight
deepened. A light breeze sprang up and stirred the spider-
webs that hung from tree to tree and went, leaving a deeper
stillness. Down the stream something was moving. There
came the sound of splashing and a low grunting. In the

branches of a tree a steely gleam showed once and was gone
as across the stream came the unmistakable black shape of a
wild pig. It was followed by another, each moving slowly and
snuffling unsuspiciously; the young pigs which followed
after showed light coloured in the patches of sunlight and
were striped vertically with brown. Following the course of
the stream, they disappeared and silence descended again.
The minutes passed and lengthened. A gold, drowsy silence
settled over the forest glade. The curled heads of the ferns
stood up in the stillness. Were they all turned to look one
way?

The tiger was crossing the glade with soundless, ponder-
ous footfalls. Where there had been only a green emptiness
the tiger colours now shone in the sunlight. The heavy swinging strides carried him forward. The low but immense shape
passed from shade to sunlight, from light to shade towards
the waiting trees.

The huge shoulders rose and fell. Carried low, the tail
with the characteristic tilted-tip swung gently. The gold eyes
were half closed and the great white-fringed jaws opened
in a protesting yawn. Heavy with meat and the warm drowsy
day, he moved away from his sleeping place, giving way
to the advancing elephants as everything in the forest, even
the tiger, does. Grumbling to himself he came, making for
the heavy forest beyond the stones where the dark shade
would close over him until the sinking sun and the first stars
sent him out again to quest through the night along the
jungle paths, covering as much as twenty miles in a night at
a slow walk, head held low and great feet placed without a
sound. The stream sang its deceitful soothing song. Not a
leaf moved. The langoors, the great monkeys, had often
spoiled his hunting with their harsh warning cries, the gut-
tural notes of alarm which were taken up by the barking-

deer until all the weaker inhabitants of the forest could be heard calling, "Danger! Tiger!" But now even the jungle crow who had fed on his kill had vanished. The betraying forest was silent and no voice spoke for him.

The soft-nosed bullet, fired from a distance of thirty yards at a slightly downward angle, entered his body behind the shoulder, a fraction too high, just grazing the heart. As the loud cracking sound exploded in the silence, he fell, knocked down and forward by the impact, to rise at once in a rear that took him backwards in a fantastic somersault. A great wheel of colour flashed in the sunlight. The forest shook to one shattering roar as two bounds carried him back the way that he had come.

A whistle sounded shrilly and a voice called loudly from the trees and was answered by shouts and one shrill trumpet as the elephants approached. The passage of the elephants was seen by moving branches and an uplifted trunk. The forest resounded with shouts and calls, but the tiger heard none of this. He had died in mid-air before his last leap was completed. He lay on his side in the shadow of a deep thicket twenty yards away. It was some time before the elephants found him lying there.

They stood in a ring looking down at him while the elephants shifted uneasily behind them in the trampled undergrowth. It seemed a long time since Manoo had fired into the ground beside the still body and had shouted that the big tiger was dead. But it had taken only a few minutes for them to descend from the machans and, easing their stiff muscles, to cross the open space to where he lay on his side, tail extended, enormous paws still in the attitude of speed. On his shoulder was a small dark puncture and from the closed black-skinned mouth oozed a few drops of blood. The soft-nosed bullet had broken up inside him, causing a terrible wound. It was a wonder that he had got so far.

Eric had not spoken since he had called out from the machans when the tiger turned. He stood, staring down with a dazed heavy look. He seemed like a man who had woken from a dream. He lifted his head and looked round their circle and said, "He's not as big as I had thought."

He bent down and touched a white scar near the neck, and looked up at Sangla. Sangla nodded and pointed. Across the hindquarters to the great hock ran an older scar, a barely perceptible furrow across the stripes. Eric traced this slowly with his finger. Murray knew what he was thinking, but the coincidence was too unlikely. A tiger probably lives to twenty years, this was a tiger in his prime. It was more than twelve years ago that Eric had lost that wounded beast. Before he could say anything, Eric straightened himself and looking past them all into the trees said: "I'm sorry. He should have died at once."

Sangla could not contain himself any longer. This was the moment that he had worked for. If Eric did not see fit to show his joy and satisfaction, Sangla would rejoice for them both. Leaping to his feet he broke into a wild short dance, drawing his knife, throwing his arms above his head, stamping his foot on the ground close to the dead tiger's head. The performance was over as quickly as it had started; it might never have been. Manoo, standing close behind Murray, murmured disapprovingly but Sangla walked away, unabashed, to superintend the cutting of bamboos.

The rough stretcher was quickly made out of bamboos tied together and the tiger was rolled onto it and carried out into the open glade, four men to each side, for he weighed all of six hundred pounds. The village headman and Puran Singh with the dog had left the truck at the sound of the two signal shots, and a small crowd of five or six unknown foresters had gathered, springing apparently out of the jungle, as happens when a tiger dies. The dog slowly advanced, hackles raised, to sniff at the still body, and then lifted his head and barked, one deep triumphant bay. He had seen many dead tigers in his time, and he knew that now the hunting in which he had no part was over. He touched Eric on the hand, and then lay down to growl watchfully at any stranger who approached too closely. They stretched the tiger out in the sunlight of the old river bed, lifting the huge head, stretching out his tail. Manoo and Sangla drove their khukris into the ground at his muzzle and tail-tip and Murray laid the measuring tape between them.

"Nine feet five inches, a huge tiger," Kay said. "Congratulations, Eric. Alice was right. He came straight to your machan."

Alice's face was flushed and her eyes were shining but, as Kay spoke, her colour went, leaving her very pale. She turned to Murray and hid her face against his shoulder.

Murray put his arm round her and looked round for Philip, but Philip, staring down at the tiger, was trying to reconcile what he had seen a short while ago with what lay before him. Here were the same tawny colours, the tiger-lily colours, the orange-red touched with black, the snowy white, of a tiger's rich winter coat. Was it the strong sunlight and the white glare from the stones that made them seem altogether different? The colours were the same, Philip decided, but something, the brightness, had gone.

CHAPTER III

By the time the tiger had been hoisted onto Sitara's back and carried by her to the truck, it was long after mid-day. Sitara had shown her usual unwillingness to do anything that was asked of her, refusing to kneel, refusing to stand still, and backing away from the dead tiger with pretended hysterical fear. Murray had insisted and all at once she had given in, resuming her nonchalant airs, carrying the tiger proudly away, head and forepaws hanging down on one side of the pad and striped tail on the other, with Sangla and Jetha perched aloft to hold the ropes in place.

Manoo and Sangla were to take the carcass back to the camp in the truck and to begin the skinning at once, that long, delicate, beautiful operation, when the skin, severed by the sharp knives from the tissues, turned carefully inside out on the pads of the great paws, the rounded ears and the lips, peels slowly off like a glove leaving a firm pink and white hand.

The rest of the small crowd drifted away. "It's late," Murray said. "Let's eat here."

The picnic baskets were carried from the car to the edge of the bank above the stones where, beyond the head of the wooded peninsula, they could see the mountains and the plain. The grass was beaten flat, the rugs spread. They sat in a half circle facing the hills, much as they sat in the dining-hut above the river. Eric and Alice with the dog at their feet sat a little apart together. The colour was in Alice's cheeks again. She talked as people sometimes do after an ordeal, a little wildly, and laughing too much.

"This is the best part of a beat," Kay said, lying back with his hands behind his head. "Where is the beer?"

"Why not stay in the truck with Puran Singh and Ebon another time?" Alice said. "Why worry about the beat at all?"

Kay heard the strained excited note in her voice. He raised himself on his elbow and looked at her. Other people are liked for good reasons, for their beauty, or charm, or wit, for their kindness and goodness, for qualities of mind and person that can be named. Alice took a shortcut to the affections. This was unfair. She did not deserve the feeling that she roused. Kay looked at her severely. What they all saw in her he did not know. There she sat, the focus point of their circle, a small, unremarkable, not very young woman who sometimes, as she did now, for no obvious reason, took on an illusion of beauty, a softness and an almost starry radiance that he had never seen in any other woman. As he looked at her, Kay could not help smiling; it was all that he could do to sit where he was and not to go to her, making some excuse to move nearer to her, perhaps to touch her hand. At the same time he was annoyed with her. What right had she to sit there so complacently with the sunlight falling through the leaves onto her hair? He would have liked to inflict some small sharp pain on her.

His quick black eyes went from her to Eric, and then to Philip. Philip, a glass between his feet and a sandwich in his hand, was staring absently across the stones at the brown distance of the plain. It was impossible to tell what he was thinking; his rather heavy, sallow face gave nothing away. Kay abruptly transferred his annoyance to him. Philip deserved all he got. It would do him good to have a thorough jolt. Kay glanced again at Alice. It was a pity that she was overdoing it. Her tactics were too obvious. Even Eric must see that she was up to something.

"Alice," he said, in the voice that she most disliked. "Do you know how well you look this morning? This blood-thirsty business seems to suit you. Look at her, all of you. Doesn't she look as sleek and plump as a good little kitten who has swallowed the canary? A little white kitten with a blue bow round her neck and yellow feathers in her mouth? But that would be a tame house kitten, not suitable here. What about a little jungle cat?"

Alice smiled kindly at him. "Poor little Kay," she said. "Did the horrid beat upset him? Eat your food and you'll feel better."

"Of course, Alice shouldn't be here at all," Kay went on. "Murray should have seen to it that this was a purely male preserve. There should be a notice half-way down the forest road saying, 'No women allowed. Keep out trouble.' "

"Now that I come to think of it," Murray said, "Alice is the only woman who has ever come to my camps."

"A great mistake," Kay said. "Alice is all wrong here. A jungle girl should be a tough, long-legged, sunburned, efficient creature. Just look at Alice, she simply asks something to come along and bite or sting her, or to be scratched and torn by thorns. You should be safely at home, Alice, sitting by the fire on a satin cushion, rocking the cradle or sewing a fine seam. Philip should never have brought you here. You are far too dangerous."

"What rubbish you talk, Kay," Eric said, but Alice was unruffled.

"Pity that we didn't leave you at home," was all she said.

Kay saw Murray looking at him and he said, smoothly changing the subject, "I wouldn't have missed this morning for anything. It all went so smoothly and easily, a wonderful bit of organisation, no fireworks, no dramatics. Now we know that it's as easy to shoot a tiger as a sitting partridge."

"Easy?" Alice said indignantly. "I didn't find it easy to sit as still as we did for nearly two hours. Ants crawled down my neck, flies sat on my nose, it felt like days. Weren't you frightened too, Kay? I trembled so much when the tiger came that I thought the tree must shake. Why was I so frightened, Murray? I was perfectly safe."

"Because it was a tiger, Alice. That was enough."

"I have heard of men who, the first time they sat up for tiger, couldn't fire when it came to the kill," Kay said. "It was as if a paralysing weight held the rifle down. Do you think that's true, Murray?"

"Ask Eric," Murray said.

"I thought today that Eric was never going to fire," Alice said. "When that pig grunted I thought that it was the tiger. After that I couldn't take my eyes off the stream. When I felt Eric stiffening I turned my head, slowly, like this. He was raising the rifle, very slowly. I looked straight along it and saw the tiger, close. I never saw it come."

"I did," Kay said. "I was the furthest away but I saw it perfectly in profile, crossing that space. What about you, Philip? At first I thought that it was going to be your shot."

Philip roused himself. He had been thinking for some time how happy Alice looked sitting next to Eric, how contented they both seemed together, how well they looked together. He asked himself why he had not seen this long ago. He looked blankly at Kay. What had he seen? He had been watching the machan next his own, trying to see through the screen of intervening branches and, because he could see very little, only an indistinct thickening in the tree and the outline of Eric's head, his mind had taken charge, that green

§ 161 §

and crooked second mind of his, showing him what his sane
mind did not accept: furtive moments, whispers, small ugly
pictures which he tried to reject. When the tiger came he saw
it without astonishment, with only relief, as if its bold strong
colours had a cauterising power to clean his mind. For the
few moments that they shone up at him from the ground the
tiger colours had filled his eyes, leaving room for nothing
else.

Kay was waiting for him to answer, looking at him
curiously. Philip said the first thing that came into his mind:
"I could have looked at him for hours. Why did he have to
die?"

"What a question!" Kay said. "Why did we all come
here this morning, all five of us, not to mention three elephants, a car, a truck, a small crowd of excited people? Why
indeed? Do you know why, Eric?"

Eric looked up. He looked from Kay to Philip and answered calmly. "He was a dangerous beast. He had killed a
man."

"And that's the unforgivable sin in the jungle. But that
was four years ago and it wouldn't have happened then if he
had been left alone. What harm has he done since? He
wasn't a cattle killer, was he, Murray?"

"As far as we know he kept to the jungle," Murray said.
"In a year or so he would have been past his prime. When a
tiger grows old he generally keeps near the villages where a
plentiful supply of beef is at hand. And a beast like this one,
who has had the bad luck to be twice involved with men,
could become an unmitigated nuisance to the villagers, if
nothing worse."

"This is a new role for you, Kay," Alice said. "You talk
like Murray or like me."

Kay smiled at her and said, "We seem to have changed

places, haven't we? Today you are all for the slayer, Alice. I wonder why?"

Murray said quickly, "This tiger is dead. He had to die, leave it at that."

He leaned against the warm stones behind him and shut his eyes. He did not want to see their faces or to hear their voices. They were suddenly unbearable to him. He could not understand why he had brought them there. At that moment it seemed to him that he would rather watch a tiger crossing a sunlit glade than see and hear all that human kind had to offer. Men are as the angels, made, they say, in the image of God. The human mind is a treasure house, a great store. Perhaps it is the terrible brightness of men's minds that dims in them the physical brightness that all other wild animals possess. Philip's mind was large and generous, Eric's was simple, noble and loyal, Kay's brain was a jewel or a polished weapon. But it seemed to him that he had heard little worth hearing in the last weeks, little except small foolish quarrels, hints and innuendoes. Must there always be some defect that spoilt the whole? As for Alice, Kay was right. One drop of woman in any mixture is fatal; she cannot help it. If Alice had not been there, if he had not had this weakness for her, would they all have had a better chance? Murray sighed. The trouble with human beings, men and women, was that there were too many of them, too many for one world. They loomed too large in the scheme of things.

Long ago tigers ruled this part of the country. In those days man-eaters, now rare, abounded and no human being dared to leave his barred door after sundown. Every living thing destroys to live, and that is right, what was intended, but was it intended that only man should go further than his need, that he should re-make the world, turning every-

thing, every beast and bird and plant and stone to his own
purpose? The balance of the living world is delicately, purposefully adjusted; take one cog away, one small part of the
whole, and that balance is upset forever. The wild pig and
the deer without the tiger, their rightful slayer, multiply
until no planted crop is safe. One answer to that is, of course,
to kill the deer, to kill everything that cannot be used or
tamed. And the birds? The birds take their share of seed
and fruit and keep the insects, man's last enemy, in bounds,
but everywhere, every day, the birds are fewer; when they
have gone there will be one last battle, a battle that need
never have been. When it has won and man is alone in the
desert that he has made will he be content or, still dreaming,
still unsatisfied, will he turn his attention to the stars?
Murray, shutting out the sound of the voices that rose and
fell round him, keeping his eyes firmly closed, contemplated
his private vision. This was a daydream that he had often
dreamt before. He saw a world where everything that lived
had its own place and its own right, a rich green world where
the desert had blossomed like the rose and the rose had learnt
to discard its thorns, where man was no longer the hunter or
the dangerous dreamer but the world's gardener, the caretaker that he was meant to be. This was a vision that he
would never tell. No one would listen to a solitary, morose
old man. No one would see.

A voice said, "Murray is asleep." He opened his eyes
and saw Alice smiling at him.

He looked back at her solemnly. He was disappointed
in Alice. Even on a day like this, a day of large happenings,
she could not keep quietly in the background but, disregarding his advice, was busy with her own small plans and
stratagems. He saw what she was trying to do and he did not
approve. This would lead to trouble; now the feathers would

fly. Luckily she was not being very subtle, poor child. Surely
Philip and Eric must both see what she was up to? He looked
hopefully at the two men, but vanity and pride make thick
blinkers. Kay had seen it all hours ago. Kay was enjoying
himself.

"I'm not asleep," he said. "You all talk too much, but
I notice that no one has asked me what I saw in the beat."

Alice said, "Don't be cross, not on a day like this. Tell
us what you saw."

He had meant to tell them at the appropriate time what
he had seen that day and no one else had seen, but now he
hesitated. Would Alice be as delighted or Philip as interested as he had thought? Eric would disapprove and Kay
would think him a sentimental old man. As the big tiger
roared and died, something had made him turn his head
and look down. There, immediately below his machan,
crouched flat in the leaf-filled depression in the ground, was
a small tigress. He could see every stripe on her anxious body
and the tensed muscles quivering under the gold skin. She
was making for the open plain that he saw on his left over
the intervening trees, using the bank of the little stream as
cover. His hands had tightened on the rifle, half lifting it.
Then, leaning forward and looking down, he had said: "Go
quickly, my girl." The eyes that were immediately turned up
to him were full of hate. He looked into them for a second
and then the tigress was gone, drawing her body silently and
swiftly away into the long grass. He had seen her once again,
a low, hurrying yellow shape, growing smaller and smaller
on the plain.

"No. I won't tell you," he said, but now no one was
listening to him. The village headman and Sangla were
standing in front of Eric.

Eric jumped up. "I had completely forgotten," he said.

"The big tiger sent it clean out of my mind. This old man will be furious with me. Murray, a tiger killed a pony almost in the village last evening, at the edge of the fields when it was still light."

Murray turned to the headman and the old, wizened man, wearing an ancient tweed coat above his white loin cloth, advanced a few steps and began what was evidently a prepared speech.

The history of the village tiger was told again and in detail. For years the village had known and tolerated him, not grudging him the cattle that for the greater part of every year he took from them, perhaps once in four days, for all must eat. But this pony, the headman's own, worth hundreds of rupees, was a different matter. And to take it in daylight, observing no decency, was not what should be. This tiger's time had come. He must go.

Murray looked at Eric.

"The kill is in the ravine below the bridge," Eric said. "They say that it was dragged only fifty yards, about two hundred yards from the village. Sangla and I should have gone there at least an hour ago."

"You mean to sit up over the kill to-night?"

"It's in sight of the village, almost on the road. But I promised that I would."

"The village would never forgive us if you didn't," Murray said. "Perhaps greed will bring the old tiger back, tigers love horseflesh. Perhaps he considers himself immune by now, one of the village Gods, and will be overconfident."

"Sangla has taken it upon himself to bring the truck back here and to leave the skinning to Manoo. I'll go straight to the village now and, if all goes well and I have time, I'll drive back to the camp for some food later. If I'm in the machan by five o'clock it will have to do. As the kill is so near the village he will probably come to it late, if he comes at all."

"Of course you will come back to the camp first. You will be frozen without a coat, for one thing. The nights are still cold."

"I shall sit up with you to-night, Eric," Alice said.

"Oh, no, you won't," Murray said quickly. "This will be a tricky business. It will probably mean a long cold wait and the mosquitoes will be bad. The only way to keep absolutely still in a machan is to be alone. You leave this to Eric."

Alice turned her head and looked up at Eric's face and said, "I brought you luck this morning, didn't I? Let me come."

Eric hesitated a moment and then sat down beside her again and took her hand in his. He said slowly, "Do you mean this, Alice?" and when, after a quick glance at Murray, she nodded, he laid her hand gently in her lap and said, "Then you shall come."

"I'll come back to the camp to fetch you as soon as I can," he said, and turning his back on them, walked away towards the truck, followed by his dog.

"Philip!" Murray said. "Don't let her do this. Stop it, forbid it. It's too much in one day. She will be overtired. She will catch cold. Philip, it's dangerous."

Philip was carefully folding the rugs. He said, "Alice must do what she likes. Don't worry, she's tougher than she looks."

Kay said lightly, in the pause that followed, "Well, what a day. It never rains but it pours. Tiger, tiger everywhere. Come on Alice, let's get back to the car."

But Alice, standing with her back to the forest, was staring at Philip. She looked so white and suddenly forlorn that Kay went to her and took her arm.

"You needn't go, my clever little Alice," he said softly. "You can always change your mind."

"I won't let Eric have the truck," Murray said.

Philip, carrying the rugs, turned towards the path that led through the trees. "How many times have you told us to leave each other alone?" he asked. "Alice isn't a child. I don't keep her on a lead. She knows what she is doing, and she will do what she must do."

Murray was left standing above the stony river bed. He shrugged his shoulders and looked up at the sky where the vultures were again making their high wheeling circles. Then, throwing his arms up in a wide despairing gesture, he walked after the others down the path.

CHAPTER IV

THE sun was still in the sky when Eric and Alice left the truck in the village street and, followed by Sangla and Jetha, walked down the raised path between the houses that led to the fields. The headman and a silent crowd escorted them to the edge of the village and then fell back. The children closed in and followed until Sangla, turning on them suddenly, sent them scurrying for home, their thin black legs twinkling across the fields. The open land between its walls of forest was a fawn jig-saw puzzle of small fields, patches of earth enclosed by foot-high mud walls that each cast its own blue evening shadow.

Sangla led the way and Jetha came behind. Their four long shadows, distorted by the rugs and coats and the two rifles that they carried, went before them. Eric turned his head. Already the village had retreated. It had turned its back on them and was busy again with its peaceful evening affairs. A feeling of unreality came over him. What were they doing, advancing, heavily laden, over the peaceful fields? What had the heavy rifle under his arm to do with this golden evening? He looked down at Alice.

Alice was watching the forest, frowning a little. It was clear that she was already far ahead, following the path that he could see winding through the undergrowth into the trees. In the camp Murray had warned Alice, "You will have to be quieter and keep more still than you have ever done before." Now she walked with exaggerated care and her expression was determined.

Eric smiled. "There's no need to be quite so cautious yet," he said.

She gave him a brief answering smile and turned her eyes to the path again. She might have been playing an absorbing game. This was not what he had expected, and he did not know what to think. He looked down at her bare head. Her small neat body in the dark warm trousers and sweater moved beside him, her shoulder touched his arm but, for all the attention she paid him, it might have been Sangla or Jetha who walked with her. During the drive from the camp, which he had looked forward to all afternoon with both longing and uneasiness, she had talked excitedly, asking questions, keeping their talk entirely to the forest and the ways of tigers, turning every opening he made back the same way, evading, exasperating him until he could have shaken her. Had he been entirely mistaken? Was he about to make a fool of himself once again? The hot blood came into his face as he looked at her.

But now they had reached the edge of the fields. Before them rose a wall of undergrowth and trees. He stepped past

Alice onto the narrow white path, motioning to her to walk behind him. This was the time for caution, although it was unlikely that the tiger was anywhere near. The villagers declared that he would lie up for the day a long way off, beyond the river. The tall pungent bushes closed round them, the mauve flowers of the ageratum caught at their clothes. It was a relief to him to see only Sangla's broad khaki-covered shoulders going before him down the path.

A jungle crow, black and sudden, flew up from the low trees at their right. The path turned and petered out. As they saw the tall red-trunked tree standing up at the lip of the ravine, a stench, faint at first, then suddenly filling their nostrils, told them that the kill was near.

Alice pulled the hem of Eric's tweed coat. He turned his head and she whispered, "Where is it? I can't see it."

He nodded towards a bamboo clump that grew on the opposite side of the ravine which at that point was not more than twenty yards broad. "Wait until you are in the machan. You will see it then."

The ground below the tree was covered with broad dry fallen leaves that crackled loudly underfoot. Looking up, Eric saw that the machan that he and Sangla had made that afternoon was well hidden. It was much higher than such machans usually are. The lowest branches of the only tree near enough to the kill were thirty feet from the ground and well over forty from the bottom of the jungle-filled ravine over which they hung. Sangla held the rope ladder that was already in place, hanging suspended from the edge of the machan. Both he and Eric looked at Alice.

Everyone in the camp knew of Alice's dislike of the swaying ladder and her hatred of heights. It was a well-worn joke of Murray's that it would take a charging rhinoceros to get her into a machan without delays and protests and sometimes even tears.

"Come on, Alice," Eric whispered. "The longer you look at it the less you will like it."

"I can't. It's twice as high as the one this morning."

"Then you will have to go back to the village with Sangla."

She looked appealingly at Sangla who made small encouraging noises in his throat, but Eric said, "Hurry up, Alice. I can't wait forever."

He spoke impatiently, looking round at the trees behind him. Then, as if he suddenly realised what he had said, he whispered again, "You must make up your mind. I won't wait for you forever."

There was nothing assumed about Alice's fear. She was pale and her forehead under the loose curling hair was damp. The grey eyes met his and filled with tears.

"Help me then," she said. "I'll never do it alone."

Eric smiled. It was a curious smile and Alice, seeing it, looked at him doubtfully, and then put out her hand, catching at the sleeve of his coat.

He stepped back. "No. I won't help you. You will have to do it alone. I won't make up your mind for you."

Alice still hesitated, but Sangla intervened. He only knew that the sun was growing lower in the sky and that the shadows were lengthening. He bent down and placed Alice's foot on the lowest rung and motioned to Jetha to hold the two ropes steady. With a re-assuring gesture he made it plain that he would climb up behind her and that he would not let her fall.

Eric stood below the tree and watched Alice, with Sangla following, slowly disappear into the branches. It occurred to him suddenly that he had never sat up for tiger with anyone except Sangla, and that he had usually made a point of sitting alone. Many years ago Murray had said to him, "Remember, you always have a better chance alone."

From aloft came a faint rustling and creaking. Sangla swung back down the ropes. He grinned at Eric and bent to hold the ladder steady again.

Eric pulled himself up by his arms, one leg dangling uselessly. When he reached the low rough platform, he saw Alice crouching on the further side, holding onto a branch and peering down into the ravine, her fears apparently forgotten. She smiled forgivingly at him and together they pulled up the bundle of coats and rugs which Jetha had tied to a rope. Sangla climbed up with the rifle, and disappeared again.

"Make yourself comfortable now," Eric whispered. "There's no time to waste."

Quickly he checked what they had brought with them. To sit still and silent and unobserved for several hours, perhaps for a whole night, is not as easy as it sounds; there is a technique for this that must be learnt. Here was the flask of hot coffee and the two separate packets of sandwiches, wrapped in banana leaves, because paper crackles, and a few sweets to suck, for sweets slowly turned in the mouth are a help against that irresistible desire to cough. The coats and rugs were inconspicuous: no patch of light or dark must show. Even the cushion had khaki covers. Perhaps the best way to keep still in a machan is to lie flat. On this particular occasion, as Murray had often done before, Sangla, remembering Eric's leg, had tied two low, ancient and soft basket chairs, that were guaranteed not to creak, firmly to the platform of cut branches which, in their turn, were supported by two large branches of the tree. This was luxurious but sensible. Their backs would be supported and from this added height they could see over the screening branches down into the bamboo clump where the kill lay. At the front of the platform a horizontal and firmly fixed branch at the height of their knees made a rest for the rifle. Quickly they put on the extra sweaters and scarves that they had brought; they did not need them now but they would as the night advanced. They smeared the mosquito cream on their wrists and necks and foreheads, and wrapped the rugs round their waists and sat down, with everything that they needed close at hand. Eric fixed the big flashlight into its grooves under the barrel of the rifle and tested it. He loaded the rifle, and carefully placed two extra, soft-nosed bullets in his breast pocket. Lastly, he bent down and released the steel hooks that kept the rope ladder in place, letting it fall back into Jetha's hands. Now they were cut off from the ground. A moment later they heard Sangla and Jetha departing over the leaves.

Eric put his arm round Alice's shoulders. "You can't go back now," he whispered in her ear. "You will have to see this out."

But Alice was shaking with suppressed laughter. "I'm sorry, Eric," she said. "I can't help it." She turned her head, pressing her face against his arm, trying to stifle her helpless giggles.

"What's so funny?" he said stiffly.

"Only us, sitting here side by side, two wrapped up mummies in the front row of the stalls. How ridiculous we must look."

"There's no one to see us," Eric said, drawing his arm away.

Alice sat up, wiping her eyes. "I'm sorry, Eric," she said again. "I'm quite serious now. Where is the kill?"

The Peacock

Above the dark tangle of the ravine the long stems of the bamboos were striped in green and gold. The long leaves cast confusing shadows onto the yellow shoots and withered leaves below. Under the shining stems, lit by the last rays of the sun, was a patch of brown, a shape foreign to the surrounding jungle.

"Yes, that's it," Eric said, "lying head on. A tiger usually begins its meal from the hindquarters."

"I can see the village. How near it is. I don't believe one word of this. The tiger will never come back here."

"He was nearer to the village when he took the pony. He will probably come from behind us, or down the ravine. Now listen, he will come cautiously, when I touch your knee you will know that he is here."

"Of course I will know. I have sat up for tigers before, lots of times with Murray and Philip. It will be impossible not to know."

"When he comes you mustn't move, not an eyelash. He may circle round for a long time. I won't fire until I hear him on the kill."

"When do you think that he will come?"

"Either quite early, directly it's dark, or much later, before dawn, but you never know. It's after five now. No more whispering, not a sound, or he certainly won't come at all. Quite comfortable?"

Alice nodded. She leant back, folding her hands on her lap. Eric tucked the ends of her scarf into her coat collar and touched her cheek gently with one finger. Her skin was cool and soft. She did not turn her head to look up at him. He sighed and turned a little away from her, staring out through the gap in the trees to the village.

He did not think that he had been mistaken. The signs that he believed Alice had given him, to one who knew her as well as he did, were surely unmistakable? But he did not understand what she was doing or what she wanted of him. He considered it strangely tasteless of her to have said Philip's name so casually a few moments ago; it made at once a space between them. If he knew Alice, she knew him, knew him too well not to know that with him it must be all or nothing. Years ago he had made his feeling for her plain. He had not changed, but if this was to happen between the three of them it should have happened long ago.

The herds were coming home across the fields drawing a low gold cloud of dust behind them. The faint lowing of cattle and the sound of cow bells drifted to the trees. As the sun sank a white mist rose from the river, and blue smoke poured from the thatched eaves. As Eric watched the evening scene which he knew so well, he slowly became less conscious of Alice's presence beside him. He felt strangely light and peaceful, suspended between earth and sky in the golden evening. In the trees close at hand birds were moving, settling themselves for the night. A striped squirrel ran across a branch in front of his eyes. The sun sank lower into its bed of trees beyond the river. Now it was a crimson ball; now an arc of fire, and now a burning line. As the sun's rim disappeared and the last light flowed over fields and sky, Eric forgot Alice. Sitting there, invisible among the branches, he had become a part of the forest scene. He had let go, given himself up to the evening. For a moment he could not remember what he was waiting for, or why he was sitting there with death on his knees.

He shifted slightly in his chair, moving his hand over the cold wood and steel of the rifle. Already the colours had faded and the shadow of the opposing wall of forest had gone from the fields. A few points of light showed where the village was, but now the houses could no longer be seen.

From the trees a night-jar called suddenly, "Tonk, tonk, tonk." The last glow had gone from the sky. The stars were showing.

The tiger came with the darkness. Although Eric was half expecting it, he was surprised almost into movement as he heard the unmistakable cautious but heavy tread on the dead leaves beneath the tree. Slowly he put out his hand, but Alice had heard the sound too. Their cold fingers met and clung for a moment and slowly separated. Below was only silence that persisted for a long time. But they knew that the tiger was there, waiting and listening.

At last the sounds were repeated, but now the footfalls were loud and purposeful; they circled the tree and paused again. When the silence was again broken it was by a crashing on their right, the sound of a heavy body moving in the undergrowth, a body that could move at will as silently as a shadow. This was a demonstration directed against them. It was clear that an intelligence in the darkness was seeking them. Again the sounds came, now to their left, followed by the same ominous listening pause. The tiger, suspicious, was forcing them to make an answering movement. One sound, the faintest rustle, would have been enough. For hours, it seemed, this went on: the feints, the pause, the fresh trial. It was a war of nerves. Eric could see nothing and the sounds came and went, advanced, retreated, flinging a circle round the tree and circling back again. A profound silence fell, which went on and on.

Eric knew that Alice had turned her head towards him. Did she think that the tiger had gone? He wondered if he dared to touch her warningly, or if a touch at that moment would be enough to break her control. As he asked himself this he heard the sound that he was waiting for, a new sound on the night: a harsh, low, rasping sound, made by a tongue as hard as a steel brush licking skin from dead flesh. It was followed by the unmistakable crunch of teeth on bones. The tiger was on the kill.

A circle of light fell onto the bamboos. For a second an immense white-edged mask, brilliant-eyed, shone up at them from the darkness. The sound of the shot rang out, reverberating through the forest, and darkness and silence closed in again.

Eric leant forward and shone the flashlight. "Well, it's done," he said. "It's over."

"Done? What's happened? Where is the tiger?"

"You needn't whisper now. It's dead. Didn't you see?"

"I saw a face." Alice's voice was now loud and unsteady. "But how can it be dead? There was no sound. I don't believe it."

"Look, down there. Don't you see? Wait, I'm going to fire again, but it's dead."

When the sound of the second shot died away, Alice saw. Among the bamboos crouched a great unmoving shape, vaguely discernible among the striped shadows cast by the flashlight.

Eric sat up, throwing off the rugs. He fired the two signal shots into the air, one immediately after the other. The wakened birds stirred uneasily in the darkness and from the village an answering tumult broke out. A drum began to beat; lights moved, running, twinkling and dancing in the darkness like fireflies. The lights streamed towards them across the fields.

Eric laughed. "No mistake this time. Straight through the forehead to the brain."

He laid the rifle carefully down between the two chairs and turned to Alice. He pulled her from her chair and put his arms round her, laughing triumphantly.

For a moment she responded, and that was enough for him. He laughed again, his doubts forgotten. Then she said: "Don't laugh like that, Eric. Don't. You frighten me."

He released her almost at once and turned to look for the flask. "You are shivering," he said. "What you need is a hot drink. Sit down and drink this before the celebrations arrive."

"I kept still, didn't I," Alice said.

"You did indeed."

"I didn't make a sound. It went on and on for hours. What's the time? It must be midnight."

"It's a quarter to eight. The tiger was there for less than an hour and a half. But thank you, Alice. One movement from you and he would have been off."

"What would have happened if you had missed?"

"A clean miss and he would have gone off, a startled tiger, but no one any the worse. But if I had wounded him here, so near the road, it would have been awkward. Are you all right now, Alice?"

"Of course, why not? Listen, here they come. Listen to Sangla!"

A long ribbon of lights was unwinding over the dark fields. Lights were moving down the path between the bushes. Sangla was calling out excitedly and from all sides voices answered him.

Sangla had spent the last hours in the village tea-shop and rest-house, which did not sell only tea. Crouched in the low, smoky hut which was lit by a couple of wicks floating in oil in the old manner, he had entertained a party of travellers and as many of the villagers as could crowd into the close small space with boastful tales and more or less untrue anecdotes of the camp. The brass drinking cups had passed from hand to hand. The home-brewed rice beer of the villagers is mild but much can be absorbed in nearly three hours. When Puran Singh, who had spent the time wrapped in his rug in the cabin of the truck with the dog beside him, or pacing the white dusty road in scornful isolation, put his head in at the low doorway to report the two signal shots, Sangla was not drunk but in a state of elation that Murray would have recognised.

Now, leaving Jetha to climb up to the machan with the rope ladder, he made a straight line to the dead tiger, hacking at the bamboos with his knife. When he stood above the body in the cleared space lit by the swinging light of hand lanterns and the red glare of torches, he looked a formidable figure.

Eric, standing once more on the ground beneath the tree, shouted orders and directions across the ravine but Sangla took no notice. The death of two of his great striped enemies in one day had gone to his head, as the mild beer had not been able to do. He gesticulated and shouted, and chanted what sounded like a psalm of praise and a running commentary on what had happened. It was Sangla who ordered a pole to be cut, who tied the enormous pale paws together and slid the pole between them. Eric could only stand and watch as the huge sagging body was carried away on many shoulders, with the excited crowd following after.

Only Jetha and one lantern were left. The darkness closed in again as the lights and the noise receded. Carrying the rugs and cushions, they started back down the path between the dark trees with the swinging circle of light going before them.

Eric was laughing quietly to himself. After the three-hour vigil he was stiff and cold and his leg was paining him, but a new and enormous exultation filled him. Nothing now could upset his good humour. He held Alice firmly by the arm, propelling her down the path in the wake of the torches.

"I can't walk so fast," Alice complained. "I'm tired and stiff. I never even saw the tiger properly."

"A brisk walk will do you good," he said. "Come along."

"What's the matter with you? Are you angry with Sangla?"

"Angry? I couldn't be angry with anyone tonight. Sangla is having the time of his life. He will come to when he reaches the village. You will find the tiger there, all laid out and ready to be looked at, not a whisker missing."

"But I wanted to see it lying where it died. I feel rather silly, don't you? Look at us, coming humbly back behind everyone else. What a way for the conquering hero to return. I'm furious with Sangla."

"No you are not. This is a special night. You mustn't be furious with anyone tonight, whatever he may do."

When they came out of the forest at the edge of the fields, they saw the lights straggling ahead. The first torches had reached the village where a drum was beating again. The torches seemed paler. The fields had emerged from the darkness into a ghostly, reflected light. As they crossed the uneven, stubble-hard ground, the moon rose behind the trees.

In the village the crowd had collected in the road in front of the truck. Eric, followed by Alice and Jetha, elbowed his way between the warm excited bodies until they stood beside Sangla above the dead tiger. Sangla was completely sober and dignified again. In front of the staring crowd he gave Eric a wide, ceremonious salute, but the old grin, what Alice called Sangla's tiger smile, was on his face. To Eric it seemed that he would remember every detail of that scene for the rest of his life. The moon, slightly out of shape and past its prime, rose up behind the roofs of the village. The red torchlight shone on the ring of dark faces and on Puran Singh's bearded head as he looked down from the truck. The tiger lay in the dust, pale and immense in death. The death of a tiger was nothing new to Eric; he had seen just such torchlit scenes before, but this moment was the culminating point for him of a long eventful day. He looked down at Alice. This day would mark the end of one phase of his life and the beginning of another. He knew, standing there between Alice and Sangla, with his dog's head under his hand, that he was himself again. Something dark had gone from him, slipping from his shoulders like a cloak. Never in his life had he felt so sure of himself, so full of power and strength. Anything was possible to him. He had only to stretch out his arms and they would reach beyond the forest to the stars.

He looked a magnificent figure. The fair head shone above every other head there, but no one, not even Alice, had eyes for him. Attention was concentrated on the tiger. A murmur came from the crowd which pressed forward. Hands were stretched out. Everyone wanted to see and touch their old enemy. Children crept between the legs of their elders and women held out their babies so that they should uncomprehendingly see the tiger and grow as brave and as cunning as he. Now came the sound of wooden wheels, and the crowd parted. They were bringing out the wooden effigy, which for so long had been a part of all feast days, to confront its original.

"Will they do away with that now?" Alice asked. "Or will it stay to point a legend?"

She bent down and touched the great forehead above the bullet hole. "He is bigger than the big tiger," she said.

"As long, perhaps, but not so heavy or so fine. These old cattle killers are often long and rangy."

"How pale he is, a fawnish cream. His stripes are faded almost to nothing. Is that because he's old?"

Sangla crouched down and, taking the hand-lantern from Jetha, showed the worn teeth and the broken claws.

"Poor old fellow," Alice said. "It seems a shame. Why couldn't we have let him end his days in peace?"

"There's no such thing as a peaceful end for a tiger," Eric said. "We have given him the best end that he could have had."

And this was true. An old tiger, if he is not killed by the sportsman's rifle or by the obsolete inefficient weapons of the village hunters, gradually grows weaker and weaker, being unable to kill the food he needs. For a time he subsists only on the small forest creatures that he still can find, rats, lizards, even frogs, and at the last meets a shameful death. In his weakness and blindness he is pulled down by a pack of wild dogs, or the jackals, who all his life followed humbly after him and lived on his leavings, discover the lonely place where he has dragged himself to die. Closing in, drawing nearer, still mindful of those huge flailing paws, they do not wait for the last breath to leave his body. When the jackals' feast is done, the cowardly and hideous hyenas laugh and fight over his scattered bones.

The headman stepped out of the crowd and offered the warm rice beer. As they drank they saw that he carried a string of large round blue beads that once circled a pony's neck.

The crowd laughed as if this grim jest were the crowning part of the evening. "He says that we should give him another pony, as now all ponies may graze in safety," Eric said.

"Only until the next tiger comes along," Alice said. "You tell him that. Can't we go, Eric? I have had enough. I'm tired. Take me home."

The Beat

The tiger was lifted into the back of the truck where he lay between the two old basket chairs that had played their part in his downfall. As they lifted him, the faithless ticks, that for so long had sucked his old blood and tormented him, fell into the dust in small grape-like shining clusters. Eric distributed the money that always changes hands when a tiger dies, and climbed into the high seat beside Alice. The crowd fell back. The last small boy swung down from the backboard of the truck as it slowly gathered speed. When its headlights could no longer be seen among the trees, the torches were extinguished and the people turned back to the village where the feasting and drinking would go on all night.

Only the wooden effigy of the tiger was left, propped against a mud wall in the moonlight. Someone had hung a wreath of marigolds round its neck.

CHAPTER V

THERE had never been as many fireflies in the forest as there were that night. They swarmed about the road, filling the darkness under the trees where the moonlight could not penetrate with their moving, dancing, cold points of light. The headlights of the slowly moving truck only dimmed their fire. The two passengers sitting silently together on the seat behind the driver were escorted on their way by a winged host, a bright triumphant horde. All round the truck the fireflies rose and fell until it moved in a starry crowd.

In the camp, where the three men sat together above the river after their evening meal, Murray, looking past the light of the fire, said, "Look at the fireflies," and Manoo, standing beside him, said that it was the new warmth in the air that had brought them out and that they foretold a change.

All through the night the fireflies shone, all through the forest. Long after the truck had passed they still gathered by the road. They surrounded the tigress who, well after midnight, walked down the road, her oval spoor falling across the tyre tracks. As she walked, tail gently swinging and her head, which was narrower and lighter than the great head of a tiger, held low, she moaned gently, the soft, low, complaining sound that a promenading tiger often makes. She was a thin young tigress, hollow flanked. Beneath her pale belly swung heavy full milk glands. That night the forest had not favoured her. She had killed late and too far from the overhanging bank under which she had left the three cubs of her first litter. Her hunger still unsatisfied, she had risen from the hot steaming deer flesh, impelled by her restless instinctive anxiety. Now she was hurrying back to the small warm bodies and the hard pulling mouths. No eyes saw her go. She vanished into the darkness and the road was empty. For the rest of the night the fireflies shone alone.

Part Five

The Plain

The Plain

CHAPTER I

At breakfast, on the morning after the tiger shoot, Murray looked at the faces round the table. Experience of many camps had taught him that it was in the backwash of a wave of excitement that quarrels rose and accidents took place. That morning it seemed to him that the danger was greater than it had ever been before. He saw that he could count on no help from Alice; for the first time since he had known her she was set against him. Her face, that morning, wore a determinedly calm expression and she would not meet his eye. Eric was obviously uneasy, fidgeting with his food and looking at once sulky and troubled. Murray found it difficult to believe that these were the same two faces that he had seen last night when Eric and Alice, appearing suddenly out of the darkness much earlier than they were expected, had stood for a moment silently together looking down at the three men who still sat round the camp fire. The

§ 187 §

firelight had revealed the exultation and glow on their faces; at that moment they might have returned to the camp from another world. Murray looked across the table at Philip and at Kay. Kay was alert and restless; his sharp black eyes were moving from face to face. As for Philip, he looked as if he had not slept for days. Murray sighed. Unless he was very much mistaken there would be trouble that day. He poured himself another cup of tea and looked thoughtfully across the river where, in the brilliant morning light, each tree stood out sharply against the blue and violet hills. He must disperse them, keep them as far apart as possible from each other all day.

Aloud he said, "What a wonderful morning. It's too fine by half. I don't trust those hills. The weather will change before to-night. Let's go out while we can."

And now, soon after eleven, dispersed they were, if not quite as Murray had planned. The camp, from the river, looked deserted. There was no one moving on the bank above the pool and, in the strong sunlight of mid-morning, the empty chairs, still in their half circle round the dead fire, had an abandoned air. Anyone watching from across the river might have thought it a camp from which everyone had suddenly fled. But deep in the trees smoke was rising from a fire behind the cook tent and an unpleasantly strong smell pervaded the camp and proclaimed to the forest that something unusual was cooking there. Murray had used the slow and odorous boiling of the flesh from the two tiger skulls as a pretext to remove his whole party from the camp for the day.

Eric had refused to rise to the bait of a fresh kill beyond the river, and then had refused to stay quietly in camp to rest his leg and to watch with Manoo the slow curing of his tiger skins. Much to Murray's exasperation, he had elected to join

Kay. Now, with Sangla and Jetha and the dog, they were advancing in line across the brown grass of the plain towards the distant hills. Ahead of them a florican, showing the black and white in its wings, rose well out of range and, further still, a flight of golden plover wheeled and dipped against the sky. The long day was before them and the great plain was alive with the small game that they were seeking. Although they were in sight and hearing of each other, they were surrounded by such an immensity of plain and sky that each might have been alone. Philip, with only Pior as a companion, was a mile away near the rim of the plain, safely embarked on a day's fishing on the great Manook river. He stood on the stones of its huge bed and contemplated the wild swift rush of its water. This river, in which their own mild river could have been lost many times, descended from the foothills in a series of rapids and tore past him across the open grasslands towards the forest. Here, between the boulder-strewn rapids, were pools that were long and deep and wide, quick and crystal clear, a fisherman's dream. As he watched, Philip saw, deep in the green cold slide, a dark fish shape making its way up-stream. He took the rod from Pior and waded in to the water, feeling the strong current pulling at his knees. Now, for a short while at least and as Murray had hoped, there was nothing in his mind except the river, nothing except its cool and healing flow.

Murray sat back in the car with Alice beside him. He felt both cross and exhausted, much, he suspected, as the sheepdog feels when his silly sheep are safely penned. That was not a jungle simile, it was out of place, but he could think of no other, for what in the jungle is ever safe or penned? Alice was driving; it would give her something to do. On the back seat sat Kancha and Kristo the cook, with several empty baskets at their feet. The car was heading up the forest road towards the border village where, that day, a market was to be held. As they passed the old Forest bungalow in the Dipsiri clearing where the plain began, Murray decided that he and Alice would eat their share of the picnic meal, which a mildly surprised Kancha had been told to put in five separate packets, on its veranda. He hoped that none of the others would join them at the bungalow, which was a favourite meeting place. After the shopping was done and the meal eaten, he meant to talk to Alice as he had never done before.

The camp was left to Manoo. The boatmen with their boats had vanished down the river towards the big village, while the remainder of the camp followers, including the water carrier who, it might have been thought, would have had enough of the river, were out of sight round the bend below the camp, washing their clothes at the edge of the water, washing themselves, and smoking their strong cigarettes on the stones in the sunlight. Even the mahouts' camp was empty. The three elephants were also celebrating their day of rest by taking a long and thorough bath. They lay on their sides in the shallow water while their naked mahouts and grasscuts, balancing skillfully on the exposed whale-like black and shining sides, scrubbed them all over with a brick. The sound of distant voices came to the camp above the sound of the river but they did not disturb the warm morning quiet.

Manoo hovered like some ancient dark male witch between the fire with its boiling pots and the place under the trees where the skins were pegged out in the shade. By now these had been scraped clean of every scrap of flesh, rubbed with wood ash, and heaped with a white compound whose recipe was Manoo's own. It would be days before they would be ready, each hair firmly fixed and the skin beneath white and clean, to be rolled up and packed with the cleaned and complete skulls, and sent by the truck and by train to a famous taxidermist in South India for their final curing and mounting.

Manoo bent down to adjust a peg, and returned to the fire where the precious tiger fat was being rendered down. This was his own prerequisite; even Sangla had no say in its disposal but, that morning, Eric had asked him to put a small jar aside as a present for the station master at Kishnagar. The empty and quiet camp pleased Manoo. Presently he sat down beneath a tree, folding his old legs under him. The whole perimeter of the camp from the river to the trees was under his eye. He took his spectacles from their case, polished them carefully on a piece of chamois leather, as Murray did, set them on his nose and opened the small paper covered book that Alice had seen. But Murray had been wrong; this was no account book: his account book was under his pillow. The dark finger with its blunt mauve nail followed the lines of devotion, the "Siva-Vakyam" of the Pattanattu Pillai in Tamil characters. Now nothing moved in all the camp. Manoo's face and hands and khaki clothes blended with the colours of the tree trunk and the ground and the camp seemed truly deserted. A striped squirrel crept down a tree and crossed the open space in front of him and sat up to look around curiously. Without raising his eyes from the page, Manoo knew that it was there, as he knew that Rama's sacred and caressing fingers long ago had drawn the stripes forever down its grey back. The squirrel vanished suddenly and Manoo cautiously raised his eyes. Something was standing at the edge of the trees behind Murray's tent, a long necked and alert shape. It moved again, advancing a few steps into the open where the glancing leaf-broken sunlight caught a brilliant gleam of colour.

The Peacock

The old man sat very still with his book spread on his knee and his finger marking his place. The jungle peacock is wary and swift and shy. Manoo could not believe in such a visitation. When he looked again, the bird had gone.

CHAPTER II

WHERE the road approached the bed of the Manook river and then ran straight on across the plain to the hills, stood the Forest bungalow and rest-house, the Dipsiri bungalow. This was a frail, two-roomed, wooden and thatched box of a building perched high off the ground on thick wooden poles and surrounded by a bare patch of ground and a ditch. The poles were wound about with barbed wire to discourage wild elephants who, every year on their way across the plain, ignored the crumbling ditch and did their best to push the whole tottering erection into the river. It had been built many years ago, perhaps as much as sixty years, which is a long time in a damp insect-infested place, in the days when Forest Officers toured their districts on pony or elephant. Before the war, Murray and Eric had been known to camp out in its bat-haunted rooms to save the trouble of pitching a tent, but, until that morning, no one except the Nepali caretaker or a Forest Officer on a tour of inspection, had climbed its rickety steps for a long time.

It looked an unlikely meeting place, no place for serious conversations or for even a picnic. Time and the white ants had done their work and the whole building leaned towards the river. Through the cracks in the wooden floor the ground and a pile of empty rusting tins and the caretaker's goat could be seen. On the walls of the veranda, above the broken cane-bottomed chairs and the table marked by the rims of long-ago emptied glasses, Government notices that were yellowed and indistinct with age, flapped gently in the stream of air which, even on the stillest day, moved continuously through the building, seeming to flow across the open grassland directly from the hills. But that morning the old place drew them each in turn across the plain and up the steps to face the wide view of the hills, which were now piled high with clouds. Perhaps this was because the building was a landmark on the plain, something dark and definite on which to rest the eye after the too large paleness of sky and waving grass. Its walls and the two simul trees in its grounds cast the only shade for miles. It was familiar to them all; they had always gone at least once from every camp to pay it a short visit, to see if the Dipsiri bungalow were still standing. To-day, although none of them realised it, they were drawn to the old building for a different reason. When they sat on the veranda where a long procession of other men had sat, they were cut off, insulated, for the time being, from the forest, and back for a short while in the outside world. Perhaps, after all, it was the best place available for serious talk, for arguments and discussions. It was a pity that Philip, as he left the river and, with Pior following him, began his long and unwise walk across the plain to the camp, only came as far as the foot of the steps. He paused there with his hand on the wooden rail, looking up at the eaves, and then, as if the sight of the old building only reminded him of what he would rather forget, he turned away.

Eric was the first to climb the steps. He had walked too far that morning over rough ground. At first he had been led on by his own obstinacy and by an unwillingness to find himself alone with his own thoughts as he had been all night. As the morning and the huge emptiness of sun and air quietened him, he had begun to enjoy himself. He was a moderate shot with a shot-gun but that morning he had shot astonishingly well. Beside him was his dog, grey muzzle quivering with eagerness, tail held stiffly. It was many years since they had been together as they were then. The black dot that was the waiting truck was soon far behind them on the road. As they advanced towards the hills, Jetha, himself, Sangla, and Kay, strung out across the plain, he forgot everything except the moving grass ahead and the sudden rise and whirr of wings.

It was when they turned on a fresh line towards the road that his leg sharply reminded him that it could never be forgotten for long. For a while he had continued to ignore it although he knew that he was keeping the others back. Their mixed bag included two florican, several couple of quail, partridge and plover and of these the greater part had fallen to his gun. He had felt his old certainty that anything was possible for him. But when Kay had suggested that they should return to the road by following one of the many green and marshy depressions that lay in the folds of the plain, he had been forced to give in. Snipe grounds, with their heavy going, their reeds and mud, would never again be for him. He and Jetha had returned alone, taking the easiest way to the bungalow where they had decided to eat their mid-day meal. He had ordered the dog to continue his work, and of course it would never occur to Sangla to leave a still firing gun, but he had felt deserted and aggrieved. It had seemed to him that the old building, perched on its stilts above the river, would never come any nearer. When at last he sank into the ancient creaking chair on its veranda and wiped his sweating face, the last shreds of his re-found certainty had gone.

Eric sat on the veranda, drinking the warm beer that

Jetha had brought him from the truck which was now parked in the shade below him, and stared at the hills. An hour later Kay found him still sitting there.

"Three and a half couple of snipe and a painter," Kay said, as he pulled up the only other chair and sat down, stretching out his muddy legs. "How's the leg? You don't look too cheerful."

Eric was looking down at the dog who, after an apologetic greeting, had thrown himself heavily down at his feet. The black coat was clogged with mud to the shoulders and the black sides heaved.

"He's done in," Eric said. "He's not the dog he was."

"What nonsense. He had the time of his life and he would go on for hours yet. Let's eat here and then, about three, try the ground beyond the sāl plantation."

"No. I have had enough."

"Just as you like. We can sit here and admire the view."

Kay leant over the veranda railing and shouted for Sangla. It was the Nepali caretaker who came, a young and plump man with a rosy face. He was carrying their small picnic basket and a large calf-bound book.

"What are you doing here?" Kay asked him. "Where is old Saidu?"

"He died years ago," Eric said. "This is his nephew, a new broom to suit the new times. He wants you to write your name in that book. I seem to remember that we did that before, but only when we stayed a night. And we are to pay two rupees each for the use of this veranda and these decrepit chairs."

"We never did that before."

"Things are looking up in Dipsiri. Quite a crowd here this morning."

Kay opened the book on his knees and took the profferred pencil. Above Eric's neat signature was another newly written name in thick upright lettering: T. K. Barua.

"Who's he?" Kay asked. "Of course, Barua, the Divisional Forest Officer. Hokgaon. So there really is such a person? He can't have gone long, the ink is hardly dry."

"Must be the new man that Murray talked about. A very different type, it seems, from that old ass Chatterjee who was here after MacDougal. Perhaps there's hope for this forest and for the work that has been done here, after all."

Kay was turning the yellowed pages curiously. "This record goes back for years," he said. "The first name, one Robinson, is dated 1888. He was a Forest Officer too, it seems. Three months on end he spent here. What was he doing? Building the place?"

"Down with malaria, more likely. They mostly were in those days, poor devils. But they had the best of it. Their world lasted their time."

"This old place won't last much longer, anyway," Kay said cheerfully. "Time it went. It has served its purpose."

"Perhaps. But what will they put in its place?"

"T. K. Barua has curious writing," Kay said. "Look, the 'T' is like a sword."

But Eric was moving restlessly round the veranda. Backwards and forwards he went over the loose wooden boards. His limp was very pronounced. Kay, watching him, thought suddenly of some large and newly caught wild anmial, who has not yet learnt the limits of its cage.

"Sit down, Eric," he said. "You will do your leg no good. What's the matter? I expected a more radiant air this morning. You are not my idea of the successful breaker up of homes. What's gone wrong since last night?"

Eric stared at him for a moment and then sat down

heavily. "You mind your own business," he said. "You keep off this."

"If Philip decides to give Alice the beating that she deserves, or to shoot you up, or, in a fit of renunciation, to go off and cut his own throat, it would be very much my business. We are cut off from everyone here."

"Philip! Can you see him? But listen, Kay. When I say keep off this, I mean it. I don't want to listen to any more of your cheap wisecracks here."

"You said that before, but this isn't the forest. Think of all the men who have sat here and of the words this veranda must have heard. We can say anything here."

"There's no need to say anything."

"Something tells me that you need a little outspoken advice. Why not talk it over? Alice doesn't try to disguise her feelings. She is right, we all know each other too well for that. And after last night when you two came back together from the village, with that starry bemused look on your faces, the situation was quite clear to everyone."

"Nonsense—there was no situation. I tell you nothing happened, nothing was said."

"You have had time to think it over and now you have cold feet over the whole business. I don't blame you. You have your life to make all over again, and another man's wife and three ready-made children tagging along won't make it easier. Alice never does anything by halves and, if I know Philip, he will fade away nobly into the background. You take my advice and run like a hare while you can."

Eric stood up and limped to the veranda railing. "What an unpleasant little specimen you are," he said.

"I suppose that means that you intend to behave as I might have guessed you would. Don't be such a fool. No one is that kind of a fool these days."

§ 197 §

The big man lifted his hand in a threatening gesture and then turned his back on Kay and leaned his arms on the railings and looked out across the plain. "What part are you playing in all this, Kay?" he asked. "Exactly why are you running round making as much mischief as possible, putting in a nasty little word here, a hint there? What do you get out of it?"

After a moment, Kay said, "Perhaps I'm trying to take my mind off my own problems. Shall we discuss them for a change?"

"Good Lord, no!"

"Believe it or not, Eric, I meant what I said. My advice was genuine. I should hate to see you adding to your difficulties. This business with Alice has gone far enough. Why not clear out, go somewhere else?"

"It's odd that you should say that. It's what I told myself all last night. But, you see, there *is* nowhere else. I came back to that every time. There's nowhere else for me."

"What complete rubbish! Do you mean to stay here, in the jungle, for the rest of your life? There's the rest of this considerable country for a start. There are other countries. There's all the world."

"Not for me. I don't see myself anywhere else," Eric said slowly, almost dreamily. "There's no future for me anywhere. No future."

Kay pushed his chair back and stood up. "Don't talk like that," he said loudly, but Eric was not listening. Far out on the plain against the blue of the foothills, a small cloud of dust had risen. It advanced rapidly on the road across the plain.

Now Kay saw it too. "The car is coming back," he said. "Murray must have thought of the old bungalow as we did. He and Alice will be here in a few minutes. We can all have a pleasant little meal together, or shall we finish this conversation elsewhere?"

"You can do what you like," Eric said. "I'm going straight back to the camp."

Kay picked up the picnic basket and followed Eric and the dog down the steps as Sangla and Jetha, in answer to a shout, came running from the caretaker's hut. As the truck bumped across the rough open ground to the gate and out onto the road, Kay turned to look back at the old building.

"What a precipitate retreat," he said. "I never liked the old place anyway. Too many ghosts, if you ask me. Enough to give anyone the willies."

"The truck has been here," Murray said. "Look at the tyre marks in the dust. The old bungalow has had visitors already."

He drove the car into the mid-day shade beneath the buildings, scattering the caretaker's brown and white goats. The caretaker was waiting for them, book in hand.

"How did he know that we were coming?" Murray said. "Old Saidu was never as prompt as this. This must be the new man that Barua mentioned."

"Barua?"

"The Forest Officer. I told you about him. The man who is so keen on game sanctuaries."

Alice stood at the bottom of the steps, looking up as Philip had done. "I don't want to go in after all," she said. "Let's sit here on the steps, that's far enough. I have had enough of the world for one morning."

"I thought that you enjoyed the market."

"I liked the hill people's flat gold faces and their clothes, and the piles of grain and vegetables. I liked being so near to the hills. But there was too much dust and chatter and staring. I soon had enough. Let's get back to the forest, Murray."

"We might as well have a look at this old place first, we always did."

Alice put her foot on the first step and quickly drew it back. "Eric and Kay have been here," she said. "Look, at the marks of blood. Sangla must have put the dead birds down here for a moment. Poor limp feathery things."

"You have seen blood before. Step over it. Kancha has put our food on the veranda table. Look at him, he's delighted to see us under a real roof again."

"He and Kristo enjoyed their morning anyway. The back of the car looks like a market stall. And now they can have a good smoke and talk with the caretaker. But we needn't stay long, need we, Murray?"

But once she had climbed the steps into the shade of the veranda, Alice examined the interior of the building with a proprietary air, running her hand over the stained teak table, touching the backs of the chairs. Murray sat down where Eric had sat and watched her moving through the two rooms. As the caretaker opened the book on the table before him, she called out, "The water jug is missing from the bathroom. Better tell your Mr. Barua that," and a moment later he heard her say, "Murray, there's a swarm of bees on the back veranda."

"Come and look at this," he said. "Talk of an angel and hear the rustle of his wings! Barua was here this morning. Here is his signature above Eric's. I wonder if they met."

Alice bent over the book for a moment. "I feel sure that they didn't," she said. "That man crops up again and again. He always seems to be somewhere about, near but invisible, like a guardian angel. He never actually appears. Write our names too, Murray."

"It's a good thing that we didn't all arrive together. The old bungalow would never have held us all. Sit down and eat, I have begun already."

Alice hung her hat on the wooden peg beside his and drew a chair up to the table. She sat with her back to the hills, facing the veranda wall. But this stratagem was defeated; the whitewash gave off a reflected light and her face was clear to him.

"I want to talk to you seriously, Alice," he said.

"Must you?"

"Do you remember that first afternoon in the camp when you said that you would just sit back and let things happen, not lift a finger? It's a pity that you changed your mind."

"Men are such fools."

"Vain, proud, dangerous fools. You are playing with fire."

Alice laughed. "Dear Murray," she said. "What a thing to say! Well, I can match it. Listen: 'All's fair in love and war!' "

"I'm serious about this, Alice. Have you really thought what you are doing? Eric is in no fit state to stand another blow. What will he do when he finds that you have let him down?"

"What extraordinary things you are saying this morning! 'Let him down.' What makes you think that I am going to let Eric down?"

"I can't believe that you and Philip— Don't sit there smiling at me, Alice. It's a sly stupid smile and it doesn't become you."

"Now, Murray. Don't lose your temper. What exactly have I done after all?"

She put her hand out and gently stroked his arm. "Dear

Murray, don't be so deadly serious," she said. "Nothing has happened. There's no harm done."

"I wish that I could be sure of that."

He lifted her hand from his arm and, getting up, walked to the veranda railing. "Look at those clouds," he said. "It's raining in the hills. We are in for a storm."

"The clouds are a long way off. It's fine enough here."

"It will be raining here before tonight. I wonder where Philip is."

"Somewhere up this river of course. You needn't worry about him. He's safe enough for the moment. Philip hasn't a thought to spare for anyone or anything when he's fishing."

"Whatever Philip is doing, he isn't fishing at this moment," Murray said. "The river was gin clear this morning but now, with this warm change in the weather and the rain in the hills, snow water will be coming down. It's no use fishing for mahseer in thick water. I can see one reach of the river from here. It looks dirty already to me."

Alice joined him at the railing and together they looked out across the plain, searching the road and the miles of grass.

"If the fishing were useless he would come to the bungalow," Alice said. "You were going to send the truck here for him this evening, weren't you?"

"Yes, but Philip wouldn't hang about an unfishable river all day."

"Then where can he be?" Alice said uneasily. "Where *is* Philip, Murray?"

At that moment Philip and Pior were half way across the plain and struggling through a belt of tall grass that shut out the hills and half hid their sky. Philip was sweating uncomfortably. His shotgun grew heavier at every step. He knew that this march across the plain was foolish and unnecessary.

The Plain

He knew exactly what kind of a fool he was being. Between him and the camp were miles of country that he did not know, grassland, scattered woodland, marsh, jungle. The long grass could easily hold rhino, still more easily, leopard or tiger, but that thought did not worry him unduly; he was far more concerned with the fear of losing his way. His life, quite possibly, depended on Pior who, rod case slung from a string round his neck, knife in hand, red head-cloth trailing over one bare shoulder, moved unconcernedly in front of him. Pior, when questioned, had been vague, agreeing cheerfully that he knew the way, that of course there would be paths, that undoubtedly they would reach camp before sundown.

Philip moved his gun from one shoulder to the other. There was still time to go back. Only a short while ago, just before they entered the long grass, he had looked round and seen the bungalow, a dark minute shape on the edge of the horizons. But he knew that he would not turn back. He would go on, taking the unconcerned Pior with him and, if they never reached the camp at all, that would be one solution of his problem. Nothing so final and dramatic would happen to him. He would reach the camp late and probably ignominiously, hot and dishevelled, to face Murray's anger or, more likely, quite unnoticed. Heroics, he knew, were not for him. Any gesture that he made in this business was doomed to be futile.

That morning, when the snow water came down and the river whitened and thickened round his knees, and he knew that his fishing for that day, at least, was spoiled, Philip reached a breaking point. It is possible to continue for a long time under a load that grows lighter or heavier often unaccountably. It is the little more that is always too much, a light and ridiculous feather more, and the load is too heavy to be borne. A short while before Philip had taken the

loss of a monster fish that he had never even glimpsed philo-
sophically enough. Its fierce rush had carried away spoon
and trace, breaking him. He had only paused to repair the
damage, to find a new trace and spoon, before moving on to
the next pool. But when he slowly reeled in his line and
watched his useless spoon coming back to him through the
thickening water which, in the space of a few minutes, had
changed unbelievably, growing darker and heavier as the
muddied rain water from the side streams came down, he
had cursed aloud, childishly and ridiculously, shouting incomprehensible words at the river before an astonished Pior.
When he stood on the bank, looking from the river to the
hills where clouds were piling and spreading out across the
sky, he had been shaken by a gust of uncontrollable rage.

By the time that he had walked the short distance down
river to the old bungalow, his rage had gone, but it was re-
placed by a feeling of black depression, a depression that was
heavier than any sorrow that he had known. He stood by
the steps leading to the veranda, one hand on the railing, for
what seemed to him a long time. When at last he looked up
at the building and saw Pior and the caretaker watching
him, he knew that he could not go on as he had done. The
time had come to make some decision. Once and for all, he
must make up his mind.

As he looked round at the vast and empty landscape that
lay between the bungalow and the hills, he knew that he
must get away by himself. He must walk until he knew the
answer to his problem. But now, as he and Pior emerged
from the tall grass as suddenly as they had entered it and he
saw ahead clumps of trees dotting the plain and a distant line
of heavy forest, he was no nearer to a solution; he saw himself and Eric and Alice as three small distraught figures who
continually changed places.

§ 204 §

"Wait a moment," he said to Pior and, resting the butt of his gun on the ground, stopped to light a cigarette. There was still time. They were still a long way from the camp. The only thing for him to do was to walk on, to look at his problem coldly and dispassionately, to stand well away from it and see it whole. He carefully stamped out the lighted end of his cigarette and picked up his gun again. The bungalow was still visible behind him, but now it was a dot, hardly to be seen at the edge of the plain. He walked on and when he looked round again it had disappeared.

CHAPTER III

THE warm close afternoon had gone. The clouds that covered the hills like a pall and stretched far out across the sky had not yet reached the sun which slid away under them towards the trees. The sound of distant thunder came from the hills but a strong gold light lay over the forest, the evening light made deeper by the approaching clouds.

Philip and Pior crossed a grassy rise and paused irresolutely. On their left was a wall of dense forest, on their right high elephant grass, but ahead were small bare rice fields, patches of still uncut mustard and, in the distance, the thatched huts of Nepali settlers. Philip had no idea where he was but, remembering that Murray had said that there were no settlements or farms to the north of the camp, he thought that they must be somewhere near the forest road and that their way lay straight on; but when he mentioned this to Pior the man only smiled and nodded and turned towards the heavy forest, following a path through the mustard fields.

"Wait!" Philip shouted, but Pior did not turn round. Already, that afternoon, they had had several arguments as to the direction to be taken. Pior had been surprisingly obstinate, not at all like his usual pliant self. When Philip had argued and expostulated and finally cursed him, he had simply walked away, leaving Philip to follow or to stay where he was. As the long hot hours wore on, it had seemed to Philip that Pior was deliberately hindering him, as the sweat in his eyes, the sharp spears of the high grass, and the thorned creepers were. It had been Pior's fault that they had found themselves struggling through a belt of jungle where every bush and creeper was an armed hand barring their way. Pior had led him into a swamp of treacherous, yielding bright green clumps of grass, channels of dark water, and patches of oily purple mud. Here they had seen several snakes, but it was when they were pushing their way through the thatch grass beyond the swamp that they heard a close, heavy, unseen body crash away from them. Pior had declared that it was only a deer, but Philip had known better and Pior's unconcerned calm, contrasting with his own shaking knees and dry mouth, had infuriated him. He had spent the next half hour plodding along, looking only at the ground and planning what he would say about Pior to Murray, when, and if, they reached the camp. The man was definitely a part of this wild hostile tract of country, no more to be trusted than its smiling, sunlit woods were.

"Wait!" he shouted again and Pior stood still on the path. He was not looking at Philip. He was watching the grass beside the path where something was moving.

Disturbed perhaps by Philip's shout, something was moving cautiously away, rippling away through the close yellow flowers of the mustard field. The field was full of movement. Half seen shapes twisted and turned through the tall stems, making for the safety of the forest. Philip saw a glimpse of blue and one raised head with the familiar crest. A flock of peacock, several cocks with their hens, were returning from their evening gleaning in the fields to the trees. It seemed to Philip that peacock were everywhere, running on their powerful grey legs away from him, as only peacock can run. He saw the peacock colours moving against the bright canary-yellow of the flowers, an astonishing, unbelievable, unforgettable display of colour, and then he saw Pior throw his arms up and begin to run.

Pior bounded like a deer down the path to cut off the birds' retreat. His red headcloth streamed behind him. He, too, had found the afternoon long and trying and this sudden movement was a release. As he ran he turned his head and shouted joyfully to Philip and pointed across the field where now the birds had wheeled, doubling back on a fresh tack. There was something infectious in the sight of his leaping body. Philip, too, began to run.

Philip never understood what passed through his mind at that moment, or what sent him running and stumbling through the fields, gun cocked and ready, after the fleeing birds. The lust of the chase was not dead in him as he had thought. It is an old deep-seated lust that, in the mildest of men, only sleeps until the right victim and the right moment appear together. He only knew that he must pursue those flying colours, to the foothills if necessary, until it grew dark.

He never knew how long that wild chase continued. He ran and turned through the fields and through the scrub jungle until he was wet through with sweat and scratched and torn, angry but determined, seeing always the elusive colours vanishing before him. Peacock seldom take to the wing until hard-pressed. They run like a racehorse, as swiftly as a deer. But the chase ended as suddenly as it had begun.

§ 207 §

The Peacock

Philip found himself, panting and dishevelled, deep in the trees, staring at a bamboo fence and a ditch. He saw the open sky, and the straw roof of a hut below a clump of wild banana trees. On all sides was the forest. Of Pior and the peacocks there was no sign.

He went up to the fence and found a rough gate and opened it. Inside the fence was a patch of cultivated ground. The evening sun shone into the hut; a brass cooking-pot gleamed. In front of the hut was a small open fire. The man and the woman paused in their work and looked at him without surprise.

Philip leant his gun against the wall of the hut and sat down on the wooden stool that the woman, answering the man's quick gesture, set for him. He did not ask himself how these people and the clearing came to be there, in the heart of the forest. To him they seemed inevitable; at the end of his long, hot, and troubled walk his feet had led him to the only possible conclusion. He took off his hat and laid it on the ground and let the evening air cool his forehead. He had not realised how tired he was. He made no attempt to speak to the man. To be allowed to sit there, at peace and still, was all he wanted of him.

From where he sat he could see into the hut. It was as bare and as poor as a hut could be. On the beaten smooth mud floor were a few cooking pots, a roll of matting, and a small tin box. A sheathed knife and a cloth hung on the wall. On the open fire a pan of rice was boiling.

The man was standing beside him holding an earthen-ware bowl of water. Philip took it and drank. The water tasted of leaves. He handed the bowl back and looked up at the broad gold hairless chest, at the muscled arms and the gold, slightly flattened face. The man turned away and,

§ 208 §

after a moment's hesitation, picked up his short wooden hoe. The woman had already turned back to her work again.

Philip sat watching them. They worked side by side, the woman a little behind the man, crouching on their heels, turning up the soil with shallow strokes. He wondered what was to grow on this patch of ground: millet, tobacco? Between them and the fence some crop was pushing up through the already sown ground, and at the side of the hut was an onion bed. The forest made a dark background to the moving figures. The woman straightened herself, lifting an arm. She wore a white and pink cloth draped like a short kilted sari. For the first time Philip saw that she was big with child.

He would have liked to sit where he was a little longer. A gold evening quiet lay over the clearing. There was no sound except the dull sound of wood beating on earth and the gentle crackling of the fire. As Philip sat there it seemed to him that now he knew the answer, although he could not remember what the question was.

It was growing late and the sun was sinking. He sighed and got up stiffly and awkwardly, reaching for his gun, and turned towards the gate. He hesitated a moment. There was something that he wanted to say. The man was standing near him, waiting politely until he should choose to leave. Philip did not look at him. He did not want to see in his eyes what he was sure was there: a restless brightness, the beginning of a dream, even if it were only a dream of a richer harvest, a milch cow, or an invention of his own, some complicated affair of trip-ropes and gongs that he was pondering on with the idea of scaring wild elephant from his crops. As for the woman, who could tell what was in her mind? Philip wanted urgently to speak to them. It was important to tell them that here, in their clearing, was everything that they needed. He wanted to ask them, very earnestly, not to look any further, not to leave the shelter of their fence to follow the tangle of paths that led through the forest where they would be sure to meet the bright dangerous bird. He opened his mouth to speak but, of course, he did not know their language.

Philip made a vague movement with his hand, which was meant to be a gesture of goodbye and of thanks, and walked towards the gate. When he reached the fence he turned his head for a last look at the clearing and the hut where the sun was going down behind the fruitful tree. He opened the gate and walked out into the forest.

Pior was waiting by the gate. Philip looked at him as if he did not see him standing there.

"The camp is near," Pior said timidly, after one look at Philip's face. "Here is a path."

Philip followed the path through the trees. The forest seemed dark after the sunlight in the clearing. He stumbled over a tree root and the small jarring shock brought him back to his own complicated reasoning world where nothing is simple and the possible answers are too many; but he knew now what he must do. He must behave like the enlightened civilised man that he had always thought he was and let Alice go to Eric as, since last night, he had known that she must have wanted to go for years.

At the thought, something hot and strong and unreasoning rose in him and protested. The rage that he felt, the desire to smash and spoil and kill, to keep by force what was his own, was an emotion as genuine as any that he had known, but it could not last. Before he had completed another step on the path, the old habit of reason asserted itself again. He saw that all these years his fears and jealousies had been a screen guarding a secret hope on which no one must lay a finger. What right had he to dream that one day Alice would miraculously become what he wanted her to be? Alice was herself as everyone is their own inviolable self, not to be made over again, changed and gilded to fit the shining pattern of a dream. He saw that all these years he had lost the substance for the shadow. And what had Alice dreamt? They all, he saw, were the victims of this unescapable human disease. They were all equally afflicted. Eric and Murray, even Kay, had dreamt their dreams, foolish unrealities, bright visions.

As Philip followed the twisting path between the trees and the thunder sounded again, nearer, almost over his head as the clouds now were, he asked himself why we are driven from what we have, what it is that continually beckons?

The trees thinned. He was out of the trees and walking across an open, still sunlit, glade. For a moment he did not see the peacock. Then he stood still on the path.

If the peacock danced as the thunder rolled, strutting and quivering before the admiring hens, the dance was over. It stood on its anthill as it had stood before, every feather glowing in the evening light. As the great train furled and sank, Philip recognised the insistent misleading colours that he had pursued all his life. As he stepped forward, the gleaming neck was turned towards the forest. In a moment, in a second, once again the bird would be gone.

The sound of the shot was loud in the glade. Something dark that Philip did not recognise rose into the air, only to fall heavily out of the sky almost at his feet. There was a flurry and commotion in the grass and a struggling heap that still gave out a fierce gleam of colour. Philip bent down, but now every feather was still.

Pior said something behind him, an exclamation, a warning. Philip looked up. He had not known that the camp was so near. He could see the smoke rising from the evening fires. He heard shouts and someone called questioningly. Voices were approaching through the trees. Now they all were there, standing between him and the camp.

As he slowly and mechanically pressed the lever of the gun over and the spent cartridge fell to the ground, he saw Manoo's dark shocked face peering out from behind Murray's shoulder.

The sight of their astonished faces made him angry again but, before he could say anything, Alice ran forward. She knelt down and lifted the peacock's crested head and held it for a moment against her breast, as she had done in his dream, before dropping it with a shudder.

Part Six

The Storm

The Storm

CHAPTER I

THE storm broke soon after the sun had set. Out of an ominous stillness the wind came in a fierce gust that tore through the camp raising a cloud of dust, snatching the loose ends of thatch from the hut roofs and lifting the tent flaps. The flames of the camp fire leant suddenly towards the river, the loose ash rose and danced, and the camp was filled with a confusion of smoke and dust, shouts and cries, and small loose flapping objects. As suddenly as it had come, the wind went. It was followed by several reverberating peels of thunder and a flash of lightning that tore the grey darkness apart. The trees across the river lifted astonished dark arms to the sky and the rain came down.

At eight o'clock it was still raining as if it would never stop. The rain drummed on the canvas of the tents and penetrated the grass roofs of the bashas. It had put out the camp fire long ago and under a hastily erected shelter, by the light of a hurricane lamp, Kristo struggled and cursed over a pile of damply smoking branches while Jetha, with a sack over his head and shoulders, refilled and pumped the two Primus stoves at the entrance of the cook tent. The rain fell heavily and vertically, turning the heavy soil to mud. Already the river had risen. It swept under the bank in the darkness with a new and threatening sound.

In the dining-hut the lamps were lit as usual. The light streamed out into the darkness and was caught by the wall of falling rain. Sitting in their accustomed places facing the dark night, they waited for what, although they did not know it, was to be their last supper under the gold straw roof.

Murray sat hunched in his chair with the collar of his coat turned up round his ears. He looked wearily round the table but made no attempt to break the silence that had settled on them as soon as they took their places. Kay, wrapped in his thick, soft coat, was looking in the direction of the cook tent and fiddling with knife and fork. Eric sat straight in his chair, staring out at the darkness; his face, under the lamp, had the grey and strangely exalted look that exhaustion gives and it was obvious that he was in pain. Murray turned his head and looked down at Alice, but all he could see of her were waves of lamplit hair, a curve of cheek, and her hands folded tightly together on the table. Philip sat next to Kay, leaning back in his chair with his hands in his pockets and his head bent. The light fell on his thinning hair and onto the high lined forehead. Murray sighed. What with Manoo sulking in his tent and upsetting all the Hindu members of the camp over this odd business of the peacock, they were in for enough trouble without the rain. Rain in camp was the very devil. If it and this sudden cold went on he foresaw bogged roads, a shortage of food, bad tempers, illness, fevers; it was lucky that he had brought an extra supply of quinine with him. Eric, the vain courageous fool, had walked too far that day, trying to keep up with Kay. A strong sleeping pill directly after supper would be the best thing for Eric; then there would be at least one of them that he need not worry about for a few hours.

"What has happened to Kancha?" Kay said suddenly. "A little warm food inside us would make all the difference. Look at us, sitting here like mutes at a funeral. For God's sake, say something, somebody."

"We will be lucky if we get anything hot to-night," Murray said. "They are having a difficult time in the cook tent. I told Kancha to open some tins."

"I'll go and see what's happening, if you like, and lend a hand," Kay said. "Come on, Alice, this should be your business."

"Kancha will be bitterly offended if you do," Murray said. "He's doing his best."

"We have had rain in camp before without all this delay and fuss."

"Not as heavy rain as this, Kay," Murray said. "I have seldom seen anything like it, even in the monsoon. We had no Christmas rains this year, as we usually do. Perhaps it has been saving up for this."

"It might have waited another two weeks until we had gone," Kay said. "Rain in camp is hell. Wet clothes, and nowhere to dry them, damp beds, cold food, cross servants, no fishing, nothing to do. My hut is leaking, Murray. Right onto my bed."

"Those roofs should have kept any rain out," said Murray. "I saw them made myself. Sometimes I think that this camp is possessed."

"This is special rain," Alice said. "What else can we expect?"

The Peacock

The four men looked at her. She met their eyes defiantly, lifting her head. Her hair fell back from her face, leaving it exposed to the lamplight.

"Now, Alice," said Murray. "Don't let's go into that again. This rain has been brewing for days. It was bound to come."

"It won't be only the rain. You wait and see."

Kay groaned. "Can't anyone stop her?" he asked. "I can't stand much more of this. Stop behaving like a silly, obstinate child, Alice. Try to look at this logically. This is a fishing and shooting camp. Say what you like, we came here largely to kill. Eric and I finished off fourteen birds between us this morning in a few hours. What about those two big tiger yesterday, and all the deer that Murray has shot for the pot in the past weeks? This is the jungle. Sudden death here is a part of every day, right and natural, only to be expected. But Philip, on some sudden impulse, which he hasn't attempted to explain, shoots one bird more and the sky falls! It was a pity, a mistake, we all agree, but the peacock is dead and buried. Leave it that way."

"Quite a speech," Eric said. "But for once I agree with you. You must forget this, Alice."

"And here is Kancha with the food," Murray said. "Hot soup for a start anyway. It would take more than a cloudburst and a leaking tent to upset Kristo, he's an old campaigner."

"Let's finish off that bottle of sherry," Kay said. "We shan't need it more than we do now."

"That's a rash thing to say," said Alice. "Perhaps you don't know what Manoo has been saying round the camp."

"Manoo is a superstitious old fool," Murray said angrily. "You don't have to listen to him."

"Come on, Cassandra," said Kay. "Drink that up and you will feel better."

Alice put her glass down and turned towards Philip.

"Why?" she said slowly. "That's what I want to know. I see that it was bound to happen, but why Philip, of all people?"

Philip lifted his head. For a moment it seemed to Murray that he was going to answer, but he only frowned irritably, as if he found the question a foolish one, and shrugged his shoulders and looked away at the steadily falling rain. An embarrassed silence settled over the table again.

It would certainly have been better if Philip had offered some kind of an explanation. Apart from any other aspect of the case, he had broken one admitted camp rule in firing a shot close to the camp. Murray looked at the averted head curiously. He, too, would have liked to know the reason for what Philip had done. That evening, as they stood in the glade round the dead bird, Philip had said in the shrill unnatural voice that had so startled them, "Don't stare at me like that. It's only a bird, I tell you." And bending down to show them, stretching out a dead wing, he had cried, as if he were trying to make them understand, "Look! Now that the sun has gone the feathers are dull, quite dull. They don't shine of themselves at all."

That strange cry could not have been called an explanation or even an apology. The whole business was inexplicable. It had better be left at that. Murray roused himself and looked round the table.

"Alice," he said, "will you pour the coffee for us, please? I have asked Kancha to bring us a charcoal brazier here. It will be a poor substitute for the camp fire, I'm afraid, but it will make us warmer and more cheerful. The rain won't last, you know. It will be fine again in a day or two. The river will soon go down. Let's make the most of the time we have left."

"We have plenty of time," Kay agreed, cheerfully. "One uncomfortable night, a day or two's fishing lost. What of it? There's no harm done."

Alice said, as if neither of them had spoken, "I see it now. It wasn't only Philip. It was all of us."

She looked round the table and cried. "The forest won't forgive us for what we have done. This rain is only the beginning. We won't be let off so lightly."

CHAPTER II

THE camp was sleeping under the steady rain. Two sheltered lanterns gave out faint yellow beams into the wet darkness but the camp, without the strong red glow of the fire, was abandoned to the night and to the forest as it had not been before.

It was two o'clock when Philip woke suddenly and lay listening to the river's angry voice. He felt light and empty and curiously peaceful. By one small inexplicable act, the pressing of a finger round a trigger, his problem had been settled once and for all. He could hear Alice breathing across the small space that divided them but he knew that she was far away, gone from him beyond recall. Perhaps every problem, long thought over and debated in the secret places of the mind, is eventually settled by one small unpremeditated act, by one word too many, by something as light and unimportant as a feather but enough to bring the balance down on one side or the other. He had thought that before, that very morning. Daylight would bring many minor problems, but he would not think about them now. He let himself drift on the darkness and waited patiently for sleep to come. When he heard the first sound that Murray failed to hear because of the loud rain-drumming on the canvas of the tent, he heard it incuriously. It was repeated: a sharp cracking sound which was followed by an alarmed squeal from the direction of the mahouts' camp. He was out of bed and listening at the doorway of the hut before he knew that he was now wide awake, and he was shaking Alice, pulling her from her bed and groping for her mosquito boots before Kay called out.

Kay woke unwillingly and for a moment he refused to believe what he heard. He knew at once what these sounds meant, but he lay still and told himself that this sort of thing did not happen in Murray's camps, that it was altogether too obvious and melodramatic to be true. Then he, too, leapt out of bed, and seized his flashlight and his shoes and ran to the doorway. He did not know that he called out loudly as he ran. His intention was to slip out of the hut and into the darkness as quietly as he could. The rain met him at the doorway and drove him back. He tore a blanket from his bed and, wrapping it round his shoulders, ran out again, only to collide with Philip and Alice.

In the open space behind the huts someone was waving a lantern. They heard shouts and cries from the cook tent and Murray's voice shouting incomprehensible directions. The beam of a flashlight shone in the darkness and they saw, for a second, the gleam of a white tusk and a circle of grey wrinkled skin, surprisingly detached against the night.

§ 221 §

"My God, it's true," Kay said. "There he is. The old devil, who would have thought it?" His voice sounded outraged and Alice began to laugh helplessly.

"Run!" Philip said. "Quick, behind the truck. He's moving this way."

As they tripped together over the ropes of the cook tent, they half saw, half sensed, an immense shape surge by.

The elephant had entered the camp from the thick trees to the north. Murray, who had heard no sound of his coming, woke at the approach of danger, as Manoo and Sangla did almost at the same time. His hand was on his rifle as he woke. The tent swayed as he slipped out of the back flaps and, as he skirted a still taut tent-rope, he heard the tent pole snap behind him. This was the second sound that Philip had heard.

It was as well that the elephant paused to knock down the tent which was directly in his path. There was time for Sangla and Manoo to rouse the sleeping servants and for them to get safely away to gather behind the tarpaulined shelter which housed the car and the truck. No one, later, could tell how this was accomplished in the confusion of rain and darkness. No one could remember in what order events took place. Pior appeared out of nowhere holding Philip's shotgun. Kristo ran back from comparative safety, making a sortie to rescue his frying-pan. The water carrier was overcome with terror and could only crouch on the ground and weep. But it was impossible in the rain and the darkness to be sure of anyone in the shivering group behind the truck. At one moment there was light on the scene. Puran Singh, who had climbed into the driving seat of the truck, suddenly switched on the headlights and, for a second or two, they all saw and retained a clear picture of an immense grey rear some seventy yards away, of a short, angry, pig-like tail, above the collapsing wall of the first hut, the hut that had been Kay's.

As the light flashed on and off, Murray and Manoo joined them.

"Are we all here?" Murray asked. "Try and check up, Philip."

"Can't we turn him? Fire a shot?"

"That would only make matters worse," said Murray. "He's keeping to the old path and only pausing to push down anything that's in his way."

"That includes all the huts. They are in a line with the tent."

"He means to go straight through the camp. If we leave him alone he will clear off after that."

At that moment they heard a crash and a rending, followed by an enormous splash.

"The dining-hut," Murray said. "He has pushed it into the river."

"Why don't you shoot him?" Kay said. "He's done enough damage already."

Before Murray could answer, pandemonium broke out in the mahouts' camp. The uneasy stamping and shuffling changed into an uproar. The mahouts' shouts were lost in a confusion of trampling and bellowing. The sound of crashing branches and of a tree falling announced that a stampede had taken place.

"Akbar won't go far," Murray said. "But we will have a difficult time collecting the two females. Curse those mahouts."

"Listen," Alice said suddenly. "That's Ebon barking. Where's Eric?"

"No one could sleep through this, sleeping draught or not," Kay said, but Alice cried:

"He's still there, in the last hut. Eric!"

"Don't go! Wait, you fools," said Murray, but Philip, with Sangla at his heels, had already disappeared into the darkness.

Philip could never remember how he reached Eric's hut. In his dash across the open ground he fell over some small obstacle, a bush, a tree root, and the shock must have dulled and shaken his mind. As he lay for a second on the ground, unable to move, the dog ran past him in the darkness, brushing against him. It was then that he heard the sound of a shot, loud and close, that sounded like the slamming of an enormous door. When he groped his way through the door of the hut, Sangla was already there, crouched over something on the ground. Sangla was before him, Sangla could have managed this alone and, once again, Philip's gesture was futile.

To the group behind the truck, the dog's barking came suddenly loud and clear. It was followed by the sound of the rifle shot.

"Keep everyone here, Kay," Murray said. "If the elephant turns this way, go up the track to the road and wait by the big tree."

"What are you going to do?" said Alice.

Murray had gone, and the watchers, peering out behind the truck into the steadily falling downpour, saw his flashlight moving behind the trees. Alice whimpered and hid her face against Kay's shoulder. He could feel her shaking against him and he put his arm consolingly round her wet shoulders, but her tears, coming so soon after her laughter, annoyed him. The scene, to him, was still unbelievable, a wild farce, not for a moment to be taken seriously, but he was puzzled. He could see Murray's flashlight moving towards the sounds that the elephant was making as he finished the demolishing of the dining-hut, but it seemed to him that the shot had come from the other side of the camp. He said, uneasily, "What is Eric doing now? He must have fired that shot." He heard Pior and Jetha muttering behind him.

Kay's uneasiness had prevented him from seeing that now the scene had changed. There was little visible except the darkness, but he could hear that now the dog was out in the open, growling and snapping, running in circles round his huge enemy. In the open space in the centre of the camp a strange shuffling dance was going on as the dog advanced and retreated round the elephant, before the enormous stamping feet, darting out of range of the single tusk and barking incessantly.

Kay realised suddenly that the sounds were nearer. He thought that he could make out a huge shifting form in the darkness. Clutching Alice's arm, he propelled her towards the track. As they began their nightmare retreat to the road they heard a shrill furious trumpeting. If they had stayed to listen, they would have heard that the direction of the sounds had changed. Elephants dislike and fear all dogs. What Eric's shot and Murray and Manoo had failed to do the dog had accomplished. The crashing and barking were growing fainter, moving away down river from the camp.

Sangla spoke to Philip in a low and urgent voice from the doorway of Eric's hut, and Philip knew what had happened. He never knew how he and Sangla carried that heavy sagging weight away from the hut, the hut that was undamaged, that was still standing above the river. Murray and Manoo were suddenly there, appearing out of the darkness. It was the extraordinary silence in the camp after the sound of the dog's barking died away that seemed important to Philip, more portentous than Murray's low hurried orders. He did what he was told, helped to retrieve the medicine chest from under the tent, held the flashlight, fetched this, held that, but even now he did not realise what had happened. Eric had shot himself, he knew that, but how or why he did not know. Murray said that they could not stay in the camp, that the elephant might come back. They must carry Eric away.

Philip walked behind Pior and the swinging lantern down the track towards the road. The light flickered over the wet shining undergrowth. The trampled mud of the track pulled at his loose boots. He could hear the progress that the small, heavily laden procession made behind him. "Go on," Murray had said. "Go on ahead and tell them." He looked up and saw a star shining between the leaves. For the first time he realised that the rain had stopped.

The luminous dial of his watch showed him that it was a quarter to three. It seemed impossible that so much had happened in three quarters of an hour. He put the watch to his ear, but it was still going. Jetha and Pior were a part of the procession behind him. What were they doing there? Had Kay, uneasy at the delay, sent these two back to the camp, or had they returned of their own accord, slipping back in the darkness, warned by some instinct of disaster, as forest creatures are? Here was the end of the track. The swinging light of the lantern showed the surface of the road that was not less deep in mud than the track had been. He turned left, following Pior, and saw a red flickering light that was still far off. As he came nearer, he saw that the huge pale girth of the tree, whose crown was lost in the darkness, was reddened by the flames of the fire at its roots.

Kay was pleased with himself. He had safely conducted his soaked and shivering party to the shelter of the tree and had caused the fire to be made of the dry litter they found between the enormous hollow arching buttresses of the roots.

§ 226 §

The Storm

It was Kancha who had produced the box of still dry matches from the recesses of his wet clothing, but everyone, even the water carrier, had helped, and he considered that now the morale of all was partially restored. Alice had not spoken since they had begun their retreat through the mud of the track. She sat obediently where he had told her to sit, wrapped in his blanket, her arms folded round her knees and her head bent. He could not see her face but, as he walked up and down in the fringe of the firelight, beating his arms together to warm himself, he was annoyed with her again. They were a strangely garbed, dishevelled, wretched looking group but she looked utterly forlorn, abandoned to misery. He was anxious himself. There had been no further sounds, no second shot, but it would do no good to show what he was feeling. When he noticed that both Pior and Jetha had slipped away into the darkness he made no attempt to call them back. He would not have ordered them to the camp but he was relieved that they had chosen to go themselves. It was about time that someone knew what was happening there.

It was Puran Singh who first saw the light of the lantern wavering towards them. Alice sprang up and Kay had to restrain her from running to meet it.

"I can't see," she said. "Who is it?" and then she cried, "It's Philip. I know that it's Philip."

Pior held up the lantern and Kay saw Philip's face. He put his hand on Alice's arm, but she took no notice of him.

"Philip," she called. "Are you all right? Oh, Philip, how could you go dashing off like that without a word?"

Philip came heavily up to them until he was standing looking down at her.

Before he could speak, she cried, "Why did you leave me? Let the others look after themselves. Anything could

§ 227 §

have happened to you and then what would I have done?"

Sobbing loudly, and stumbling over the fringe of the blanket, she threw her arms around his neck.

Philip looked over Alice's head at Kay. He could not speak. It was Kay who said, "Hush, Alice. You must be quiet. Eric is dead."

CHAPTER III

IT was a grey hazy morning three days later when Murray walked down the still muddied track to the camp. No heavy rain had fallen since the night of the storm but for three days they had been cut off from everything except the immediate forest; this was the first day that the forest road had been open. Murray was returning from the road where he had said goodbye to the Police Officer from Kishnagar and to the Forest Officer, Barua, and had watched their cars crawl slowly back down the road towards Hokgaon.

The interview had been less painful than he had feared. The policeman, a middle-aged, soft-spoken Bengali, had asked only what it was necessary for him to know. After a few words with them all he had asked to see the rifle and the hut, and he had put a few questions to Sangla in his own tongue. He had agreed with their theory of the accident, nodding his head when Philip showed him where the body had lain in the doorway and the rough woven wall of the hut on which the trigger must have caught as the lame man, roused suddenly from a heavy sleep, fell. He had asked Murray to describe the wound in the chest. "You are a doctor," he had said. "Was death instantaneous?" Eric had been breathing when Sangla first touched him, but he was gone before Murray could examine him. "There was nothing that I could do," Murray had said. "It would have made no difference if I had reached him before I did." Barua, standing beside him had said gently, "You must be glad of that."

Murray was grateful to Barua. He must write to him—send him a letter of thanks. There had been no real reason for him to come to the camp and when he had arrived, following the Police Officer's khaki clad figure down the track, he had given an impression of sternness, almost of anger, but when he left the atmosphere in the camp was lighter and less strained. With Manoo he had examined the prints of the enormous circular feet that were stamped deep in the mud all over the camp. He had bent down to measure them. Twice the circumference of an elephant's foot gives its height at the shoulder. "Ten feet," he had said to Murray. "I didn't think that he was as big as that." And then he had volunteered the information that the Ganesh had been seen making for the border. "He has gone. He will trouble you no further," he had said with authority, as if he really knew.

When Murray had told him that they, too, were going the next day, the Tallents and Kay to catch the mid-day train and he to the Dipsiri bungalow where he meant to move the camp and stay until his leave was up, Barua had only nodded. But as he was walking back to his car he had said, "Dr Coombes, I will be on tour from to-morrow, but when I get back I will do my best to see that the grave remains as you leave it. Before you go, to prevent the jackals disturbing what is there, see that it is heaped high with stones."

They had made the grave on the bank high above the river facing the wooded island above the camp. Murray had been glad that, with the road closed, there could be no question of anything else. Only Kay and Manoo had objected.

Manoo had come to him with a long rambling request; fire, he had said, was the cleaner way, the better way and, although he had refused to listen, Murray was not sure that Eric would not have agreed. Kay's attitude had been more difficult to understand. Kay had quarrelled sharply with Alice when she had said that Eric would have been glad to stay where he was. "We should take him back to be among his own people," he had said. "We can't leave him in this strange wild place. We can't go and leave him here. We shall never be able to forget him if we do." Kay's behaviour had been altogether surprising. Who would have thought that he would feel this so much? He was like someone who had lost his way and he had wandered aimlessly round the camp until he was on all their nerves. Sangla's behaviour was more understandable. He had been devoted to Eric. Sangla had been present at the burial, standing impassively a short distance away, and when it was over he had gone straight to the salvaged heap of stores, stolen the last two bottles of whiskey and remained drunk in his tent for two days.

The camp, as Murray entered it from the track, looked much the same as it had done before, although, from the trees across the river the empty space where the dining-hut had stood and the one hut left standing were more noticeable, as was the new shelter that Manoo had made for Philip and Alice, using the tarpaulins from the truck. When daylight came and they knew that the long night was over, they had returned to the camp, straggling back down the road to find that the damage was surprisingly small. The car and the truck were untouched, the cook tent was still standing and, although the two huts and the tent were flat, most of their belongings were retrieved from under them. The fishing rods were smashed and the barrels of Murray's shotgun were bent. All the cutlery and china and many of the stores had gone with the dining-hut into the river. The chairs that they had left standing round the fire were chairs no longer and no one could have said how many once sat there. If only the sun could have shone again, the camp might slowly have become something like its old self, but the sad grey weather continued, although the cold that had come with the storm soon changed to a warm heaviness. Even if Eric had been with them, if this swift and final thing that they still found difficult to realise had not happened, they would have felt oppressed.

Now, as Murray walked towards the bank, Alice ran to meet him.

"Murray, come quickly," she cried. "Ebon is back. We found him lying by the fire. He's terribly thin and dirty, but unhurt."

The dog had not been seen since the night of the storm. Akbar had returned of his own accord after twelve hours of freedom and, with his help, the two female elephants were found grazing peacefully in the forest not far from the road. But the dog had vanished into the darkness and, although they searched the surrounding forest and kept a watch for him on the road, they had found no trace of him. As the hours went on they had given him up. Perhaps it had seemed to them that this was a fitting end for him. They had told each other that the dog had always been a shadow of himself when Eric was not with him, and that their brief reunion should mark the end of his days.

He had appeared suddenly in the long grass on the opposite bank of the river, drunk deeply of the pool, and, crossing above the rapid, had climbed slowly up the water carrier's path to stretch himself out by the newly lit camp fire. They stood round him, looking down at him, as if this resurrection disconcerted them.

§ 231 §

The Peacock

"Where can he have been all this time?" Philip said. "He must be starving but he won't touch anything."

"Trapped in some hole, or lost. Perhaps he had to wait for the river to go down before he could cross."

"He has made no attempt to look for Eric," Kay said. "He just lies there."

"He knows," Alice said. "Perhaps he knew before we did."

"That couldn't be. He was out of the tent and barking round the elephant before we heard the sound of the shot."

Alice knelt down and touched the dog's black head. A tremor of acknowledgement ran through his body but he did not open his eyes. "Poor old Ebon," she said. "He's done in. Let him sleep. We can see to him later. Of course he knew. He would have been back days ago otherwise to see what had happened to Eric."

"What shall we do with him?" Kay said. "He will remind us all of Eric. He's old. It would have been better if he had not come back."

Alice looked up indignantly and Murray said, "Unfortunately death doesn't always arrive at the appropriate moment. The old have a way of lingering on long after it would have been better for themselves and everyone else if they had gone. You had better leave Eric's dog with me."

Alice stood up. "I shall keep him with me as long as he lives," she said. "I shall be glad to be reminded of Eric." She pushed her hair back from her face and, turning to them, cried, "Look at us all, alive and standing here while Eric is dead. Philip and I are happy. How dare we be happy? Murray is bitter, thinking of being old. He is lucky to have had the chance to grow old, Eric didn't. As for Kay, he is thinking how quickly he can forget all this and get on with his own affairs. I hate us all, I tell you!"

§ 232 §

Murray went to her and held her hands in his. "Hush, Alice," he said. "Eric had come to a dead end in his life. He couldn't go on. He was the sort that never bends, in this world he was bound to be broken. Perhaps he was lucky. It was a quick way out."

Kay said, "He told me himself that he had no future."

Alice pushed Murray away. "Do you know what you both are saying?" she asked. "Don't you see, this is what I'm afraid of? It wasn't an accident. He meant it to happen."

"That's not true, Alice," Murray said.

"Eric wasn't the kind to do such a thing," Kay said. "You should know him better. And if he had been, he wouldn't have done it then."

"It was an accident," Murray said. "Everything in the hut made that clear."

"It was my fault. The whole thing has been my fault," Alice said. "I let him think that I was in love with him. So I was, in a way, and always have been, but not as he thought. I must have let him see that I didn't mean it, that I was only using him."

"On the contrary, he was afraid that you did mean it," Kay said. "I didn't like to disillusion him. I advised him to run like hell."

Alice turned to him. "What had it to do with you?" she said. "Why must you always be there, putting your little monkey hand into everything?"

"Now listen to me, Alice," Kay said. "You can't have it every way. The vanity of you women! Don't you know yet that men are willing to die for almost anything on earth, for money, for greed, for honour, for friendship, out of sheer obstinacy, but never, never for love of a woman? You have an outrageous idea of your importance. You come a long way down in our scheme of things."

Alice turned her back on him and began to cry. She stood in front of them all and wept without making any attempt to hide her tears. The three men watched her without moving, until Murray said:

"That's enough, Alice. There's no reason for you to blame yourself, my dear. None of us is guiltless."

"It's time that we got away from here," Kay said. "We are growing morbid, all of us. It's time that we picked up our lives again. I know what I'm going to do with mine. While we have been standing here talking and thinking about Eric, I made up my mind to do it. I never liked him much, you know. He seemed to me to be a conceited stiff kind of fool, but it's what he would do."

"What are you going to do, Kay?" Alice said, drying her tears.

"I shan't tell you now, the atmosphere is too emotional. I will tell you to-morrow, just before we leave."

"You will change your mind before that."

Philip had moved a little away from them. He stood looking up the river, and now he said, "This haze is lifting. The sun is trying to come out. If it does the road will be dry to-morrow."

"Are you afraid that you won't be able to get away after all?" Murray said.

Philip turned quickly towards him, but Alice cried, "We don't want to go, Murray. Don't think that."

"What about Kay?" Murray asked. "He seems eager enough."

"It's time we went," Kay said. "If you must know, I have always thought that this was a dangerous place in more ways than one. We knew that when we came, we came with our eyes open, but if we had the chance, would we come again?"

"I should come again," Alice said, putting her arm through Murray's. "The place is exactly as it has always been. But we won't have another chance."

"How do you know that, Alice?" Philip asked.

"We have spoilt it. We had our chance, and now we must leave the garden."

"The garden?" said Kay. "What *do* you mean?"

"Never mind, Murray knows. Look, Philip is right. The sun is coming out. It will be a fine afternoon but we must pack."

Part Seven

The Road Back

The Road Back

THE sun was shining when they drove down the forest road. From the newly washed and refreshed jungle came the loud shrill singing of the cicadas and a green and delicious scent. Every leaf sparkled in the sunlight. The sky behind the trees was blue and without a cloud.

At first, near the camp, their progress was slow. Where the trees arched over the road the ground beneath was deep black mud in which the car wheels, in spite of their chains, sank and laboured. Twice Philip and Kay were forced to cut branches to lay across the road, and to push and heave at the car while Alice drove. Once the truck, following them with the luggage, caught them up and with the help of ropes and of some friendly carters, dragged the car out of the mud. Several times the car skidded off the road into the shining wet grass. It seemed as if the forest did not mean to let them go easily, if at all; but, as they drew further away from the

§ 239 §

foothills and the camp, the road dried and hardened. Here little or no rain could have fallen, and the car hurried on, putting mile upon mile between itself and the camp. The trees fell back, leaving the road clear before them, and closed in quickly again, barring the way behind. To Philip it seemed that now the forest could not get rid of them quickly enough. It was hurrying them on, spewing them out. The grey tree trunks leant away from them. The leaves flashed by.

Philip was driving with Alice beside him. Kay and the dog shared the back seat.

Only an hour or two had gone since Kay had made the announcement that had astonished them all. They had been sitting on the car cushions on the bank above the river on the spot where the dining-hut had stood, eating their breakfast. In the background the car and the truck stood waiting. All was ready and in a few minutes they were to leave the camp for the last time.

"You, Kay?" Murray had said. "I should have thought that you were the last person."

"A farm? But you are a lawyer, every inch of you. An Italian farm. You must be mad."

"Why didn't you tell me before?" Alice had said. "What is she like? Oh, Kay!"

Kay had smiled and shrugged his shoulders in a gesture that made him seem already foreign and far away from them. "Why not? I'm half Italian," he had said.

As he drove, Philip was remembering Kay's small fastidious hands. Kay did not mean it. He would change his mind when he was back in his own world; but there were worse things than living close to the earth, so close that there is no view. Kay had said, "It will be a wonderful life. I shall beget six children in six years. I shall have a horde of in-laws who will do all the work. I shall strut about in the sun and rule the roost." Now Philip pictured a small fierce gaily coloured cock crowing from the height of his dung-hill, and he laughed aloud. Alice made a small protesting movement beside him.

He glanced down at her and saw that she was looking at him reproachfully. Her eyes were full of tears and he knew that these were not only for Eric. He, too, would not soon forget their last glimpse of Murray: a small, upright lonely figure that grew smaller and smaller behind them on the road. Sangla had not been there to see them go, but Manoo, seeming even darker and more bent than he usually did, had made them a ceremonious speech of farewell; his eyes, peering up at them, had seemed to have become suddenly grey and filmy, like the eyes of a very old tortoise. Philip put his hand re-assuringly for a moment on Alice's knee. He would have liked to tell her about this new incarnation of Kay's; she had often called him a cocky little man, even in the days when she had seemed most taken with him. It was strange to think that he had once been jealous of this same ridiculous small Kay. It was a humiliating thought.

Philip looked quickly at Alice again. This was the face that he had never been able to see clearly for long. Now the mists of jealousy and fear were gone and he saw it exactly as it was from the low, white, slightly bulging forehead to the round obstinate chin. At the corners of her mouth were a few faint wrinkles that he had not noticed before. This was Alice. He knew her now. There was nothing more to see and nothing that he could not guess. Now there was no dream.

Alice met his eyes and smiled at him. Her eyes behind

the film of tears were transparently grey but, as he looked into them, the brown lashes came down and her look slid away under his. He knew that nothing had changed.

As he stared fixedly at the road again, Philip was smiling, a little wryly perhaps. The act of acceptance is always faintly bitter, as dry and astringent to the mind as a cleansing medicine is to the mouth. If he did not know Alice and would never know her, at least he knew himself.

But now something was moving on the road. He saw it from a long way off and, as the car rushed forward, he kept his eyes on it. Now Alice had seen it too. It was a deer. It was a chital stag: the sunlight shone on a gold-red hide spotted with white and caught the polished branching antlers. In the grass at the side of the road a doe lifted her head to stare at the oncoming car. And here was another doe and another. A herd of chital, the most graceful and shapely of all the deer, was grazing on the new bright grass that edged the road. As the car approached, the deer stared for a moment, and then flashed into movement. They bounded across the road and back, leapt into the air in graceful high bounds.

Perhaps it was the new freshness in the air and in the morning sunlight that filled them with this leaping joyful movement. The air in front of the car was full of flashing, leaping shapes. The small red shining bodies, that were spotted with white as if by snowflakes, gambolled and danced before the car as lightly and gaily as a company of antlered fairies. Philip's delighted eye picked out one small perfect stag as it rose from the ground, horns back on the spotted shoulders, great eyes staring, all four tapering but steel-strong legs lifting it high above the shining grass. For a moment he saw it, as it would always be for him, fixed and held by an invisible frame in his mind.

"What a picture?" he cried. "Look, what a picture!"

With a flash of white-lined tails the deer were gone.

When she said goodbye to Murray, Alice had said, "There will be another time. One day, somehow, we will come back?" In Philip's pocket there was a letter from Murray addressed to T. K. Barua's office at Hokgaon. Barua, as Murray knew, had that morning set out to complete his interrupted tour of inspection of his domain. He was busy somewhere behind them in the forest, but he would find the letter waiting for him at his Headquarters when he got back. How much Barua would have to do with Alice's question Philip was not sure. There would be many reasons why they would not come back.

Hokgaon, which marked the end of the forest road, was still many miles ahead but, if they had looked back down the road, they would have seen that now the forest was a dark green impenetrable wall behind them. Was it some trick of the sunlight slanting through the leaves, or was there in the sky the flashing arc of a great moving sword?

CHAPTER II

MURRAY stood with his back to the river and watched the two loaded elephants disappear down the track. He had sent Sangla, now sober but a shadow of himself, ahead to the old bungalow. Everyone else had gone with the elephants, Kancha and the cook riding on Sitara and the rest walking. The last that he saw of them was Pior's red headcloth vanishing between the trees. Now there was no camp, only a bare patch of ground.

Akbar and Manoo were waiting for him where his tent

had once stood. It was time to go, but first he would walk round the camp-site once again to make sure that the last traces had been removed.

He saw that the rubbish pits and the latrines had been filled in and the ashes of the fires raked and scattered. Not a scrap of paper, not a tin or shred of sacking remained, nothing foreign to the forest except a few scars on the ground. This is how a camp-site should be left. In a week, even in a day, the jungle would begin its effacing work and soon there would be nothing to show that a camp had been there. There is nothing that the earth will not accept and hide away: bury the bones, bury the faeces, leave no mark, no human trace.

As Murray completed his inspection and walked towards the waiting elephant, he stopped at the edge of the bank and looked down. But there was no glimpse to be had in the dark swirls of water of the great fish who lay there, head up river, fins moving gently to hold himself steady in the stream. Akbar knelt and rose. From the height of the elephant's back Murray turned for a last look at the pool and at the ranks of the trees on the further bank. Then he touched the mahout on the shoulder and pointed up the river. There was one thing more that he had to do.

When they reached the piled white stones of the grave that faced the wooded island and the hills, he did not dismount. He glanced briefly at the place, which was high above the sands of the river bed and clear of the trees, to make sure that his last orders had been carried out. All was well, and he looked away at the hills. Once again, above the hills, the snows were showing. They shone in the sky, white, serene, remote.

The elephant turned back to the trees. Murray intended to join the road where it met the plain. At Akbar's swinging,

§ 244 §

comfortable, unhurried pace, they would reach the Dipsiri bungalow by mid-day. The trees closed round them again. The white stones of the grave were hidden. Now to the north, between them and the foothills, was nothing except untouched forest. Murray crossed his legs comfortably on the pad and let his body swing to the movement beneath him.

Manoo touched his arm and he roused himself reluctantly and looked down. He saw a small enclosed field, a hut beneath a clump of wild banana trees and two bending figures. He had forgotten the clearing.

"Still here?" he said aloud, and the mahout, taking this for an order, checked the elephant.

"What are you waiting for?" Murray said angrily. "Turn back, you have missed the way. Join the road by the big tree. There's nothing here that I want to see."

As Akbar swung round obediently and they moved on again, Murray looked back. He could still see the clearing but now the hut was dwarfed almost to nothing by the dark wall of the forest. Unwillingly he raised his hand in salutation.

On their way back through the trees they crossed the green and sunlit glade where now no bird walked.